"It's not weird," Wells said. He turned, smiled. "Honestly. We had a moment, but like all moments, it passed."

He seemed to recover from her rejection quickly. Sinead wasn't sure how she felt now. Relieved? Disappointed? Both?

Before she could say anything else, the crack of a whip ripped through the din. A concrete pillar next to Wells exploded with dust and bits of rock. The scent of gunpowder was strong over the smells of body odor and motor grease.

Without thinking, she knew it was gunfire. Her gut threatened to turn to liquid, but her training was stronger than her fear. "Gunman," she yelled. Sinead withdrew her sidearm.

Wells already had a gun in his hand.

"This way." She moved forward, sweeping up people from behind and ushering them toward the stairs. And yet Sinead knew one thing to be true. It wasn't a random shooter who had fired a random shot.

Whoever fired the gun had been aiming directly at Wells.

Dear Reader,

There are a few things in life that I love as much as a good romance novel. And one of those things—or rather, places—is New York City. There are great restaurants, iconic landmarks, interesting people and the city has a unique energy like nowhere else. I'm fortunate to live within driving distance of the city and enjoy each and every visit. So, it will come as no surprise to you that I was thrilled to be a part of The Coltons of New York continuity.

More than getting to set a book in a city I love, I adore the characters. FBI special agent Sinead Colton is smart, funny, dedicated to her work. Yet she has always felt that she isn't good enough—no matter how good she really is. Detective Wells Blackthorn is a rising star in the NYPD, but his life has recently been upended. Wells became the guardian of his ten-month-old nephew following the death of his brother and sister-in-law. Sure, he's busy learning how to take care of a child, but with a serial killer loose in Manhattan, duty calls.

As a writer, I just had to put Wells and Sinead on the page together, and the chemistry between the characters took care of the rest!

I hope you enjoy reading this book as much as I enjoyed writing it!

Warmest regards,

Jennifer D. Bokal

COLTON'S
DEADLY AFFAIR

Jennifer D. Bokal

Special thanks and acknowledgment are given to
Jennifer D. Bokal for her contribution to
The Coltons of New York miniseries.

Recycling programs
for this product may
not exist in your area.

ISBN-13: 978-1-335-59366-5

Colton's Deadly Affair

Copyright © 2023 by Harlequin Enterprises ULC

For questions and comments about the quality of this book, please contact us at CustomerService@Harlequin.com.

Harlequin Enterprises ULC
22 Adelaide St. West, 41st Floor
Toronto, Ontario M5H 4E3, Canada
www.Harlequin.com

Printed in U.S.A.

Jennifer D. Bokal is the author of several books, including the Harlequin Romantic Suspense series Rocky Mountain Justice, Wyoming Nights, Texas Law and several books that are part of the Colton continuity.

Happily married to her own alpha male for more than twenty-five years, she enjoys writing stories that explore the wonders of love. Jen and her manly husband have three beautiful grown daughters, two very spoiled dogs and a cat who runs the house.

Books by Jennifer D. Bokal

Harlequin Romantic Suspense

The Coltons of New York

Colton's Deadly Affair

Texas Law

Texas Law: Undercover Justice

The Coltons of Colorado

Colton's Rogue Investigation

Wyoming Nights

Under the Agent's Protection
Agent's Mountain Rescue
Agent's Wyoming Mission
The Agent's Deadly Liaison

The Coltons of Grave Gulch

A Colton Internal Affair

The Coltons of Kansas

Colton's Secret History

Rocky Mountain Justice

Rocky Mountain Valor

Visit the Author Profile page at Harlequin.com for more titles.

To John, Now and Forever

Prologue

Andrew Capowski drew in a deep breath. Up here, the air was clean and cool. His work shift was almost over. He'd made it through another night guarding the Empire State Building. Not that there was much to the job, or at least not much to do when the building was empty. Sure, there were other security guards and the overnight cleaning crew—less than two dozen people in total.

He stood on the eighty-sixth-floor observation deck and rested his elbows on the railing. Sure, there was another observation deck that had been added to the 102nd floor. But Andrew was old-school and liked the original deck best. A narrow concrete walkway circled the perimeter of the building. The entire outside area was enclosed with a metal fence high enough to stop anyone from trying to jump. During the day, this space was crowded with tourists taking pictures but never really seeing the city.

It was 4:45 a.m. and the deck was blessedly empty. The sun had yet to rise, but the sky was starting to lighten on the eastern horizon. Right before sunrise was his favorite time of the day. At his feet, the greatest city in the world slept. Fog rolled off the Hudson River. He could see lights in the apartments across the same river in New Jersey. If he looked to the left, the gentle hills of Pennsylvania were visible in the distance.

He exhaled a contented sigh. Up here, he really was king of the world.

Andrew had to admit that life treated him pretty well. Sure, he'd never get hired by the NYPD. But he had a job he liked. He was married to Vanessa, a woman who he loved more than life. They were expecting their first baby in the fall. It was a boy, the doctor said. He and Vanessa had just agreed on a name—Andrew Capowski Junior.

Him, a dad. Who'd believe it?

One day, he planned to visit this exact spot with his son. From up here, he'd show him the city that the Capowski family had called home for generations.

A door from the elevator bank opened with a whoosh and he froze. Nobody else was assigned to patrol the deck. Had there been an accident? Was there an emergency with his wife? He turned to face the doors and just like the first drop on a roller coaster, his stomach fell to his shoes.

A person stood on the walkway. They were dressed in black—black hoodie, baggy black jeans, dark sunglasses, surgical mask, gloves, and a black book bag was slung over one shoulder.

Standing straight, Andrew lifted his chest. It was a posture he practiced in the mirror every day. He knew that the joker who stood near the doors would get a good look at the badge he wore.

The person removed their sunglasses and stared at Andrew.

This high up, a constant breeze buffeted the building. Despite the wind, Andrew started to sweat. Maybe they were new to the cleaning crew. "You lost your way or something?"

"I'm right where I'm supposed to be," they said. "You're the one who's lost."

"What're you doing out here?"

"Looking for you, Andrew."

The use of his name hit him like a slap. He stepped back. "You ain't supposed to be out here." True, having a person on the observation deck was troubling. But more than that bothered him. "How'd you get in here in the first place?"

The person's eyes crinkled with a smile under their mask and gooseflesh rose on Andrew's arm.

It wasn't that Andrew was afraid of taking a punch— or giving one, for that matter. But there was something very wrong with the scenario.

"I asked you a question," he said. "And you need to answer me. Who in the hell are you? And how'd you get into the building?"

Shaking their head, the person gave a quiet laugh. "You really are an idiot."

Now Andrew was mad. "What'd you call me?"

"An idiot—you idiot. You said you asked me one question. Obviously, you can't count because you asked me two questions."

"Aren't you the self-righteous little punk? How'd you like to get charged with trespassing?" He wasn't sure what other laws had been broken, but Andrew would make sure they got charged with it all.

He reached for the walkie-talkie that was hooked to his belt. Lifting it to his mouth, he depressed the talk button. "Burt, are you there?" he asked, calling his supervisor. "This is Andrew on the eighty-sixth-floor OD. We got ourselves a problem up here."

"Yeah?" He let go of the talk button. Burt's voice cut through the static. "What kind of problem?"

Before he could say anything, he saw the gun. His heartbeat thumped against his chest. There was a flash of fire. The boom of thunder. The scent of gunpowder hung in the air. A flock of pigeons took flight, their wings beating against the gray sky. Andrew fell backward and hit the deck. He couldn't breathe. His chest burned. That was when he saw the blood soaking the front of his uniform shirt. He touched his chest and his palm turned scarlet.

"You shot me," he gasped.

His vision closed in from all sides.

In the distance, he heard Burt's voice. "Andrew? You there? What kind of problem you got?"

He wanted to answer all the questions, but he couldn't remember how to speak. His last thought was of the son who he would never meet.

Chapter 1

Wells Blackthorn held his nephew and paced. He went around the sofa, into the kitchen, down the hallway to the front door and back to the living room. The apartment he'd inherited when his brother and sister-in-law passed away was bigger than the studio he'd lived in before. But it was still too cramped for a cop and a cranky baby.

"Hey, little man." Wells jiggled ten-month-old Harry on his hip. "What's the matter with you? Why don't you want to sleep—like ever?"

Harry regarded him with watering eyes. Dual rows of snot ran from his nose.

"That's not a great look, you know." Wells tucked his hand into the sleeve of his NYPD sweatshirt and wiped Harry's nose. The baby went rigid and then shrieked.

Wells made a shushing noise, bounced the baby and wished that the kid would go back to simply crying.

"You want to run the SoHo 500?" It was named for their South of Houston neighborhood and the five hundred times that he ran the route every night. He made motor sounds and then let off his pretend brake with a screech. He zoomed around the apartment, pretending to be a car. Harry quieted and snuggled into his arms.

Was his nephew about to fall asleep?

He'd had been up with the baby since 2:00 a.m. He was exhausted and ready for a few hours of shut-eye. The sun was starting to creep above the skyline. But what time was it?

His phone sat on the kitchen counter. He glanced at the screen as he passed, and he stopped. It was already 5:07 a.m.

What's more, there were several notifications on the cell. Three missed calls.

How had he missed three calls? Then again, he knew. There was no way he could hear a phone over the racket that Harry had been making. True, he loved his nephew. And he'd always take his responsibility as guardian seriously. Since the death of his brother a few weeks earlier, Harry was the only family Wells had left.

But he was a thirty-two-year-old bachelor. Wells didn't have a dog. Or a cat. Hell, he didn't even own a cactus. Now he was supposed to raise a baby by himself?

He picked up the phone and opened the voice mail app.

Harry started to cry again. His wails were so loud that Wells couldn't hear the message.

"Dude." He looked down at his nephew. "Do you mind?"

His nephew rested his head on Wells's chest. He kissed the top of the baby's head. "Thanks, little man."

He pressed Play again. "Wells, this is Colleen." She was his boss at the 130th Precinct. "A body was found on the eighty-sixth-floor observation deck of the Empire State Building. I need you on the scene ASAP. Call me back when you get this message."

The other two messages were also from Captain Reeves. He pressed Play and listened to them both.

"Wells, this is Colleen. I need you down at the Empire State Building."

Then: "Wells, have you gotten any of my messages? You need to call me back."

Using the contact from the missed calls, he placed a call of his own to the captain. She answered on the third ring.

"Sorry," he said before she even got a chance to say hello. "I didn't hear the phone. Harry's been crying all night."

"Poor baby," she said, her voice tinged with sympathy. "Do you think he's teething?"

Teething? He glanced down at Harry. The kid was finally asleep. His head rested on Wells's shoulder. "I have no idea. When do kids usually get teeth?"

She ignored his question. Turning the conversation to work, she said, "I need you in Midtown, ASAP. You got childcare straightened out for Harry, right?"

"My neighbor takes care of him when I'm at work." A playpen sat next to the sofa. He set Harry down on his back. His arm was numb from holding the kid for hours. His fingers filled with pinpricks as blood started to flow down to his extremities. Moving back to the kitchen, he searched through several drawers. Finally, he found one with a pen and a stack of sticky notes. "What can you tell me about the victim?"

"Andrew Capowski was shot in the heart. His body was found on the observation deck of the Empire State Building by his supervisor."

One month earlier, the body of Mark Wheden had been found in the Ramble in Central Park. Wheden, a city employee, was discovered by an early morning bird-watcher along with a note. *Until the brilliant and beautiful Maeve O'Leary is freed, I will continue to kill in her name. M down. A up next.* Maeve O'Leary was her own set of problems for the city and its police force. O'Leary had killed her lover, Humphrey Kelly. The murder led to a citywide manhunt that ended with Maeve in jail.

From the little that Wells knew of this latest victim, he didn't like it. "Do you think this is the same person who killed the guy in Central Park last month? After all, they threatened more killings. Andrew Capowski. The name is right. He's also an employee at a New York City landmark—just like Mark Wheden."

"I was thinking the same thing," said Reeves. "Crime scene investigators are already on-site. I've been in touch with the FBI. We're putting together a team to investigate and you'll be the lead. I don't have to tell you, Wells, this is a big responsibility."

Wells's career with the NYPD had been smooth from

the beginning. But he was always hungry for more. Bigger cases. More responsibility. Higher rank. His pulse thrummed in his ears. "I can handle it."

She continued, "I don't have to tell you this either, but everyone will be watching you and this case. The police commissioner included. There are some lieutenant slots opening in the fall. If you do well, you'll be on the short list."

She paused, her silence saying more than her words ever could. *If you don't do well, forget about a promotion, now and later.* "I understand what you're saying. I won't let you down."

"That's what I want to hear. How soon can you get to the ESB?" ESB was a New Yorker's shorthand for the Empire State Building, one of the most visited tourist sites in the entire city.

Honestly, Wells would have liked to sleep for several hours and then take a long shower before going to work. But he didn't have time for either. He opened his messaging app and sent his neighbor Deborah Horowitz a text.

You up? I need to drop off Harry early.

Her reply was immediate.

I'm awake. Bring him on over.

He sent a thumbs-up emoji. Julie had stayed home with Harry. But more than once his brother and sister-in-law had used the neighbor for childcare when they went out for the evening. Deborah also helped out when Julie ran errands during the day or simply needed a break.

The fact that she'd become his primary source of childcare was a godsend—and not just for him. He sensed that having Deborah around was helping the kid adjust to life with Wells.

To his captain, he said, "I'm on my way."

The call ended. Wells took a few minutes for basic hygiene, like brushing his teeth and changing out of his snot-covered sweats and into a suit. He shoved a tie into his pocket and checked the diaper bag. Diapers. Formula. Two jars of food and a bib. Wipes. A change of clothes. Harry's favorite toy, Mr. Elephant. He tucked a blanket into the bag and slipped the strap over his shoulder. He thought enough to grab a banana for his own breakfast.

He hated to rouse the sleeping baby, but he had no choice. Gently, he lifted the child from his playpen and walked to the front door. Harry leaned his entire small weight on Wells, smiling as he slept.

He exited the apartment and pulled the door shut. As was his habit, he checked the door to make sure the lock was secure. Then he took a few steps to the next unit. Always aware of the sleeping child in his arms, he knocked lightly on the door.

Deborah flung the door open, her smile wide. If Wells had to guess, he'd say that his neighbor was in her midseventies. Yet she was far from old. She kept her silver hair short—a testament to her years in the Marine Corps. She wore a baggy Marine Corps T-shirt and a pair of shorts. The muscles in her arms and legs were wiry and unmistakable. "There's my two favorite boys." She clamped a hand over her mouth. In a loud whisper, she asked, "Is he sleeping?"

"Finally." Wells was suddenly exhausted. How was he supposed to make it through a new murder investigation on only a few hours of sleep? Then again, he knew. He'd power through, like always. "I've packed up everything you need," he said, holding out the bag.

"You know I live next door. I also have a key to your apartment. If there's anything missing, I can get it."

"I know, I know. It's just..." Wells let his words trail off, not sure how to explain his emotions. He hadn't been close to his brother, Dan, since he graduated from high school. Wells had attended John Jay College of Criminal Justice and majored in psychology. Since he was a kid, he'd had a single dream of one day joining the NYPD. Dan went to Stern, NYU's school of business, and majored in finance. After graduation, Wells joined the force. Dan went to work for a money manager. Wells got a civil servant's salary while Dan made the big bucks. By the time Dan and Julie died in a car accident, the only thing the brothers had in common was their last name and childhood memories. Maybe it was fidelity to that name and those memories that made Wells worry he was failing with Harry. Since Julie had no family, Wells was all the kid had left. "I like to pack his bag is all." He paused. "What do you know about teething?"

"Back when I was a kid, my mom put whiskey on our gums to make them numb. I don't think that's considered acceptable now. There's medicine that does the same thing. You want me to pick some up?"

"Only if he gets crabby."

Deborah opened her arms. "I'll take him. You get to work."

Wells handed over the child. Harry gave a contented sigh as he settled onto the sitter's shoulder. To be honest, he couldn't decide how he felt. He was relieved to have a few hours out of the house—even if it was to investigate a grisly murder. Then guilt hit him like a fist to the gut. Was he a horrible person for wanting to get a break from his nephew?

Placing his hand on the back of the baby's head, he said, "Be good."

"You're doing a good job with him, you know," said Deborah.

"Maybe you can add mind-reader to your resume. I was just thinking how bad I am at the whole parenting thing."

"All parents think they're doing a horrible job—trust me."

He wasn't sure that he agreed. "I didn't spend a lot of time with Julie, but she always had a schedule for Harry. Play dates. Baby swim lessons. She even had some app that was supposed to teach Harry how to speak French."

"Just remember, there are a lot of different ways to raise a happy kid."

He grunted. "I've gotta get going."

While holding Harry, she backed up in her apartment and closed the door. Wells walked down the hallway. Built in the 1920s, the brick apartment house wasn't luxurious by Manhattan standards, but it was nicer than anything he could ever hope to afford. He'd stayed because the apartment came with Harry's inheritance, and really, the kid should be in his own home. What the building lacked in luxury, it made up for in charm. Each floor had four apartments and the whole building had seven floors. Wells lived on the second floor. A spiral staircase wound up through the middle of the building, complete with a wooden railing that was kept polished by the building's manager.

He took the steps two at a time. After crossing the tiled entryway, he pushed the front door open and stepped onto Watts Street, a narrow side street filled with similar apartment buildings. His SUV was parked, like always, at the curb. Using the fob, he unlocked the door and started the engine. Slipping behind the steering wheel, Wells tried to turn his mind to the task ahead. Was this latest murder the work of a serial killer? And if it was, would Wells be able to stop them before they struck again?

Special Agent Sinead Colton looked down at the body of Andrew Capowski. The corpse stared at the sky. His eyes had already turned milky. A pool of blood covered the concrete. A ragged hole was torn in the front of his shirt. It was black with blood and gore.

Before she even had time to eat breakfast, she'd received a call from the assistant director in charge, or ADIC, of the FBI's NYC Field Office. A body had been found on the observation deck of the Empire State Building. This morning's victim had a similar physical description to another man who'd been murdered a month before.

Sinead worked as a profiler for the Bureau and the ADIC wanted her observations.

A crime scene unit from the 130th Precinct was on hand, collecting evidence, along with the investigators and several patrolmen who'd run crime scene tape around the area. Sinead was one of the few representatives from the FBI.

A brown leather backpack was slung over her shoulder. Inside were the tools of her trade. A notepad and pen. Latex gloves. Tablet computer. Evidence bags. She'd never arrested anyone in the five years that she'd been with the Bureau, and still, she carried several sets of flex-cuffs.

She wore her typical attire—a pair of jeans, a blue polo shirt with the FBI's seal embroidered on the breast pocket, an FBI windbreaker and leather sneakers.

Kneeling next to the body of Andrew Capowski, she studied the single bullet hole to the chest. There were powder burns on his blue uniform shirt. "Looks like our killer was close to the victim when they fired their weapon. Andrew was no more than four or five feet away when he was shot. There are also no defensive wounds." She glanced up at lead CSI investigator, Patrick Colton. Patrick was one of Sinead's many cousins who worked in law enforcement. He was thirty-three years old, just a year older than Sinead. Even as a kid, he'd been the smart one. So she knew he'd have a theory when she asked, "What does that mean to you?"

Patrick knelt next to Sinead. He bent down to examine the black residue. "Usually, it means that the victim allowed the murderer to get close. Most likely, he knew his killer."

Anything was possible. "Maybe." The lip of the observation deck was less than four feet away. Sure, the edge was surrounded by fence with a crosshatched metal railing. She scanned the skyline. The sun had risen over the Atlantic Ocean and now the city was bathed in gold. The Hudson River unfurled like a carpet of diamonds.

Even Sinead had to admit, it was an awe-inspiring sight.

"Maybe he was distracted." She rose to her feet. Standing at the railing, she could imagine it all. "Our victim comes up here on his rounds. Maybe he's here every day. But why at this exact time?" she asked. "I think it's for the view. He likes to watch the sunrise."

Patrick came to stand at her side. "You might be right. How does that help us?"

She looked over her shoulder. The door that led from the bank of elevators was less than a dozen feet away. "If he was distracted, someone could get in close before he even knew."

"Do you really think that's possible?" Patrick asked. "I'm not saying you're wrong. He is a security guard, after all."

"Yeah, but the building was closed. Why would he expect anyone else to be on the observation deck— or anywhere they didn't belong for that matter? Or, if someone came out that door, he expected it to be a coworker and he wasn't afraid at all."

"Both could be true at the same time," Patrick suggested. "Mr. Capowski could have been both distracted by the sunrise and familiar with his killer. Or even expecting them." He paused. "He could've been here for a liaison…"

Sinead had another theory in mind.

Last month, when Mark Wheden was killed, the murderer promised that there'd be a new victim. She recalled the macabre note left by the killer. *Until the brilliant and beautiful Maeve O'Leary is freed, I will continue to kill in her name. M down. A up next.*

Andrew Capowski's name did begin with *A*. Was he the promised victim?

"Has he been searched yet?" Sinead asked.

"Not yet. What're you hoping to find…" Something near the bank of elevators caught Patrick's attention.

Sinead looked in the same direction. The doors leading to the elevators, brass and glass, opened. A tall man with dark hair stepped onto the observation deck. He wore a dark suit, white shirt, and tie. She pegged him for a cop from the minute she laid eyes on him. But that didn't do the guy justice. His hair was short and mussed. It was only 7:00 a.m., and already, a five-o'clock shadow covered his cheeks and square chin. He had dark eyebrows over his dark eyes. He was, without question, one of the most handsome men Sinead had ever seen.

That was saying a lot. After all, she'd lived in New York City for years. It was a place filled with actors and models.

The new cop spoke to a patrolman who was guarding the crime scene. He bent in close, a mischievous smile on his lips.

The patrolman roared with laughter. "That's funny, man. Real funny."

So, he had a sense of humor, too. Now Sinéad was truly intrigued.

"Who's he?" she asked her cousin.

Patrick leaned toward her. "That's Wells Blackthorn. He's a detective in the 130th."

"Talk about New York City's finest…" she said, before clamping her jaw shut. It wouldn't do for a special agent to be ogling a detective—even if it was in front of family.

Patrick gave her a side-eye but made no mention of her comment. "You've seen him in the news before. He's a big hot shot with the police department. Everyone loves him."

She watched Wells. He moved like a predatory cat, somehow both languid and alert. Who could blame the world for loving a guy like that?

Chapter 2

Sinead had to focus on the murder investigation—and not think of the handsome Detective Blackthorn.

She said to Patrick, "We need to search this body." After all, Mark Wheden's killer had shoved a note into his pants pocket. If this was the work of the same murderer, there'd be a note as well. She continued, "And there has to be video footage from security cameras." She glanced over her shoulder. Right above the door was the round dome of a lens.

Bingo.

Wells Blackthorn approached. "Morning, Patrick," he said. "What have you got for me?"

"Andrew Capowski," he said before giving a run-down of the facts as they were known. He ended with,

"The medical examiner is on her way, but I think the cause of death is a single gunshot wound to the chest."

"Has the body been searched? Have you recovered footage from the video camera?"

Sincerely, Sinead liked interagency cooperation. It made sense for everyone in the law enforcement world to work together. But she'd been sent to this crime scene by the ADIC of the New York office personally. She'd be damned before being sidelined on this investigation. "We were just about to do both," she said, stepping forward.

"We?" Wells echoed. "Who are you?"

"Special Agent Sinead Colton, FBI."

Folding his arms across his chest, Wells regarded her for a moment. "Thanks for stopping by, but this crime is being investigated by the NYPD. We've got everything covered."

Oh, hell no. "Or maybe it's the FBI who's got this crime scene covered and we don't need your help." Although, what Sinead had suggested wasn't exactly true. At the moment, she and her cousin were the only two from the Bureau on the observation deck.

"Listen, you two, I'd love to continue this pissing contest," said Patrick, his voice filled with sarcasm. "But I've got a crime scene to process. There's plenty for both of you to do and I'd like to search the body before the medical examiner comes to collect the corpse."

Giving a terse nod, Wells said nothing.

"You're right." Sinead promised herself she'd play nice with the detective.

They all knelt next to the body to get a better look.

Wells pointed to black powder surrounding the bullet wound. "Looks like our victim was close to his killer when he got shot."

"Yeah, we noticed that already," said Sinead, her words laced with snark. Sure, she'd promised to be nice. But she had yet to decide how nice she would be. She continued, "It looks like our victim was shot and fell to his back immediately. He bled out from the exit wound. Otherwise, there'd be more blood on his chest."

Patrick said, "I concur."

Sinead looked at the corpse from head to foot. There was something about him. "Does he look familiar to you?"

"Familiar how?" Wells asked.

"He just looks like someone I know…"

"Blond hair. Blue eyes. I know who he looks like to me."

Then she saw the similarity. "He looks like Mark Wheden."

"That's exactly what I was thinking." Wells bent closer to the body. "What's up with this?" he asked. The uniform shirt had two breast pockets, both closed with buttons. A badge, complete with an outline of the Empire State Building, was affixed to one pocket. The other was unbuttoned. After slipping a pair of blue surgical gloves from his pocket, he put them on.

He lifted the flap. The rough edge of a paper was visible. "Patrick, you got an evidence bag?"

"I do," Sinead said. She swung her backpack to her chest. Resting it on her knees, she unzipped the front compartment. There, she found several transparent bags. The words *Evidence* and *FBI* were stenciled on the plastic. She removed one and held it up for Wells. He took the bag, his gloved fingertips grazing hers. An electric charge danced up her arm. He looked up at her. His eyes were wide with surprise.

Had he felt the connection, too?

The last thing that Sinead needed was to get involved with a colleague. Never mind that he was handsome or charming—make that charming to everyone but her. She pulled her hand away. "Before you take that out of his pocket, we need photographic evidence," she said.

A camera hung around Patrick's neck. He snapped several pictures. "Got it."

Sure, Patrick was taking photographs of the letter for the case file. But Sinead wanted pictures of her own. She removed her phone from her bag and took several photographs of the note and the body.

Using the tips of his fingers, Wells withdrew the sheet of paper. Carefully, he unfolded the note. It read, *Until the brilliant and beautiful Maeve O'Leary is freed, I will continue to kill in her name. M A down, E up next.*

"It looks like we have a bigger problem than a single murder," said Wells. "The killer from a few weeks ago has struck again and it doesn't look like they're done yet."

The security for the Empire State Building was managed in a suite of cramped offices in the back corner of the fifty-second floor. Wells sat in one of those offices. Sinead was in a chair beside him. He wasn't sure why the fed was nosing around in his investigation. But he did know that he couldn't get rid of her without causing a stink. So, when he came to interview the victim's supervisor, he invited her to join him.

They faced a cluttered desk. On the other side of the desk was a tall Black man with graying hair. Burt Stanley was the security shift supervisor and the one who had discovered the victim's body.

Burt wore the short-sleeved light blue shirt of all security guards and held a ceramic mug. He lifted the cup to his lips. His hand shook slightly, and coffee sloshed over the rim. Liquid dripped off his wrist. He set the cup back on the desk and blotted his arm on the leg of his trousers.

Picking up the cup again, he took a sip. "I probably don't need the caffeine. My nerves are already fried. What'd I like is a harder drink, but I was with the state police for more than a dozen years. I don't figure you want a witness who's drunk."

"State police? Where'd you work?" Wells asked. Sure, it was inconsequential information, but this was an interview. He'd get more information if the two of them had bonded a bit.

"I worked all the troops in and around the Buffalo area. My wife is a costume designer and she worked for one of the theaters in our area. Then she got a call from a theater company in the city. Kind of like getting pulled up from a minor-league team to play for the major league. With an offer like that, you don't say no." He took another sip of coffee. "I decided to take this job instead of transferring within the state police. The pay is about the same. The hours are better, and the work is easier." He set the cup down on his desk. "Or usually it's easier."

"Tell us about Andrew," said Sinead. "What was he like?"

"Good kid. Wanted to be a cop. He couldn't pass the physical due to a heart condition." Burt leaned back in his chair and rested his hands on his ample stomach. "He was always a strict follower of the rules and he loved to enforce them. Sometimes it was a bit much. A tourist would break a rule and he'd get madder than he needed to."

"So, you'd say he had a temper?" Sinead asked.

Burt leaned forward. "Now, I didn't mean to imply that he was a hothead or anything. It's just that he really wanted to be a cop and viewed himself as the ESB's police officer." He sat back in his seat. "For a while, it was bad. There was a complaint about Andrew every day it seemed. That's when he got transferred to working nights. Me? I never had a problem with him."

Wells nodded. "Let's talk about this morning. What happened?"

Burt sniffed. "It was a little before five. I was here, in my office, and Andrew reached out to me via walkie-talkie. He said something like, 'I've got a problem up here.' I asked him what kind of problem and he didn't answer. I was worried because of the heart condition and all and got there as quick as I could. By the time I showed up, he was dead."

For a moment, nobody spoke.

Sinead was the first to break the silence. "How did Andrew get along with his coworkers?"

"Fine. During the night shift, there's only a handful of people in the building. There's a cleaning crew, but we don't interact with them. Then there's me and nine other officers. Everyone has a section of the building they patrol at different times. They've also got to sit in the video room and watch the security monitors for a few hours."

"Same schedule each night?" she asked.

Burt nodded. "I've used the same schedule for close to a year. If it ain't broke, don't fix it. Ya' know." *Ya* came out as a flat *yah*. A testament to his time in Western New York.

"Since you've worked with Andrew for years, do you have any idea who might want to kill him?" Sinead asked.

Burt sighed. "Like I said, Andrew was a good kid. He and his wife are expecting their first baby in the fall." He drew in a shaking breath. "Poor Vanessa. She's gonna be devastated."

Wells knew they didn't have much more time before the supervisor became too emotional to speak. Still, there were things he needed to know. "Any idea how someone might get into the Empire State Building?"

"None. The front doors are locked and monitored by a guard all night. The side entrances—those used by employees—are controlled by a code. There's no way a random person could just walk in here."

Was the killer an employee at the ESB? What would be the connection to Mark Wheden? Maybe Andrew Capowski was the intended target all along. Maybe the other killing and the note were simply a ruse to kill one man. But why?

There were still more clues to be found, Wells knew. "You said there are cameras throughout the building. I'd like to get a look at the video."

There were more than a hundred cameras in and around the Empire State Building. All the footage was sent to the security office that took up the back corner of the fifty-second floor. More specifically the video was stored in a small windowless room. A table sat in front of a wall of twenty monitors. The only light in the tiny room came from the glowing screens.

The NYPD had sent their own tech expert. It was another of Sinead's cousins, Ashlynn Colton.

Ashlynn sat at one of the tables. She looked up as they entered the room.

"Hey, you two." She gave a wan smile. "I'd say it's good to see you both, but it's never great to be on a murder investigation."

"We're here to see what was caught on camera," said Wells.

Ashlynn made a face.

"Nothing good, I'm guessing," Sinead said. An empty chair sat next to Ashlynn. She dropped into the seat.

"Can I ask one thing before we get started?" Wells stood behind Sinead. She had to turn in the chair to see him. "How many of you Coltons work in New York's law enforcement community? I've seen three of you already today—and it's not even eight o'clock yet."

Ashlynn laughed.

His comment even earned a smile from Sinead. There was a serious reason that she and so many of her cousins had gone into law enforcement. But the story was Ashlynn's to tell. Since Wells had asked a glib question, Sinead gave him an equally glib answer. "We're a big Irish family, what do you expect?"

"It's more than that," Ashlynn said, her tone serious. "My dad was killed by a serial killer."

"Oh, crap, I'm sorry," said Wells. His eyes pinched with concern. "I didn't know."

She shook her head. "It was years ago. We were all kids. But it affected us all. Me, Sinead, my two brothers, Rory."

Rory. The mention of Sinead's half-sister left her uncomfortable. She had to guess that Wells knew Rory, too. The last that she'd heard, her baby sis had been assigned to the 130th Precinct. Opening and closing her palms several times, she let go of the painful emotions that arose whenever Rory's name came up in conversation.

"My condolences on the loss of your father," said Wells again. He looked at Sinead. "To you all."

"Thanks," Sinead mumbled. Then, she added, "We all know the kind of damage a serial killer can cause—not just for the victim, but their families as well. Because of our personal history, we'll all be laser focused on finding this killer." She continued, speaking to Ashlynn, "What kind of video have you found for us?"

Ashlynn said, "We've got people looking at all the video we have. Due to the number of cameras, there are hundreds of hours to review—and that's just for early this morning."

"I can imagine," said Wells.

"So far, this is what we've found." She lifted the lid on her laptop and clicked the mouse. An image appeared on the screen. It was a street view of Fifth Avenue. The time stamp on the video read 4:27 a.m. It was still dark outside, and the streetlamps shone a halo of light. A person in baggy jeans and a black hoodie walked up the street. They stopped beneath a camera and stared into the lens. They wore a pair of sunglasses, even though it was still night. A surgical mask covered the lower half of their face. They also wore a pair of latex gloves.

"This is the first time we see the suspect," said Ashlynn. She clicked the mouse and froze the suspect on the screen.

"They're savvy about the cameras in and around the city," said Sinead, putting voice to her thoughts.

"Sure," said Wells. "Because you can't see their face."

But it was more than that. "Not only have they hidden their face, but their body as well. With the baggy jeans and hoodie, it's impossible to tell their gender. Their hands are even covered, so we can't even guess at a particular race or ethnic group. We might be able to figure out an approximate height. But the suspect could put a pair of lifts in their shoes, giving them an extra inch or two of height."

Wells cursed. "They've thought of everything."

He was right. She said, "My guess is that they're well above average intelligence. I put their age between twenty-five and thirty-five."

"That's pretty specific," he said, a definite challenge to his voice. "How do you figure that?"

"Someone under thirty-five years old has grown up in a world where cameras are everywhere. If they were older, they wouldn't be as aware. And younger?" Sinead shrugged. "This crime took a great deal of planning and patience. The brain's frontal lobes aren't connected until at least twenty-three years old. So, someone younger might not be able to think through a crime to this detail."

"That's a good insight," Wells said. She wasn't certain if he was being sincere—or not.

Sinead asked, "What else do you have for us, Ashlynn?"

"If you thought I didn't have much before," she began, her tone warning, "it's about to get worse."

The picture on the screen began to move again. The suspect stopped at the corner. They pressed their back into the building and blended with the night. At the edge of the screen, Sinead could see a door open. Seven people exited. Each was pushing a large plastic bin on wheels.

"What's going on there?" She touched the image.

"That's the cleaning crew. Garbage is in those bins."

"Let me guess," said Wells. "They take out the trash every morning at four thirty."

"That's my understanding," said Ashlynn.

On the screen, the killer sprinted down the side of the building. They stayed in the shadows, making it impossible for them to be seen. The door had been left open by the cleaning crew. The killer slipped inside and disappeared. A moment later, the crew returned and pulled the door closed.

"Are there any other shots of the killer while he's in the building?" Sinead asked.

"Sure are," said Ashlynn, typing on her keyboard. She brought up a twenty-second clip. "See that?" She touched the screen. "That's an arm." Then she brought up another clip. "You can see a shadow move here." Another clip. "There's a reflection of the killer here…"

"They've definitely done their homework," said Sinead, starting to get a sense of the killer. "They know where all the cameras are located. How hard would it be to get that kind of information?"

"It's not on the internet," said Wells. "The Empire State Building is still considered a terrorist target. Having the security plan accessible to the public would pose too much of a risk."

Sinead reasoned, "But parts of the building are open to the public. The murderer could've done his own reconnaissance."

Wells nodded slowly. "How long does the Empire State Building keep their video?"

Ashlynn sighed. "The system's cleared every twenty-four hours at midnight. All's we've got is today."

"Can you get me high-resolution images of the perp?" Wells asked. "I want to see if we can find anything on pictures. Hell, a label on the backpack would be more than we have right now." He paused. "Though I doubt it. It seems like this person thought of everything." He glanced at Sinead. Her cheeks warmed under his gaze. "You might be right about our doer having above average intelligence."

Before she could reply, her phone pinged with an incoming text. She took the cell from the front pocket of her backpack and glanced at the screen. It was from Xander Washer, the assistant to ADIC Roberta Chang. It read: Chang needs to be briefed on case at Empire State Bldg. Come to the 130th Precinct building. 8:00 a.m. Avoid the media. Direct orders.

Make no mistake, she'd been summoned. There was only one way for her to reply.

On my way.

Chapter 3

Sinead checked the time. It was 7:24 a.m. The 130th Precinct wasn't far away. In fact, it was an easy walk, so long as she left now.

"I have to go." After stowing her phone in her bag, she stood.

Wells looked up from his cell. "Thanks for your help. I gotta get going as well." To Ashlynn he said, "Send me everything you find."

"I'll be done going through the video in a few hours," she said. "I'll send it to you once I'm done."

Giving a smile and wave to both Sinead and Ashlynn, Wells left.

Once he was gone, Sinead leaned on the table where her cousin worked. "What was up with that guy? He was like a tornado. Shows up on the crime scene, blows hard. Then he leaves."

Ashlynn rolled her eyes and shook her head. "I've worked with Wells before. He's not usually intense."

"It's more than being intense. When we first met, he basically told me to get lost. He's rude." She bit off her last word, knowing full well that she was close to complaining. Especially since she lived in New York, a place known for its blunt speaking. And yet, she said, "But to just show up at a murder investigation and leave before the crime scene was processed…" Sinead let her words unravel.

Ashlynn asked, "Didn't you say that you have to go as well?"

The text from Xander. How had she forgotten, even for a minute? "Damn, you're right. It's good to see you."

Ashlynn stood and gave Sinead a quick hug. "Don't take anything Wells says too personally. I heard that his brother died over the Fourth of July weekend. He might still be dealing with that loss."

Sinead wasn't close to her own family, but she knew other families that were very tight. Even other branches of the Colton family tree had groups of siblings who were inseparable—kind of like Ashlynn and her brothers. Did Wells come from one of those close-knit families?

She opened the door and paused on the threshold. "Thanks for everything, including the information about Wells."

After working her way out of the security wing, she hustled down a hallway and toward the service elevators. She rounded the corner and stopped short. There, waiting for the doors to open, was Wells Blackthorn. Her stomach filled with an excited fluttering. What was it about this guy that had gotten her so rattled?

She smoothed down the front of her shirt. "I'm surprised to see you still here." Her words came out with more frost than she intended.

"I was stopped on my way out of the building." He paused. "What about you?"

She shrugged. "Ashlynn *is* my cousin. We chatted for a bit."

He gave a small smile and Sinead's heart betrayed her, beating in triple time. "Oh yeah, I forgot. You Coltons are everywhere."

He wasn't wrong. She shrugged.

The doors opened and he gestured for her to enter the car. She stepped into the elevator, and he followed. She reached out for the button to the first floor at the same instant as Wells. Their hands met, fingers touching, and she froze. She glanced over her shoulder. He was right there. His eyes were more than dark brown. They started off black at the outer edge of the iris and lightened to chocolate before turning golden near the pupil. His scent surrounded her. He smelled of minty toothpaste, musk and—interestingly—milk. The combination was intoxicating.

He let his hand drop and stepped back.

Sinead swallowed and pushed the button for the ground floor. The doors closed, leaving her alone with Wells. She was keenly aware of his presence. The back of her neck tickled, and she glanced over her shoulder again. He was watching her. Their gazes met and held. He was so close that she could reach out and touch him if she wanted—and that was exactly what she wanted to do.

But to what end?

She turned back to face the door. Her reflection was caught in the metal doors. Her blond hair hung around her shoulders. She hadn't bothered with makeup this morning, but she rarely wore any cosmetics. Her blue eyes were bright. Her figure was trim, and her muscles were toned. In short, she liked the way she looked.

Truthfully, she never had issues finding men to date—even if her ex-husband had turned out to be a bastard. So, why the nerves around Wells? He was a good-looking guy. But he was still just a guy.

Maybe she needed to try dating again. Her last foray into dating had been through an app with disastrous results. The "selfies" that guys seemed compelled to send... *Ugh.*

Or maybe she should just focus on her job, like she'd been doing for the past several years.

The elevator stopped and the doors slid open. She exited the car and Wells followed. Walking down another corridor, she wondered what to make of their moment in the elevator. If she turned to look at him again, would he still be watching her?

Once more she glanced over her shoulder. His eyes were glued to the screen of his phone. The fact that he wasn't interested at all stung.

"I suppose I'll see you around."

He glanced up. "Oh, yeah. See you around." As soon as he spoke, he dropped his gaze back to his device.

Sinead walked faster, creating distance between herself and Wells. The hallway led from the service elevator toward the front of the building. A wall separated the working part of the Empire State Building from the public entrance, complete with the building's outline, crafted in metal, on the floor. She pushed open the door and stepped back.

From where she stood, she could see 34th Street, and a gaggle of reporters.

Xander's message from ADIC Chang had been clear. *Avoid the media. Direct orders.*

Now what was she supposed to do? Her shoulders pinched together.

Wells approached her from behind. She could hear his footfalls before he spoke.

"You okay?" he asked.

His scent surrounded her again. It was a combination of clean, sexy and homey. If she were completely honest, it hit all the right notes. She opened the door again and pointed toward the sets of exterior glass doors. "Reporters."

"Damn. How'd they get the scoop so fast?" She didn't think he wanted an answer, so she said nothing. Wells continued. "You know the drill, I'm sure. Just walk past them and tell them, 'No comment.'"

She stepped back from the door and let it shut. Turning to look at Wells, she said, "That's just it, I've been ordered to avoid all media contact. I think that walking through a scrum of reporters would count as contact."

"Then you have yourself a bit of a problem." He wiped his hand over his mouth. "Come with me." He grabbed her wrist. His fingers were warm and strong. "I have an idea."

He led her out of the door and past the security desk. To the left were the public elevators. To the right was an escalator that led to the mezzanine. The horseshoe that overlooked the entrance, one level up from the ground floor, was home to a coffee shop and a two-story drugstore.

Wells jogged toward the escalator and stood on the bottom step as it rotated up. Sinead followed. "Where am I supposed to go from here?" she asked, as the escalator delivered them to the mezzanine.

He gestured to the drugstore. "That has a side entrance onto Sixth Ave. There won't be any reporters waiting outside that door."

"That's brilliant," she said.

He gave her that smile. Her middle filled with excitement again. "I know."

Gripping her elbow, he led her toward the entrance. They entered the store and Sinead let out a long exhale. "Thanks so much." She slipped out of his grip but could still feel the imprint of his palm on her arm. "You've saved my butt."

"Anytime."

They made their way through the cosmetics department and past the row of vitamins and supplements. Another set of escalators—one up and one down—bisected the middle of the store. They took the down escalator to the ground level. Sinead tried to think of something to say. Nothing came to her.

Wells asked, "Can I run a theory by you?"

They stood in the drink aisle. Since nobody else was nearby to overhear their conversation, she asked, "What's up?"

"I think that the killer might've been only after Andrew Capowski."

"And Mark Wheden? What about him?"

"Maybe his killing was a ruse."

Sinead took a moment to think through Wells's supposition. She shook her head. "There are easier ways to kill Capowski. A fake mugging when he leaves work. A hit-and-run at the same time. Besides, who'd want him dead? His boss said that he got along with his coworkers."

"What are your thoughts?"

"I can't figure out the fixation on Maeve O'Leary. But if you want my professional opinion, this is a serial killer in the making. And they aren't going to stop until we stop them."

"I was afraid that's what you were going to say." He handed a bottle of water to Sinead. "Buy this."

"What's this for?" she asked.

"To drink. It's hot outside and you need to stay hydrated," he said. "But it's also a decoy." He pointed to the drugstore's exit. "Without a purchase, some observant reporter might see you walk out empty-handed and wonder why."

"Looks like our killer's not the only one who's good

at problem-solving." She paused. "What's next in the investigation?"

"Hopefully, there's more on the video than Ashlynn's found so far." He checked his phone. "I really do have to get going. Thanks for the insights on the case."

Without another word, Wells left. Sinead shouldn't care. She didn't know the guy—and he certainly didn't owe her anything. She was only doing her job by showing up at the crime scene and examining the evidence. All of that was true. But it was also true that Wells stirred an emotion that she didn't have the courage to examine.

Taking her bottle of water, she walked to the self-checkout and scanned the barcode. After paying with her watch, she walked out of the drugstore. The morning was already hot. The air, humid. She took two steps and perspiration began to cling to her back. Her shirt stuck to her like a second skin. She checked the time. 7:45 a.m. Damn, she'd dawdled too long. If she walked fast, she could make the meeting on time. But then, she'd be a sweaty mess. She couldn't wait for a rideshare, either. Stepping up to the curb, she lifted her hand to hail a taxi.

A yellow cab slid up next to the sidewalk.

She opened the back door and took a seat.

"Where to?" the driver asked.

"46th and Lex," she said. The precinct was located on 46th Street and Lexington Avenue—close to Grand Central Station. At this time of the morning, the streets would be clogged with morning commuters. Sinead worried that she'd be tardy to the meeting. "And take the quickest route."

"Will do," said the driver. He pulled into traffic, his tires squealing.

The acceleration pushed her into the seat, and she relaxed a bit. With a little luck, she'd make it to the meeting on time. Because Sinead was many things—but late to an important briefing was never one of them.

Wells stood in the baby care aisle and scanned the shelves. Diapers. Wipes. Baby food in jars. Baby pain reliever and fever reducer. Hell, there were even picture books. But he couldn't find any teething gel. A woman in a red apron walked past. The store's name was stenciled across the chest.

"Excuse me," he said, stopping her with his words. "Where's the gel for teething babies?"

She looked at the shelves with him. "It's usually right here." She placed the tips of her fingers on the empty shelf. "But it looks like we're all out."

Wells had the whole day ahead of him to find something to help Harry, so he was neither disappointed nor frustrated. After thanking the clerk, he paid for his water and left the store.

A truck for a national media organization was parked on the sidewalk. That was one thing about living in New York City—local news quickly became national news. He could already tell that this newest murder was going to be the main attraction in what was sure to become a media circus.

So, yeah, Wells had a lot of problems to occupy his

thoughts. A killer on the loose. A cranky baby at home. The need to handle the media. What's more, he'd been called back to his office for a special meeting. So, the last thing he needed was to have something else on his mind.

But he did.

Walking down the street, he couldn't stop thinking about Sinead Colton. The special agent was smart, proficient, and sexy as hell. He'd like to get to know her better. What was he thinking? He didn't have time for a personal life, not with Harry needing so much of his time.

It was best if he put his libido on ice for a while.

He'd parked his unmarked police car at the curb. To keep from getting ticketed or towed, he'd placed an NYPD placard on the dashboard. After unlocking the door, he slipped into the driver's seat. His phone pinged with an incoming text.

Wells glanced at the screen. The message was from his precinct captain, Colleen Reeves.

You on your way?

He replied.

Be there soon.

Then, he sent a second message.

The media's already gotten wind of this story. News vans are all over 34th and 5th.

She replied.

Just get back to the office. We're all here and you're going to be late.

Wells didn't care much for punctuality. To him, the important thing was that the job got done right. He tossed his phone onto the passenger seat and pulled into traffic. As he drove, he wondered what kind of meeting was so important as to pull him off a homicide investigation.

Thanks to the taxi driver, Sinead arrived at the home of the 130th Precinct with five minutes to spare. In all honesty, she'd have preferred extra time, but at least she wasn't going to walk into the meeting once it was underway. The precinct was housed on the bottom seven floors of a high-rise on Lexington Avenue.

She pushed open the door and entered a small waiting room. A woman sat behind a pane of thick, bulletproof glass. She wore an NYPD uniform and name tag that read Margaret Chase, Duty Sergeant. "Can I help you?" she asked.

"Sinead Colton." She held up her FBI credentials for the woman to see. "I have a meeting."

"They're expecting you." The duty sergeant pointed to a door next to the window. "Pull on the handle when you hear a click."

She heard the latch release and opened the door. Next to the door sat the duty sergeant's desk. Margaret pointed down a hallway to the right. "The conference room is on the third floor. You can use the elevator, but it's slow."

"I'll take the stairs."

The other woman pointed to a door on the left. "The stairs are right there."

Her phone pinged with an incoming text. It was Xander Washer, the ADIC's assistant.

Where are you?

She typed out her reply.

Coming up the stairs.

He sent another text.

I'll meet you.

She walked up to the third-floor landing and opened the metal fire door. The door led to a large room. It was filled with workstations that were partitioned off with half walls. Even at 7:55 a.m., almost every desk was filled. Agents and analysts spoke on the phone, the din of conversation making it impossible to hear a single word.

Xander Washer, ADIC Chang's assistant, met Sinead by the door. He was twenty-nine years old, only three years younger than Sinead. Yet to her, it always seemed like the age difference was more. He wore his light brown hair short and had blue eyes. For the day, he'd donned a slim black suit, gray shirt and no tie. "Thanks for coming in so early." He walked down a side corridor and she followed. "They're all in the conference room and waiting for your presentation."

Nobody said anything about a presentation. She stopped. "Who's waiting for what?"

He walked a few steps before turning to regard her. "Chang's there along with Colleen Reeves," he said. "She's the captain at the 130th Precinct. They're putting together a combined NYPD-FBI task force and you need to provide them with a briefing."

"You can't drop something big like this on me at the last minute. I need time to organize my presentation." A knot dropped into her middle. She hated being unprepared—it was almost as bad as being late. Then again, bowing out was the last thing that she'd do. "I'm okay," she said. "Just give me a minute."

Xander started to walk again.

Taking her phone from her pocket, she pulled up her contact list. She found Ashlynn's number and typed out a text as she kept pace with Chang's assistant.

Can you send me the video of the killer sneaking in through the opened door? It's important.

Ashlynn replied.

Done.

A second message appeared on Sinead's phone. It was a file with the video.

She replied.

Thx.

Since her phone and tablet computer shared files, Sinead should be able to bring up both the photographs from the crime scene, along with the video. It wasn't much, but she was always prepared to do her best. Certainly, what she had to say would suffice.

But in the back of her mind was the same old voice that always told her that same thing. *No matter how hard you try, you'll never be good enough.*

Chapter 4

Xander opened the door to the conference room and held it as Sinead crossed the threshold. The conference room sat in a corner of the building, with narrow windows that looked onto Lexington Avenue. A screen, which was remotely connected to a computer, hung on the back wall.

A large table sat in the middle of the room with seats for a dozen. Only two of the chairs were occupied. Roberta Chang sat at the head of the table. Her black hair was swept into a bun at the nape of her neck. She wore a black silk shirt and black slacks. To Chang's left was another woman with white-blond hair and bright blue eyes. A NYPD badge hung from a chain around her neck. She wore a linen blazer over a silk T-shirt. Sinead assumed that the second woman was Captain Reeves, of the 130th Precinct.

"Ms. Chang," said Xander. "Sinead Colton's here to give the briefing."

Nodding at Sinead, Chang said, "Thanks for coming by on such short notice."

Sinead didn't have much of a choice beyond showing up and giving the briefing. Still, it was kind of her boss to say thanks.

She removed her tablet computer from her bag. "Is there any way I can connect this to the screen? There are some things I'd like to show you all."

Xander stepped forward. "I can get you connected."

Maybe she shouldn't have snapped at him. A small pang of guilt struck her in the chest as she handed over her computer.

"Thanks," she whispered.

"No problem," he whispered back. And then, he said, "I'll have this set up in just a second."

Reeves waved her hand. "Take your time. We're still waiting for the head of the task force to arrive."

It took less than five minutes for Xander to get Sinead connected to the computer system. "Are we ready now?" Chang asked of Reeves. "Or do you want to wait for your detective?"

Reeves blew out a long breath. "Let's just get started."

The ADIC looked at Sinead. "You may begin."

Using her tablet computer, she chose a photograph. The image of the note found at the crime scene appeared on the large screen.

"To begin with, this was found on the body of Andrew Capowski, a security guard at the Empire State Building. The letter is with the NYPD crime scene unit, and they will have a more in-depth analysis of the paper, handwriting, etcetera. Also, they will be able to compare it to the letter that was found with Mark Wheden's body. But the wording on this letter matches the one found with the victim in Central Park. Furthermore…" She brought up another photograph, this one of Andrew. "Both men have similar *looks*." She hooked the last word with air quotes. "They're Caucasian. Blond hair, blue eyes. Age and build are both similar…"

The door opened and all heads turned. Sinead's words dried up like a stream during a drought.

Wells stood on the threshold. He gave a grin. "Am I late or something? Parking around here is a nightmare."

She held her breath. The blowback to his flippant comment was sure to be swift and severe.

Reeves just shook her head. "Nice of you to join us, Wells," she said, like an overly indulgent aunt. "Have a seat and we'll get back to Agent Colton's briefing. Unless you have something to add."

Was that it? Her jaw went slack for a moment. Then, she ground her teeth back together. Wells was one of *those people.* Good looking and charming, he relied on both to get what he wanted. He was the kind of person who flitted through life, never taking any responsibility, yet somehow always getting positive attention from their higher-ups.

Sinead loathed *those people.*

Maybe it was a good thing that she was done with

this case after her briefing. Then, at least, she could put Wells into her rearview mirror and never look back.

He took a seat at the end of the table, next to Sinead and the screen. As he moved, his scent wafted over her. Her heart skipped a beat. She couldn't help herself. She was drawn to Wells.

Chang said to Sinead, "You can continue. What's your assessment? Is this the work of a serial killer?"

She glanced at the screen. What did she think? "Technically, there need to be three killings by the same person that are similar—either in MO or the types of victims selected. Right now, we're only at two. But it's my assessment that the killer isn't done. They plan to spell out the name of Maeve O'Leary in victims, that is unless they are stopped."

"What is it about the Black Widow Killer that's so appealing?" Roberta Chang asked, using the media's nickname for Maeve O'Leary.

"Most serial killers have childhood trauma and dysfunctional families. Maybe Maeve reminds the killer of his mother. Perhaps, in his mind, he's protecting her," she said before adding, "Then, the victims would be a father figure."

Xander grunted and rolled his eyes.

Yep, he really was immature.

Nobody else seemed to be bothered by his antics. Sinead made no comment.

"You said *he*." Captain Reeves emphasized the pronoun. "Is there any reason you've assigned a gender to the killer?"

"We don't have evidence that the killer is a male,"

said Wells. "Other than the statistic that most serial killers are men."

"Do you have any clues to help identify the killer?" Chang asked.

"In all honesty," said Sinead. "No."

Wells spoke again. "We do know that the killer is above average intelligence and very careful to conceal their identity."

Yep, he really was one of *those people*. It seemed like Wells was ready to take credit for her analysis.

He continued, "They were caught on camera. Because they wore a surgical mask and sunglasses, their face is completely hidden. They also wore loose-fitting clothing, hiding their shape."

Sinead added, "They could be any gender, race, or age." Although her comment added nothing new to the conversation.

Wells continued, "I'd estimate their age to be between twenty-five and thirty-five. The killer is thoughtful, which means that their brain is fully developed. On the other hand, they're technologically savvy enough to know where all the security cameras are located at the ESB and avoid being photographed."

Oh, hell no. Was Wells really going to take credit for all of Sinead's ideas? Or maybe that wasn't a question she should be asking at all—because he obviously had.

"That's very astute of you," said Chang.

Sinead tried not to glare. She tried not to judge Wells. Although, he deserved both a dirty look and her low opinion.

"It wasn't me," he said, giving his easy smile. "It was Sinead Colton who came up with all the brilliant ideas."

Okay, so maybe he wasn't that bad of a guy.

"What else have you found?" Chang asked. "Have you figured out how he knew when the cleaners were going to leave the door open?"

"My assessment is that he's done a good bit of reconnaissance. That's how he knew when the cleaning crew took out the trash and when Andrew Capowski would be alone."

"I hate the smart criminals," said Reeves. "The dumb ones are always easy to catch."

Wells added, "This one seems especially intelligent."

"Thanks to both Agent Colton and Detective Blackthorn for their preliminary investigation," said Chang. As she spoke, Xander unplugged Sinead's computer and handed it to her. She took a seat next to Wells. The assistant hooked up another device. Then Chang continued, "We have one more problem to discuss before the task force meets to get started on the case."

On cue, Xander pulled up an article that was just posted in the online edition of the *New York Daily Herald.* It was accompanied by several pictures. There was one with crime scene tape across the doors of the Empire State Building. Another showed a line of police vehicles parked on Fifth Avenue. The final one was of two shadowy figures standing in a doorway. It was a photograph of Sinead and Wells looking at each other.

Sure, the image was grainy. But she could see the interest in her face as she looked at Wells. The question was, what did everyone else see?

The headline read: *Killer Strikes Again at NYC Landmark*. The byline was given to a reporter named Nadeem Alvi.

Wells made a noise that could have meant anything.

"What?" she asked.

"Nadeem," he said with a groan. "Speaking of intelligent people who are easy to hate."

As a profiler, she never dealt with the media. But the *Daily Herald* was a widely respected publication—not just in the city but around the world. "What's the matter with Nadeem?"

Wells said, "For starters, he'd publish a critical story about his mother just to get clicks."

"So, he's ambitious," said Sinead.

"He's a journalist," said Reeves, her tone salty. "And he's doing his job, Wells. Don't let him stop you from doing yours."

Sinead guessed that there was a history between the detective and the journalist. What was it? She hadn't a clue. Wells was proving to be quite a puzzle. Her opinion of him had changed more than once since he arrived on the crime scene. Slipping her tablet computer into her bag, she figured that the real Wells Blackthorn could remain an enigma. She'd done her job and shared her findings. The only thing left was for the briefing to officially end, and she'd be free of the handsome detective.

Reeves continued, "Roberta and I have assembled a task force of FBI agents from the New York Field Office and detectives from the NYPD. Like we discussed, you're the leader, Detective Blackthorn. Everyone on the task force—including those from the Bureau—will report to you. You'll report to me. I'll be in contact with Roberta." She stood, ending the meeting. "Wells, we've given you a conference room on the fifth floor. The rest of your team is upstairs and waiting."

Sinead stood and slung her bag over her shoulder. "If you need anything else, you can reach me at Twenty-seven Fed," she said.

ADIC Chang got to her feet. "I think you've mistaken your role on this case, Special Agent. You aren't simply consulting on this morning's crime scene. You're part of the task force. If we are going to stop and catch this killer, it's going to take the best law enforcement minds in the city—yours included."

The fifth-floor conference room consisted of three tables that were pushed together to make a large block. Chairs surrounded all four sides. A TV monitor was affixed to one corner. A row of whiteboards stood along one wall. On the opposite side of the room was the single door. There were no windows and fluorescent lights were tucked into the ceiling.

The setup was supremely uninspirational. But as Wells crossed the threshold, his blood began to buzz. It wasn't just because he was following Sinead Colton and had more than once noticed how nicely her rear and hips filled out her jeans.

The team was already gathered. Eight people were seated around the table. Five men. Three women. Four feds. Four detectives from the NYPD. Wells knew them all. Stan Wojcik, Jayden Clarke, Kiri Nang, and Pedro Rocha were from the police department. Mateo Lopez,

Ilia Federov, Jane Griffiths, and Dave Tkachuk were the representatives from Team Fed.

Sinead hooked the straps from her bag over a chair back and sat.

The quiet chatter stopped as he walked to the front of the room. Wells picked up a dry-erase marker and wrote four words, in two-word pairs. He pointed to each set of words as he read. "Mark Wheden and Andrew Capowski. I want you to remember their names. These men are the reason we are here today. Their lives were cut short through no fault of their own. What's more, we have reason to believe that their murderer isn't done killing yet." He paused to let the gravity of his words sink in. "Bringing justice to these men and their families is your first priority. This killer needs to be stopped before anyone else gets hurt. You men and women are the best of the best." He pointed to a few people around the table. "All except you all from the FBI, but those of us with the NYPD will let you ride our coattails to the top." He smiled wide to show that he was joking. His comment earned him quiet chuckles from the audience.

"Now, let's start brainstorming on a plan of action." He paused before asking, "What do we know about the killer? Or the victims?"

"According to the letter, the next victim's first name will start with *E*," said Sinead. "Combine that with the physical description—blond hair, blue eyes, Caucasian. Age is roughly early to midthirties."

On a second whiteboard, he wrote down the facts that she'd shared. "Good start. Do we know anything else?"

Pedro said, "Both victims worked at a New York City landmark and were killed at work. That could be a connection."

While nodding, he wrote that on the whiteboard as well.

Ilia, one of the agents with the FBI, said, "It looks like we have enough specifics to get a list of possible victims. I say that we find out who else might be on the killer's list and warn them."

Wells had to admit, he loved the exchange of ideas that came from gathering a group of highly talented investigators. Ilia was right, they needed to get in touch with potential victims. "Any idea how we can get a list of employees at city landmarks?"

Stan said, "I doubt there's a single database. It's not like they all work for the city of New York or anything."

"Still, everything's on the internet," said Sinead, typing a message on her phone. "We just have to know where to look or who to ask." She set her phone aside. "I just sent a text to Ashlynn Colton. She'll see what she can find and get back to us."

"While we wait for that," Wells began, "Sinead, can you share what you found at the Empire State Building? There are cables to connect your tablet to the TV." He pointed to a small round table that sat beneath the TV. Atop the table were several cords.

It took her only a few minutes to connect her computer and another ten minutes to give her briefing, complete with photographs of the letter and the victim, and video of the killer. She went over the same information that she'd shared with Reeves and Chang, so Wells was able to study Sinead without being too obvious.

He'd already noticed that she was attractive. But there was more to her than beauty. She was smart, observant and perceptive. Sure, she was a perfectionist—something that Wells was not. But she was definitely someone he would trust. Could there ever be any more between them?

Then again, he didn't have space in his life for romance. Slipping his phone from his pocket, he checked to see if Deborah had texted anything about Harry. She hadn't. He supposed that the adage about no news being good news was true.

"Any questions?" Sinead asked, finishing her briefing.

There were none.

Sinead continued, "While I was talking, Ashlynn texted me. She has a list of people who fit the criteria for a possible victim."

"Send the list to everyone on the task force. We need to warn these men that they might just end up in a killer's crosshairs—literally."

She used her tablet computer and forwarded the message.

Everyone around the table looked at their phones.

Mateo said, "I can talk to the first two on the list. The Intrepid and the Javits Center are right by each other."

"I can go with you," Kiri added.

Two things made sense to Wells. "The task force should be broken into teams of two. One NYPD detective. One agent from the FBI." He went around the room, matching agents with detectives. "Meet with your partner and make a plan for the day."

Chair legs scraped across the floor as people traded places. The din of conversation filled the room.

Once everyone was seated with their partner, it left two people. Wells and Sinead.

He glanced in her direction. Their gazes met and locked. Even if he'd wanted to, he couldn't look away. Her eyes were more than blue. They were bright and brilliant like sapphires but a million times more beautiful than any gem. Even in the dingy conference room, her blond hair shimmered with gold. Her lips were a shade of musky red and oh so kissable.

Leaning his elbows on the table, he said, "Looks like it's just you and me."

She smiled and his pulse raced.

"Looks like it," she said.

"Will you be okay with that?"

She sat back in her chair and folded her arms across her chest. "Of course," she said. "I'm a professional. I can work with you or anyone else in this room."

He was glad that she was a professional. Because the way she sat, leaning back slightly, forced her breasts against the fabric of her shirt in a tantalizing way. Images filled his mind that were not professional in the slightest.

He dropped his gaze to the table. "It seems like we got off on the wrong foot at the Empire State Building."

"What gives you that idea? Because you tried to kick me off the crime scene?" Her tone was filled with sarcasm. "I'm not going to hold a grudge—not even for you trying to pass off my findings as your own."

"Hey," he protested. "I told Reeves and Chang that all the ideas were yours. I also told them that you were the brilliant one—not me."

She gave a wry laugh and shook her head. "You really are charming."

He gave her his best smile. "You say that like it's not a compliment."

"It's not," she said while shoving her phone into her backpack.

Wells should be happy that Sinead wasn't attracted to him in the slightest. Leaning back in his chair, he stretched out his legs. How many times this morning had he decided that a relationship with Sinead was a bad idea? Or maybe he should be asking another question. How many more times would he have to remind himself that he needed to avoid getting tangled up with her before he believed it?

Chapter 5

Sinead needed to draw some boundaries with Wells if they were going to be partners.

He watched her with his amazing brown eyes, and she started to sweat. She'd never let him know that he'd gotten under her skin. Raising her chin defiantly, she asked, "There something you want?"

"Yeah," he said. "I want to start over." He held out his hand to her. "My name's Wells Blackthorn, NYPD detective from the 130th. And you are?"

She couldn't help it and laughed. "Oh, you are smooth, aren't you?" She reached for his outstretched palm. Her hand touched his and her flesh warmed. A current danced along her skin.

She gazed at Wells. The vein at the base of his throat

thrummed with the same energy that raced through her veins.

She swallowed and tightened her grip on his hand. "Special Agent Sinead Colton. FBI. Profiler."

"Nice to meet you," he said with a smile.

Now what? She withdrew her hand from his. "Thanks for the reset."

"I hope that we're good now," he said.

"We're good."

He said, "Being the task force leader's partner comes with the dubious honor of getting all the grunt work. Let's see who's left on our list of potential victims."

Sinead had already put away her tablet. She withdrew it from her bag. "We should create a document to share," she said. "That way everyone can enter up-to-the-minute information."

"Good idea," said Wells. "And it wasn't a false compliment what I said to Reeves and Chang. You are brilliant and organized—two things I am not."

Her face warmed with his compliment until Sinead worried that she'd started to glow. She opened the list of names she'd received from Ashlynn before transferring them to a new document. Wells read off the list of the teams tasked with interviewing each one. He concluded by saying, "That leaves Edward Pendleton at the Metropolitan Museum of Art and Edgar Goldman who works as a ticketing agent at Grand Central. We can speak to both of those men. Anything else?"

She held up the device so he could see the screen. She said, "I've sent the team a link to a document. It has a list of our potential victims, along with those who've been assigned to make contact. We all have editing access to enter case notes. That way, everyone will know what's going on in real time."

"Another good idea from a brilliant lady."

She gave an exaggerated eye roll. "I bet you say that to all the women."

He smiled. "Only the ones who really deserve it."

Her cheeks warmed, but she said nothing.

"It's time to get to work." He stood and waited for the conversations going on around the room to stop. "Everyone's been sent a link to a document by Sinead. You have editing access. Enter any case notes so we're all on the same page—literally. We'll meet back here at four thirty for a briefing. If you need anything in the meantime, I've got my phone." He slipped it out of his pants pocket as if to prove a point. He glanced at the screen, pausing for a moment. It was the second time in less than ten minutes that he'd looked at his phone. Was he addicted to the device? After all, a lot of people had a compulsion to look at their phones constantly.

Or was he expecting an important message?

She didn't like the idea of Wells being distracted, especially during such a critical time in the investigation. She also didn't like the nagging feeling that he was hoping to get a message from a woman. And what she really didn't like was the fact that she cared at all.

Looking around the room, Wells continued, "Whoever murdered Mark Wheden and Andrew Capowski is a danger to our city. I have confidence in each and every one of you. We can find the killer and keep New York safe."

In pairs, the members of the task force left the conference room. Sinead stood and slung her bag over her shoulder. Wells wiped away a bead of sweat from his brow with the side of his hand. Sure, it was hot as hades outside. But the thermostat in the conference room was set at arctic. What had left him sweating?

"You okay?" she asked.

Without bothering to meet her gaze, he gave a small smile and shook his head. "I try to be inspiring, but I never know exactly what to say."

"You did good," she said. And he had. "I can see why you were selected as the task force leader. You're a natural in the role."

"Thanks."

More than the sweat on his brow, Wells had dark smudges under each eye. Was he ill? "I noticed that you keep checking your phone…" Maybe he was waiting for test results from a doctor.

He looked at Sinead and her breath caught in her chest. God, he was good looking. That five-o'clock shadow she'd noticed already covered his cheeks and chin. Far from making him look unkempt, it gave Wells a rugged air. "It's nothing like that…" His words unraveled.

She waited a moment and then a moment more. He said nothing. She stepped toward the door. "I'm ready to get started, if you are."

"Wait," he said, his one word stopping her.

She turned. "What is it?"

"Right now, my life is complicated. I'm exhausted and I am distracted."

So, she'd been right. It was another woman. Even though she expected the blow, disappointment was a sucker punch to the gut. "Your personal life is none of my business."

"I guess that you're right about that, too. For now, you're my partner and I wanted to let you know about my headspace. But I also wanted to let you know that my problems won't interfere with the investigation— not anymore, at least. I meant what I said. Finding the killer is my top—and only—priority."

Sinead wasn't sure if she liked Wells or not. She did, however, admire the hell out of him. "I appreciate your candor."

Wells straightened his tie and nodded toward the door. "All right then, let's roll."

They left the conference room. New York City was a study in contrasts. While developers were tearing down old buildings all over the island to put up gleaming new skyscrapers, many other buildings were ignored. The 130th Precinct was in one of those long-ignored buildings. The hallway was narrow and dark. Paint that at one time might have been mint had faded to a bile green. The floor tiles were swept clean but, after years of use, they were stained and chipped.

At the end of the hallway was a set of stairs behind a fireproof door. They took the steps to the ground floor. The landing ended in a massive workroom that was filled with desks, ringing phones and working uni-formed officers.

The duty sergeant's desk sat behind a wall with a pane of bulletproof glass. On the other side of the wall was a waiting room, and beyond that the door outside. It was the same door Sinead had used when she arrived at the precinct little more than an hour earlier.

Wells approached the duty sergeant with a smile. It was the same person Sinead had seen earlier. "Morning," he said to the woman who sat behind the desk. "How're the kids? The little one feeling better?"

"He's right as rain," she said, smiling back. "But now his big brother is sick."

With the shake of his head, he said, "I hope he gets better soon."

"It's hard when your babies are sick. Thankfully, their dad can work from home this week."

Wells lifted his chin toward Sinead. "Margaret, I want you to meet Agent Colton with the FBI. She's working with me on a task force, so you might see her around."

"I met the special agent when she arrived, but it's nice to have a formal introduction. It's a pleasure to meet you."

Sinead wished that she had a tiny bit of Wells's interpersonal skills. Still, she managed a smile and said, "Same here."

Wells said, "We have to go. People to meet. Criminals to catch. You know the drill."

"I do indeed," said Margaret.

Pushing the door open with his back, he spoke to Margaret. "You stay healthy, you hear me? I won't want to come into work if I can't see your happy face."

She laughed as he crossed the threshold. "You have a good day and be careful out there."

"Will do," he called over his shoulder.

A narrow room that served as a waiting area sat beyond the duty sergeant's desk. On the far side of the room, a set of doors led to the street. She and Wells crossed the small space, and Sinead pushed the door open. Wells stepped outside. She stole a glimpse of his nice rear as he passed by. Then, she followed him. The air was heavy with humidity, and heat radiated off the pavement. Sun reflected off the surrounding windows; the glare was blinding. She looked in her bag for her sunglasses. As she slipped on her shades a woman rounded the corner.

As if Sinead had been bolted to the steps, she stopped walking. Sweat gathered at the nape of her neck and it wasn't entirely because of the oppressive heat. The woman climbed two steps. She glanced at Sinead and stopped.

"Hey, Rory," she said, trying to smile. How long had it been since she'd seen her half sister? Weeks? Months? It definitely hadn't been more than a year since they'd last spoken. Or had it?

"How are you doing?" Rory wore a pair of sunglasses as well. She slid them onto the top of her head, holding back her wavy hair. Looking into her half sister's eyes was like looking into a mirror. Then again, their eyes were about the only thing they had in common. "Been a long time."

"I was just thinking the same thing." She paused. "You look good." Rory did look good. She wore a pair of jeans, leather tennis shoes and a short-sleeved blouse.

"Look at you, you're not even sweating. Me, I look like the public waterworks."

Rory laughed. "You don't look like you're sweaty at all. But this heat. Ugh."

"Yeah, ugh." Jeez, the conversation was so lame that it had already moved on to the worst topic ever. The weather. Now what was she supposed to say?

Rory asked, "So what're you doing here? I thought you were working out of the Federal Building?"

Wells stood nearby. She nodded toward the handsome detective. "I'm assigned to a joint FBI-NYPD task force."

Rory gave a quick smile. "Then maybe I'll see you around."

"Maybe." As always, she was conflicted whenever she saw her half sister. It wasn't Rory's fault that Sinead's dad was a cheating rat-bastard. Nor was it Rory's fault that their dad left Sinead and her mom for another woman. Even if that other woman was Rory's mom, and the fact that she was pregnant with Rory was why he left.

She drew in a deep breath. Muggy air filled her lungs. Sinead felt like she was drowning. "Well, I better go." Skipping down three steps, she passed Rory. "I'll see you around, okay?"

"Okay."

She walked down the final two steps. True, their dad had died years ago, but the fact that he'd chosen another family—another daughter—over her was a wound that never healed. Gripping the strap of her backpack, she strode down the street.

"Hey," Wells called out. "Wait up."

She stopped and turned to face him.

"My car is over here." He pointed to a black SUV that sat at the opposite end of the block. "It's hot as blazes out here and the Met is more than forty blocks away. I guess we could walk, but honestly, I'd rather not."

"A ride is definitely better." Her face flamed. "Thanks."

As she followed Wells, she wondered how often she'd run into Rory. True, her sister was assigned to the 130th, but it was a big precinct. Maybe they'd never see each other.

Oh, who was Sinead kidding—other than herself?

She was bound to see her sister now more than ever. She hated that each time they met it was hella awkward. But was it even possible to reconcile a relationship that never was?

"What's up with my ride?" Wells asked.

It was a question that he did expect to have answered. Sinead moved closer to him, to see what he saw. "What do you mean?"

Pointing to his car, he asked, "Do I have a flat or something?"

He was right. The left rear bumper was lower than the other four. They jogged to the SUV and examined the tire. Yeah, the tire was flat. But there was more. A gash was opened on the sidewall.

"You think the inner tube exploded?" she asked.

A screwdriver, the head sharp and gleaming in the sun, lay under the rear axle. Wells nudged it with his toe. "I don't think this was an accident. Someone deliberately slashed my tire. You'd think that being so close to a police station would keep punks from playing stupid pranks." He cursed. "I don't have time for this. We have to get to the Met." He pulled the phone from his pocket and placed a call. "Margaret, it's me, Wells," he said, talking to the duty sergeant. "I need someone to fix a flat tire. My car's at the end of the block." He paused. "Thanks. You're the best," he said, ending the call. "My SUV will get taken care of, but for now, I'm without a car."

She pointed across the street. A railing surrounded a set of stairs that descended under the sidewalk. "We're New Yorkers. We take the subway."

He gave her that smile and her belly flopped. "Let's go."

They waited for a break in traffic. Side by side, they jogged across the street. Taking the stairs to the subway station, they paused at the gate. Sinead kept her Metro card handy by stowing it in the front pocket of her backpack. She swiped the card. A light in the turnstile turned from red to green and she pushed through the security arm. Wells followed.

The platform was empty, save for the pillars that held up the ceiling. She checked her watch. It was 10:43 a.m. At this time of the day, the service was sporadic. "Who knows when we'll see a train," she said. The air on the platform was as heavy and hot as the air on the street level—maybe hotter. "But at least there's no sun."

Wells gave a snort of a laugh. "Ain't that the truth." He paused a beat. "So, you Coltons really are everywhere. I saw you chatting with Rory. She's another cousin, I assume."

Sinead gave a quick shake of her head. "She's my sister."

"Sister. No kidding. I don't know her well, but I never heard Rory mention having a sister who played for Team Fed."

"She's my half sister," Sinead clarified. "We've never been close. Funny we share half our DNA and a parent, and at the same time, she's not much more than a stranger." She wasn't sure why she'd shared such an intimate detail with Wells. Maybe it was because on the empty platform, there was nobody around to hear her—other than the detective. Or maybe she was starting to fall for his charm.

"Sibling relationships can be hard," he said.

Then she remembered what Ashlynn had said about his brother's recent death. "I heard what happened to your brother. I'm sorry."

"Yeah, thanks. It was a real shock. Dan and his wife were staying with friends in the Hamptons for the July Fourth holiday. They were coming home from another party and a distracted driver failed to yield at a stop sign. I'm not even sure that Dan knew what hit him."

"Jeez, it just happened on the Fourth?" It was only a few weeks ago. "Are you okay to be back at work?"

"I can't sit around my apartment and mope. I need to do something. Besides, being a cop is who I am. It's not just what I do."

Sinead felt much the same about her job with the FBI. "It's a calling."

"I knew you'd get it."

Yeah, she was definitely starting to feel something for him. She wanted to touch him. To rest her hand on his arm. Or to stroke the side of his face. To offer him some sort of comfort.

Yet physical contact wasn't appropriate. Clenching her hands into fists, she pressed them to her side. "I am sorry about your brother."

He pinned her with his gaze. "I appreciate that. Sincerely."

The rumble of a distant train came from deep inside the tunnel. The sound grew to a roar—a giant waking from a deep sleep. Hot air was pressed out of the concrete tube and blew across the platform.

"That's the B line." The brakes screeched as the train came to a stop. Wells had to yell to be heard over the noise. "It'll get us close enough to Central Park. From there, we can walk to the museum."

"There's just one thing I want now, though," she said.

"Yeah? What's that?"

The doors opened with a whoosh and cool air poured out of the car. "I just want that air-conditioning."

Chapter 6

The subway car was half-full. All the seats were attached to the car's wall and faced the center aisle. A family—two dads and a toddler in a stroller—sat across from the doors. An elderly couple sat at the far end of the train. A group of college-aged kids consulted a paper map and their phone. She recognized enough of their words to know they spoke Spanish. But she didn't speak enough Spanish to offer her help. Several other seats were taken by single riders. One man read. A woman swayed to the music only she could hear through wireless headphones. A man in a suit sat next to a woman in sweats.

It was people from all walks of life—and from all over the world.

This was one of the many things that she loved about the City.

She took an empty seat and Wells sat next to her. He nudged her with his elbow. "Happy you got air-conditioning?"

"Ecstatic." She paused a beat. "Is it just me, or do the summers seem hotter than when we were kids?"

"I dunno. My parents owned a cottage on Cayuga Lake. It's one of the Finger Lakes near Ithaca. When I was a kid, we headed to the lake as soon as school got out and didn't come back until right before Labor Day."

After her dad left, Sinead's mother had to struggle to make ends meet. There was no extra money for a summer home. Her mom couldn't go for more than a week without earning a paycheck—much less months on end. Still, a childhood of summers swimming in a cool and clear lake sounded idyllic. "I bet it was nice."

"It was." He laughed. "We had a wooden dock that led from the yard out to the lake. Dan and I used to run across that dock doing the Tarzan yell and then see who could jump farther into the water. It was fun. The neighbors probably hated us."

She laughed, too. "What'd your parents do for work that they could take off the whole summer?"

"Mom taught third grade at a private school in Midtown. She had all summer off. Dad taught economics at NYU. He taught summer classes at Ithaca College and Cornell."

"Where are your parents now?" she asked—partly being nosey, partly making conversation.

"They passed away three years ago. A sailing accident off Long Island."

"I'm sorry. Any other siblings?"

He shook his head. "Nope."

Both of his parents and his brother were dead. That meant that Wells was all alone. Her heart ached for him.

"You want to know what sucks the worst?" he asked. His story sounded pretty awful to begin with. Sinead had a hard time imagining what might be worse.

Still, she asked, "What?"

"After my folks died, Dan and I had to decide what to do with their property. He wanted to sell the cabin. I wanted to keep it." He rubbed the back of his neck. "I mean, I hadn't been to the lake in years. But of all the places out there, the cabin was home. Dan was insistent. The market value had gone through the roof. We'd make a ton of cash. Mom and Dad wouldn't want us to fight. Blah, blah, blah. I wanted to keep the place, but it wasn't worth the hassle. I caved. We sold."

"I can see how that would be upsetting."

"No, really. It gets worse. Dan took his share of the money and bought this sleek sports car. Some Italian thing that looked like sex on wheels." She could guess where the story was going. "It was that damned car he was driving when he died. The thing was totaled and now, even the car's gone."

Sinead's throat tightened, like a closed fist.

She opened her mouth. He held up a hand. "Please don't tell me that you're sorry again. I can take a lot—but not pity."

He looked at her. Her heartbeat began to race. She

dropped her gaze. Their hands sat on the plastic bench, so close they could almost touch. She reached out with her pinky. "I don't feel sorry for you," she said, without raising her eyes.

He covered the back of her hand with his palm. His hand was strong and warm. He leaned in close. Again, she was surrounded by his scent. He spoke, his whispered words washing over her shoulder. "What is it," he asked, "that you feel for me?"

The last time Sinead had allowed herself to care for another person, it was her ex-husband. He'd left her because she wasn't enough. Her marriage had been like living with her father all over again. She couldn't let herself get sucked into another bad relationship. Moving her hand from under his, she looked him in the eye.

"I definitely don't pity you. I don't feel anything for you, beyond the respect owed to a team member."

He smiled and shook his head. "Thanks for making that clear."

They rode for several minutes in silence. A prerecorded voice announced the next stop.

Wells stood. "That's us," he said, his tone reserved.

Sinead stood as well. What she'd said to Wells wasn't true. She did feel something for him beyond the bond she felt for most who worked in law enforcement. But those feelings were dangerous. She wouldn't jeopardize her career for an office fling.

Still, they couldn't work as a team if there was a misunderstanding between them.

Wells walked to the doors. He held on to a rail as the train slowed to a stop. She followed, looping her arm around a pole. "About that hand-holding thing," she began.

The doors slid open. He glanced over his shoulder, meeting her gaze. Turning forward, he exited the car.

"What about it?" The train settled on the rail and let out a metallic groan.

She followed him into the subway station. Posters, advertising shows on Broadway, lined the walls. Gang tags had been painted onto the pillars and the walls. The platform was filled with people. Most wore shorts and T-shirts and she guessed that they were tourists. An entire family of fifteen people had donned the iconic I Heart NY shirts. The sound of a hundred voices speaking at once mixed with the ding as the train made ready to leave.

Wells's question had gone too long unanswered.

She got close to his back, raising her voice to be heard. "I just don't want things to be weird."

"They're not weird," he said. He turned, smiled. "Honestly. We had a moment, but like all moments, it passed."

He seemed to recover from her rejection quickly. Sinead wasn't sure how she felt now. Relieved? Disappointed? Both?

She crossed the platform, heading toward the stairs. Looking over her shoulder, she saw that the crowd had slid between her and Wells, leaving him several yards behind. He was next to the wall, trying to slip by the knot of people.

Before she could say anything, the crack of a whip ripped through the din. A wall behind Wells, exploded with dust and bits of rock. The scent of gunpowder was strong over the smells of body odor and motor grease.

Without thinking, she knew it was gunfire. Her gut threatened to turn to liquid, but her training was stronger than her fear. "Gunman," she yelled. "Everyone, exit the platform now."

Sinead withdrew her sidearm.

Wells already had a gun in his hand.

She scanned the crowd. People were wide-eyed with terror. Some cried. Others prayed. A few held up their phones and took video. Others ran for the stairs. But she didn't see the one person she sought—the shooter.

"This way." She moved forward, sweeping up people from behind and ushering them toward the stairs. Yet, Sinead knew one thing to be true. This wasn't a random shooter who had fired a random shot.

Whoever fired the gun had been aiming directly at Wells.

A piece of flying concrete had sliced open Wells's scalp. His head burned like it had been branded. Hot blood oozed from the side of his head and into his collar. The wound throbbed with each beat of his racing heart. Sinead was herding people toward the exit. But there was still a shooter on the loose.

As a plainclothes detective, he didn't carry a walkie-talkie with him. He did have his phone. With his gun in one hand and his cell in the other, he placed a call.

"This is Detective Wells Blackthorn with the 130th Precinct. We have an active shooter at a subway station.

B line, 86th and Central Park West. We need backup now."

"Backup is on the way," said the dispatcher.

He ended the call with a press of his thumb and slid the phone back into his pocket.

A row of people raced up the stairs. The panic was thick in the air. A young man shoved the person in front of him. The rest of the line teetered on the narrow steps.

"You," Sinead barked, calling out the guy. "I need everyone to hurry but shoving people over won't help you get out of here faster."

The guy glared at Sinead. She glared back. The young man slid into the line heading to the exit.

The evacuation of the station was going as smoothly as Wells could hope. Now he had to find the shooter. Another shot rang out. The bullet slammed into the concrete floor near his feet. A figure in a black hoodie and dark pants shoved a woman aside.

"Get him." Wells sprinted toward the staircase. He shouted to Sinead. "The guy in the sweatshirt."

People started screaming. Crying. Wells shut out all the distractions and focused only on the shooter's back as he slogged through the crowd on the steps.

Sinead was right behind the subject. "Stop," she yelled. "FBI."

The shooter stopped. Sinead lifted her gun. "Raise your hands where I can see them."

For a minute, Wells thought that the perp was going to comply. Then he grabbed a girl who stood next to him on the stairs. The child shrieked as the perp lifted her into the air and threw her at Sinead.

She dove for the girl, catching her before she hit the concrete steps. The shooter sprinted up the stairs and onto the street.

Wells ran to Sinead's side. She held the crying child.

"You okay?" he asked.

Standing, Sinead handed the girl to her mother. "I'm fine. Let's go catch this bastard." With the perp on the street, evacuating the subway station was no longer a top priority. Wells bellowed, "Everyone, stand aside."

The crowd of people pressed themselves to the railing, creating a narrow passage for him and Sinead. He ran up to the top of the steps. She was on his heels. The stairs ended on 86th Street. Traffic ran in both directions. Tall buildings rose on one side of the street. Central Park, a carpet of green in the ultimate urban jungle, spread out on the opposite side of the road. A pair of uniformed police officers sprinted from the direction of the park.

Wells turned in a circle, taking in everything.

The perp was gone.

"Where in the hell did he go?" he asked.

Sinead stood at his side, breathing hard. "What's that?" She pointed across the busy avenue. A wrought iron railing surrounded Central Park, separating it from the rest of the city. A black piece of cloth hung from the fencing.

"You think that belongs to the shooter?" Wells asked.

"I think we need to get a better look and see what it is," said Sinead.

She was right.

A traffic light at the corner turned red. For a moment, the street was free of all cars. They sprinted to the park.

As they got closer to the fence, he could tell that the dark object was a black hoodie—exactly like the one worn by the perp. Frustration roared through him like a locomotive. "The shooter could be anywhere by now."

Sinead stood. "Worse than that, since they ditched their jacket, they could be anyone."

"It's like he freaking disappeared." He pulled a pair of latex gloves from his suit coat's pocket and slipped them on. He picked up the hoodie and patted down the fabric. "Nothing in the pockets," he said. Sure, he didn't expect to find anything. But he never knew when he might get lucky.

"Could be that our perp wore this jacket just to ditch once he got onto the street," said Sinead.

"You said *he*." Wells emphasized the single word. "Did you get a good look at the shooter?"

Sinead drew her lips through her teeth again. Damn, that look really was sexy.

After a beat, she shook her head. "It's more of an impression that the person was male. I only caught a glimpse of his profile. He's light-skinned. Probably Caucasian. That's all I can say for sure."

"Round up whatever witnesses you can find. They need to be interviewed. Maybe one of them got a better look at the guy." Wells thought of the perp picking up the kid and hurtling her at Sinead. That'd take a good deal of strength. Not that a woman couldn't be physically strong enough to throw a small child. But he agreed with Sinead, the shooter was most likely male.

He still held the sweatshirt. If they were lucky, there'd be DNA on the fabric. Although that would take time to analyze. "You wouldn't happen to have an extra evidence bag in that backpack of yours, would you?"

"Actually," she said with a wry smile, "I do." She flipped the bag around to her front and opened one of several zippers. She removed another translucent bag. *Evidence, FBI* was stenciled on the plastic in black lettering. She held the bag open. "Here you go."

He placed the sweatshirt in the evidence bag, then paused as a new thought occurred to him. It left him chilled, despite the heat. "Do you think we just saw the same perp from this morning?"

Sinead sighed. The sound was sexy, too. Was everything about her a turn-on? Then again, there was no sense in torturing himself with something—or make that someone—he couldn't have. He looked away.

"I don't think that the subway shooter is the same person who killed Wheden or Capowski," she said.

He turned back to look at her. Behind Sinead, the street was clogged with patrol cars, their lights strobing. At least the uniformed officers had taken control of the situation. He returned his attention to Sinead. "Why would you say that?"

"The modus operandi is wrong," she said. "There weren't any witnesses to the murders of Wheden and Capowski. This guy tried to shoot you in a packed train station. Both earlier victims share a strong physical resemblance—one that you don't have."

"Me? Are you joking?" He studied her for a moment.

Her face held no hint of emotion—except in the eyes. "You think I was the intended target?"

"They shot at you twice. So, yeah. I think the subway shooter was after you."

She was right. Two bullets had been fired. They'd both been aimed in his direction. Adrenaline still surged through his system and his pulse raced. The wound at the back of his head still throbbed. He raised his hand to the cut on his scalp. His hair was sticky and wet. He looked at his fingertips. They were covered in blood.

"You're hurt." Sinead gripped his arm hard. "You need medical care." She glanced over her shoulder. An ambulance was parked on the sidewalk. "Can you walk?"

He'd chased down a would-be assassin. "Of course, I can walk." He paused and touched his head again. The bleeding had stopped but the bruise hurt like hell. "I think it's just a scratch. I'm fine."

"That's not for you to figure out." She kept her hand on his arm. "Let's go see the EMTs at least."

"I'm not going to be sidelined by a cut to the head. Especially since it's already starting to heal." He touched his scalp again. The flesh was tender, raised and warm. "I'll have an impressive bruise, but I don't need a doctor."

"Impressive," she echoed with a snort. Raising her palms in surrender, she said, "It's your head, so it's your call."

Beyond the bruise, Wells had one hell of a headache. The continual pain in his skull made it all but impossible to think. It was bad timing because he needed his brain power now more than ever. If Sinead was right, two violent and dangerous people were loose in the city.

And both of them needed to be stopped.

"Detective Blackthorn?"

Wells turned to see who'd called out his name. A tall man with dark hair, jeans and a linen shirt approached. His phone was in his hand. "Damn," Wells muttered. "See that guy? It's Nadeem Alvi."

Looking over her shoulder, she asked, "The reporter for the *Daily Herald*?"

"That's the one."

"Detective Blackthorn," said Nadeem. The recording app on his phone was open. Seconds clicked off on the timer. "I have a few questions."

"No comment," Wells growled. As far as he was concerned, Nadeem was the worst person in a city filled with millions of people.

"I haven't even asked any questions yet," said the reporter. "How do you know that you don't have a comment?"

"Because it's you who's asking the questions." He had to get some distance from the reporter. Turning up the sidewalk, he walked away.

Chapter 7

Wells tried to get away from the reporter. But the man wouldn't give up and followed as he and Sinead walked up the street.

Nadeem yelled a question. "Detective, is it true that someone fired a gun twice on a subway platform?"

"No comment."

Nadeem tried again. "We have a report that one man was murdered at the Empire State Building this morning. Now someone fired a gun on a subway platform. Were these crimes committed by the same person?"

He stopped walking. Sinead stood at his side.

"There's nothing connecting the two cases," Wells said, knowing full well that he was giving Nadeem a comment. "I don't want you to create hysteria in the city."

"So, there are two separate shooters loose in the city?"

"I didn't say that either..." His frustration rose. After drawing in a long breath through his nose, he exhaled. "Call the precinct and talk to the media coordinator. She'll have an official statement for you."

"With all due respect, I'm not looking for a statement. I'm looking for what's really happening." He paused a beat and tried again. "Is it true that you were the intended target of the subway shooter?"

The pounding in his head grew. Now he felt as if he was being struck by a hammer. "Where'd you hear that?"

Nadeem scrolled through his phone. "There's a video. A bystander caught it all on his phone and posted it to his social media." He flipped the screen around for Wells to see. Sinead moved closer and stared at the phone as well. The image was jerky, as if the person filming had also been running. But even then, it was clear enough.

The crowded subway platform.

People screamed and ran. Wells was in the picture. He held his phone in one hand and his gun in the other. Into the phone he said, "This is Detective Wells Blackthorn with the 130th Precinct. We have an active shooter at a subway station. B line, 86th and Central Park West. We need backup now."

From off camera came Sinead's voice: "You. I need everyone to hurry but shoving people over won't help you get out of here faster."

And then there was another crack of gunfire. The

floor in front of Wells filled with dust as the bullet drove into the ground at his feet. The look on his face changed from shock to fury in an instant.

Using his thumb, Nadeem stopped the video. "Looks like they were aiming at you."

His pulse thundered in his ears. Sinead was right—Wells had been the target. Clenching his teeth, he said, "No comment."

"Detective, is that blood on your collar?"

Wells pulled on his shirt to look for a stain. A red streak ran from the top of the band to the endpoint. "No comment."

"Who's your friend?" Nadeem used the phone to point in Sinead's direction. "Is she a new detective at the 130th?"

Sinead stepped forward. "I'm Special Agent Sinead Colton. FBI, New York Field Office," she said, her tone friendly. "And I have to say, I read your online column every morning, Mr. Alvi. You're a great writer—truly gifted. But you know as well as we do that we can't comment on any investigation or incident. I know you're trying to do your job. But asking us questions that we can't answer keeps us from doing ours." She paused. "The official statements might be lame, but it's all you're going to get from either the NYPD or the FBI." Then to Wells she said, "We should go."

"One more thing," said Nadeem. Despite his urge to just walk away, he paused. "I noticed that Mark Wheden and Andrew Capowski look alike."

Wells should have guessed that someone would connect the two murders. He just hated that it was Nadeem.

"There are eight million people in the metro area. I'm sure that a lot of people look like those two."

"Yeah, but how many of them have been murdered?"

He glanced at the reporter. "I don't know. But you're the investigative journalist. Why don't you investigate?" Turning his back on Nadeem, he scanned the street.

A perimeter of wooden barricades had been set up around the subway exit. Witnesses were being interviewed by police officers. Wells needed to get to the scene and take charge. Turning his back on the reporter, he walked away.

"One more question," Nadeem yelled at Wells's back. "Why's an FBI agent working with an NYPD detective?"

Looking over his shoulder, Wells glared at the reporter.

Nadeem held up his hands. "I know what you're about to say. 'No comment.' But I can't help thinking that there's a lot more to this story."

Nadeem was right. There was a lot more to the story. Wells refused to think of himself as a victim, but he was undoubtedly the subway shooter's target. If he'd let it, the idea would have left him shook. But for now, he had bigger problems—and someone aiming at him was problem enough. A serial killer was on the loose in NYC. He also had to keep Nadeem Alvi from printing something that would lead to confusion or alarm.

And true, all those problems were more than enough.

But he suspected that his biggest problem might be his growing feelings for his FBI partner. And that wasn't good at all.

* * *

While at the early morning briefing with ADIC Chang and Captain Reeves, Sinead wondered if there was something that connected Wells and the *Daily Herald* reporter, Nadeem Alvi. Now that she'd seen the two men interact, she suspected they had a personal story with an unhappy ending.

"What's up with you and the reporter?" Sinead asked. Before he could deny any past relationship, she added, "Don't say *nothing*, because I know that's not true. Also, as your partner on this case, I'm entitled to know if you have issues with a local reporter—especially if that bad blood might taint our case."

For a moment Wells said nothing.

It left Sinead with a difficult choice. Did she press him for more information? Or did she let the subject drop?

"Back when I was a new cop, Nadeem was just getting started as a reporter." He leaned close, his mouth near her ear, so he could be heard over the noise of the city. "We struck up a working relationship. I told him what I could about interesting crimes. He did all the follow-up on his own. He let me in on any gossip that might lead to a case. He wrote good stories. I made good arrests. After a while, I considered him a friend."

Working with a reporter would get her fired from the FBI. The NYPD played under different rules, so she knew that everything Wells had done was legal.

He stopped walking and turned to face Sinead. "One fall, there was a spate of drug overdoses in the city. Turns out, some smack was laced with rat poison.

Nadeem was the one who came up with a name for the dealer. He told me, I told the Narcotics Division. I was on patrol one evening when Nadeem called. The dealer had been spotted. The information had gone through a few people before it reached the reporter, so I didn't think it was enough to pass onto my superiors. I figured I'd stop by the location and see what I could. Ya' know?"

"I know."

"The dealer was outside this club, smoking a cigarette. I had him in cuffs before he had time to react. The department made a big deal out of the arrest. The mayor gave me a medal and a promotion. I sat down with Nadeem for an interview. The article made him a known commodity in New York media. Then, he got picked up by the *Daily Herald*."

"Sounds like it worked out well for the two of you," said Sinead. "So, why the animosity now?"

"I was just getting to that." Wells scanned the street and sighed. "I was assigned to a homicide investigation. It was grizzly, that's all I'm going to say. Even though I'd been a detective for a while, I was personally affected. I called Nadeem, my friend. We met for a drink. I told him everything I'd seen. Everything I felt. The next day, the story's on the front page of the damned print edition. Not only did he use my words, but he also attributed my quotes." Tightening his jaw, Wells spit out, "Ambition I can handle. Disloyalty, I cannot."

"Ouch." That was a harsh way to end a friendship. "I can see why you don't like or trust him."

"He tried to apologize. Said he was sorry. Said his

editor threatened his job if he didn't print the story." Wells gave a disgusted grunt. "I don't trust anyone in the media now. They're all a bunch of rats, as far as I'm concerned."

Sinead knew that the media could be a powerful ally to law enforcement. Who, other than the news, could reach so many people so quickly? All the same, she didn't blame Wells for his personal dislike. "Thanks for sharing your story with me." True, she had pressed him for what had happened with Nadeem. But she hadn't counted on getting such a detailed accounting.

"I don't talk about it with anyone," he said with a wry laugh. "Sorry to dump so much on you. I'm usually more pulled together than this. It's because I'm so freaking exhausted."

It's the second time that Wells had mentioned his lack of sleep. "Problems at home?"

"You could say that." And then, "We have more to worry about than me. Let's go check on the witnesses to the subway shooting."

Sinead and Wells approached the police barricade. The first person she saw was Detective Sean Colton.

He smiled when he saw them. "You two are having a busy day."

Sean was tall, athletic and a few years older than Sinead. He worked at the 98th Precinct and was yet another Colton cousin—so long as a person knew how to follow all the branches in the Colton family tree. He continued, "First, I heard you were both called in to the scene at the Empire State Building this morning, and now this." He nodded toward the group of witnesses to the shooting who were being interviewed by the police.

"Yeah." She gave him a quick hug. "Busy day and it's not even noon. How's Orla?" she asked, mentioning Sean's new love.

He smiled. "She's great." The smile vanished and he regarded Wells and Sinead, his eyes narrowed. "Tell me what happened."

She and Wells spent a few minutes covering the basics. The shooter. His description. The fact that Wells was definitely the shooter's target.

"We found this across the street," said Wells, handing over the evidence bag that contained the sweatshirt. "Neither one of us saw the shooter drop it, but it matches what he was wearing."

"We're going through video footage now," said Sean, taking the bag. "Hopefully we get an image of the guy on his way to the station. But I have two questions. Why were you two on the subway in the first place? Wells, doesn't the 130th give you a car?"

"It does, but my tire was slashed."

"Oh, really?" Sean said. The random act of vandalism to Wells's SUV didn't seem so random anymore. "You think that slashing your tire was deliberately done to force you onto the subway?"

Wells scrubbed his cheek with a palm. "Could be." He paused a beat. "What's your second question?"

"Is that blood on your collar?"

Wells touched the bloodstain. "A piece of flying concrete cut my scalp. It bled a little but it's okay." And then, "We have to talk to someone at the Met concerning what happened this morning. Do you have this scene under control?"

"I got this," said Sean. "And I'll do you one better. I have an NYPD shirt in my car. I was gonna wear it to the gym, but I don't see any workout time in my future. You can borrow it for now. It's clean. And then, you aren't trying to conduct an interview while covered in blood." Sean took a key fob from his pocket and pointed it at a sedan that was parked at the curb. The lights flashed and the horn beeped. "It's in a duffel on the back seat. You can get it back to me whenever."

"Thanks, man," said Wells. "You'll keep us posted on the subway shooting?"

"Will do, man," said Sean.

Wells and Sinead made their way to the car. She could feel heat rising up through the soles of her shoes. Wells opened the back door of Sean's car. As promised, a black duffel bag sat on the seat. He opened the zippered compartment. A black T-shirt with the NYPD seal on the right breast sat atop a pile of workout clothes.

Wells took out the shirt. He looked up and down the street. "You okay if I change here?"

He didn't seem like the kind of guy to be shy, so she assumed he was asking to be polite. Besides, he was just stripping down to his waist. "Be my guest," she said.

Wells loosened his tie and shoved it in the pocket of his jacket. Next, he slipped the jacket from his shoulders and arms.

Sinead held out her hand. "I can stow your stuff in my bag for now. You can get it cleaned later."

He handed her his suit jacket. "Thanks."

After folding the suit coat, careful not to touch the bloody stain, she slid the jacket into her backpack.

Wells started unbuttoning his shirt. For Sinead, time slowed. The first button undone exposed a sliver of his chest. The next two gave her a view of his firm pecs, the sprinkling of dark hair that covered his chest. Three more buttons unfastened. She got a glimpse of his rock-hard abs, and the line of hair that dove straight into the front of his trousers. She imagined her lips on his chest. Her mouth went dry. Sweat gathered at the nape of her neck and trickled down the back of her shirt.

She dropped her gaze to the blistering pavement.

Before now, she'd obviously realized that Wells was a handsome man. And yes, she already guessed that he was fit.

What she never could have predicted was her reaction. Sinead's pulse raced. Her hands itched with the need to touch his chest, just to see if the muscles were as hard as they looked. She was drawn to be closer to him. Yet just being by his side would never be close enough.

Sinead had to steer clear of thoughts of Wells. Because if fantasies about him kept sneaking into her mind, she'd never be able to do her job.

The Metropolitan Museum of Art sat on Fifth Avenue, surrounded by Central Park. It occupied a stretch of road affectionately called Museum Mile, and was fronted by impressive steps that spanned 154 feet. Pillars, etched with scrollwork at the top, ran along the entrance of the building.

Halfway up the staircase, a brass-and-glass sign was

affixed to an ornate post. It read: *The museum will close today at 3:30 p.m. for a private fundraising event.*

"As a kid…" Sinead said, leaning in close to Wells. As she spoke, she kept her tone low and conspiratorial. "I always watched the Met Gala red carpet." The gala always took place in the spring, so this event was something else. Still, she imagined the party would be filled with famous people looking fabulous. She loved the idea.

"You?" The surprise was evident in his tone. "No offense, but you don't seem like the high fashion-slash-high society type to me."

Maybe she shouldn't have shared her love of all things glamorous about New York. But she'd started the conversation and felt compelled to defend her opinion. "Obviously, I'm not into couture, but I do love to see all the celebs dressed up. Besides, it's a fundraiser and is always for a good cause."

"Or they could save all the money they spend on getting dressed up and send it to the charity…"

It was a criticism she'd heard more than once. In fact, "I think Nadeem Alvi wrote a column with that same sentiment last year."

He gave her a side-eye but said nothing.

At the top of the staircase, they approached the door. A uniformed security guard sweltered under a sun umbrella. "I need to see what's in that bag." He slowly stepped forward and wiped sweat from his brow.

Sinead removed her FBI credentials from the front pocket of her backpack. Wells already held his NYPD badge and ID.

Sinead said, "I'm Special Agent Colton with the FBI. This is Detective Blackthorn of the New York City Police Department. We need to speak to one of your employees, Edward Pendleton."

The security guard's eyes went wide. He pushed the door open and pointed inside. "Go straight to the security desk. Someone there can help you."

Sinead entered the foyer and a blast of ice-cold air hit her in the face. The foyer was a large rectangle that led to four different sections of the museum. Large signs hung above each gallery.

The security desk sat in the back left corner of the foyer. A female guard stood as Sinead and Wells approached. They both lifted their IDs so the guard could see their photos and badges.

Introducing themselves was like a well-rehearsed script. It was Wells who delivered the lines this time. "I'm Detective Blackthorn with the NYPD. This is Agent Colton with the FBI. We need to speak to one of your employees, Edward Pendleton. He's an assistant curator for photography."

"Can I ask why you need to speak to him?" She wore a name tag. E. Baltra.

"We need to talk to Mr. Pendleton about a private matter," she said. "It's best if we do it here and not downtown."

The woman looked nervous. Then again, a visit from both the FBI and NYPD was never to deliver good news.

A phone sat on the guard's desk. She lifted the handset and pushed several buttons. After a moment, she spoke into the receiver. "I have people here who need to speak to Edward Pendleton. It's the police and the FBI." She paused again. "I'll send them down."

A clear plastic container was filled with folded maps. It sat on the edge of the desk. Ms. Baltra removed a map. After unfolding it, she picked up a pen and marked a spot with an X. "We're here. And the photography offices are here." After drawing another X, she pointed across the foyer. Egyptian Wing. "Go all the way through the exhibit. It ends at the Temple of Dendur. At the back of the room there's a door marked *Employees Only* but there's a call box. Use that. They're expecting you."

Chapter 8

Sinead walked next to Wells as they wound through the labyrinthian Egyptian exhibit. One wall held pottery artifacts. Behind a thick pane of glass, there were tools used by farmers in the Nile River Valley. There was a case filled with jewelry. Everything caught her eye. Sinead had to fight the urge to stop and read the descriptions. Finally, they came to the gallery, a huge windowed room that contained the tomb. Surrounded on three of the four sides with a shallow water-filled trench, the stone structure stood more than twenty feet high. Every time she saw it, her heart skipped a beat.

For an instant, she wondered what it would be like to spend a lazy Saturday afternoon with Wells at the museum. She shook her head, clearing away the thoughts. And still, the image stayed with her.

"I think the employee door is over there." She pointed to the back corner of the room.

Staying on the walkway that surrounded the shallow moat, they found the door. Like the security guard had promised, a call box hung on the wall.

Wells pressed the button on the box.

A static-filled voice came from the small speaker. "How can I help you?"

"Detective Wells and Special Agent Colton to see Edward Pendleton."

"Pull the handle," said the voice.

The lock disengaged with a click. Wells pulled the door open. A tall man stood in the corridor. He had blond hair and blue eyes. He looked to be approximately thirty-two to thirty-five years old. Without being told, she knew they'd found Edward Pendleton.

"I heard you wanted to see me," he said, folding his arms across his chest. "What's this about?"

"You Pendleton?" Wells asked, clarifying that they'd found their man.

"I am," he said, his tone indignant. "What's this about? I haven't done anything wrong—and what's more, you're interrupting my work."

Sinead didn't like the guy already. After putting her personal opinion aside, she asked, "Do you have a place where we can talk privately?"

He sighed. "I share an office, but my colleague is at a conference in Paris." Turning, he said, "This way."

The corridor was narrow and long. Overhead, lights buzzed. The hallway was lined on both sides with doors. Edward stopped. A small sign hung on the wall. *Jackie*

Fontaine. Edward Pendleton. Assistant Curators. Photography.

He opened the door and stepped inside. Sinead and Wells followed. The cramped room was filled. Two desks sat facing opposite walls. A large set of shelves filled the third wall, and it was covered in files. Boxes littered the ground and a stack teetered precariously in the corner.

Pendleton dropped into a desk chair. "Sorry, I only have the two seats. I wasn't expecting you or I could've booked a conference room."

"We can stand," said Sinead. "This shouldn't take long."

Wells said, "We have reason to believe that your life is at risk."

Pendleton blinked several times. "My life?" he echoed. "Who'd want to kill me? And why?"

"Have you seen any of the media coverage concerning the two men who were murdered?" Sinead asked. "One body was found at the end of June. The other was found this morning."

"I really don't pay attention to what's *reported*—" he hooked the word in air quotes before continuing "—in the *infotainment* world." Another air quote was placed around *infotainment*. "But this is New York City. People get murdered all the time. What makes these men so special?"

"These victims have a very specific profile." Sinead didn't want to share too much information that hadn't been released to the public. But she knew that Edward wasn't going to take them seriously unless he realized that the danger was very real. "You fit that profile."

"You're here to warn me that the city is a dangerous place? The world is a dangerous place, but that doesn't mean we stop living."

Wells said, "We'd like you to leave town for a few weeks…"

Edward was already shaking his head, "No way." He swept his arm in front of him, taking in the entire cluttered office. "Do you know what's in these boxes?" He didn't wait for an answer. "A heretofore unknown collection of Eadweard Muybridge photographs. He was one of the pioneers of motion photography from the nineteenth century. His great-great-niece died. The estate sold the house in Surrey, England. The new owners found three steamer trunks filled with these. The pictures need to be authenticated, cataloged and preserved. I can't leave now."

"If you're dead, then none of this will matter," said Sinead.

"If I don't pursue my life's passion, then I'm not really alive, either," said the museum curator.

Sinead knew they weren't going to convince him to take his safety seriously. Still, she said, "You can always come back to this work later. We have reason to believe that you could be the next target of a serial killer."

Rubbing the back of his neck, Edward repeated, "Serial killer?" His voice trembled.

"This killer has already killed two men and has warned of more murders. We don't know much about the perp," said Wells. "But we do know what kind of victim they're looking for. Male. Midthirties. Caucasian. Blond hair, blue eyes. Works at a New York City landmark. Initial of first name begins with *E*."

"That's very specific and very much me." Edward swallowed.

"If it's an issue of money, the FBI can help with a hotel out of town and protection," Sinead offered. She recalled Wells's stories about summers spent in the Finger Lakes region. "I heard that Ithaca's nice this time of year."

"I can't live in fear," Edward said, speaking more to himself than to Sinead or Wells. "Besides, if I don't make a dent in this project in the next two weeks, Jackie will come back from Europe and take credit for my work. Just like last time." He looked up, meeting her eye. "I have to keep working."

She keyed in on the comment about his colleague taking credit for his accomplishments. "I get that your job here has complications. If this killer gets to you before we find them, what kind of credit will Jackie get for your sacrifice then?"

"You said you have evidence that I fit the killer's profile. Do you know for a fact that it's me?" Edward asked, a quaver in his voice.

Wells said, "We do not."

Edward sat in silence for a moment. After squaring his shoulders, he said, "It doesn't matter what's out there lurking. I have my work. It's important to me—and to the world. I'll lock my doors at night. I'll look over my shoulder when I walk down the street. But I'm staying in the city."

Wells and Sinead exchanged looks. He shrugged. She took the gesture to mean, *What else can we do?*

She asked, "What can we say to convince you to take your safety seriously?"

Edward stood. "I take everything seriously," he said, his tone resolute. "I'm staying put."

Wells removed a business card from his pants pocket. "Call us if you change your mind."

Edward took the card and tapped it on his palm. "I don't think I will make a different decision. If I do, I'll reach out." He opened his office door. "I need to get back to work. We all have to be out of the museum by three thirty today. The Met's hosting some kind of swanky event. I'll walk you out."

He led them down a straight and narrow hallway. At the end, Edward opened the door. "I do appreciate your warning," he said. "I'll be careful, I promise."

After crossing the threshold, she turned to face Edward. "This killer is smart, cunning and lethal. Careful might not be enough."

Nodding slowly, he stared at the business card he still held in his hand. "Still, I'm going to take my chances. Like I said, if I change my mind, I'll call you." Then he let the door shut.

The fact that the assistant curator had refused help shouldn't have surprised Sinead. But it did leave her reflecting on how someone could be so cavalier about their own safety.

The gallery was surprisingly empty. Then again, it was the middle of the day. She imagined that many of the visitors were getting lunch.

She walked to the back of the temple and paused. Hieroglyphs had been carved into the stone. There was an eye. A figure of Isis. Another figure, this one was Osiris. "Thousands of years ago, someone took the time to scrape away the rock bit by bit. Do you think that they knew their work would last for centuries?"

"The Ancient Egyptians believed that those prayers had magical powers that kept people safe," said Wells.

Sinead had heard the same explanation over the years. "Maybe someone should carve a hieroglyph for Edward Pendleton."

He snorted. "Maybe."

They moved slowly around the temple. It was almost like the date she'd imagined. Her finger twitched, pulled closer to his hand like a magnet to steel. "It feels like there's more we should be able to do."

"Do you want to take him into custody for his own safety?" Wells asked.

"That's an extreme option. I doubt it would work for long." With a shake of her head, she could already imagine how the scenario would unfold. She continued, "He'd hire an attorney who'd petition a judge. Edward would be released before we were even done with our paperwork."

"Sounds cynical."

"Let's just say it's been a rough day."

Wells nodded. "And you weren't even the one who was shot at."

He was right. She asked, "How's your head?"

He touched his scalp. "It hurts but I'll live." They continued around the temple. Their footfalls echoed in the silent room.

She enjoyed the quiet company with Wells. Still, she couldn't be lulled into thinking she didn't have a job to do. "There are more names on the list of possible victims," said Sinead. "We should find the next person on the list and follow up."

Before Wells could speak, his phone rang. He pulled the cell from his pants pocket and glanced at the screen. "It's Captain Reeves. I have to take this." He swiped the call open. "Hello."

"When were you going to call and tell me that you were the subway shooter's target?" Even without the speaker function turned on, Sinead could hear the captain's words clearly. "You want to know how I found out? Nadeem Alvi called me and asked for a comment."

Since the room was empty, she assumed he was fine taking such a sensitive call in a public place.

"You don't sound pleased, boss," said Wells.

Now, that was an understatement.

"I'm not pleased—in fact, I'm freaking pissed." She paused and drew in a shaking breath. "Why were you on the subway in the first place?"

"My tire was slashed. At the time, I thought it was just random vandalism. I asked Margaret to take care of my vehicle."

Reeves was silent for a moment. "We need to figure out who's after you and why. Come back to the precinct. Pronto."

"We have another possible victim to visit," he began.

"Send someone else. You can't be out on the streets—not with a target on your back," she said.

The thing was, Captain Reeves was right. What's

more, Sinead was at Wells's side. If the shooter came after him again, she might be caught in the crossfire.

Wells rarely visited the captain's office. But whenever he entered the space, he wondered what it would be like to be the one in charge. Captain Colleen Reeves had a corner office with one set of windows that overlooked the street on one wall and another set of windows that faced a parking lot. Since the room was flooded with natural light, she rarely used lamps during the day.

Today was an exception.

"It's too damn hot," she complained, drawing wooden blinds across the window. "All the heat rises from the street and turns this place into an oven."

The workplace itself was larger than many Manhattan apartments. Her desk sat at the far end of the room. A bookcase filled one wall. A single-serve coffeemaker and variety of pods sat on a table in the corner between the sets of windows. Next to the door, a sofa and two chairs surrounded a coffee table.

Wells sat on one end of the sofa. Sinead was on the other. Ashlynn Colton sat on one of the chairs. A laptop was balanced on her knees. Colleen closed the final set of blinds and came to sit in the final open chair.

Ashlynn began, "We've pulled up traffic cam footage from around this building. Unfortunately, your SUV was parked in a blind spot. We didn't get any video of the damage done to your car. We did however find this…"

She set the laptop onto the coffee table. The screen was filled with the image of a street. Wells recognized it as the road that ran in front of the building. A delivery van rumbled past the camera and then, a person appeared. They wore a dark sweatshirt with the hood pulled up. Their back was to the camera.

"That's the first image we get of the subway shooter," said Captain Reeves.

Wells watched as the person sprinted across the street and down a set of stairs that led to the subway station. "I'm sure you caught him on video on the platform," he said.

"We did." Reeves nodded to Ashlynn.

The computer tech leaned forward and tapped on the keys. Another image filled the screen. It was an overhead view of a subway turnstile. The person in a dark hoodie came into view. Head down, they swiped a Metro card and walked onto the platform. Sprinting to the far side of the platform, they slipped behind a pillar.

"At least they paid the fare," said Wells with a sarcastic snort.

"The subway shooter is careful. Jumping the turnstile would draw unwanted attention." Sinead said. She paused a beat before asking her cousin, "Anything we can learn from the Metro card used?"

Ashlynn shook her head. "Nothing yet but we're trying to find out if a credit card was used to purchase the Metro card." She clicked the fast-forward icon on the screen. "I'm going to speed up the video now." The timestamp sped up, several minutes passing in only seconds.

Two figures walked onto the platform. Wells and Sinead.

"Damn," said Wells. His gut burned with anger and frustration. "He was there the whole time."

"What are your thoughts, Sinead?" The captain leaned forward in her seat. "You've seen the video. You were a witness to the shooting. What kind of person would target Wells? Is this connected to the other case?"

She shook her head. "Wells and I have already discussed that possibility. But no, it's not the same person who killed the other two men."

"How can you be sure?" Captain Reeves asked.

There was one thing that Wells noticed. "The subway shooter is a lot taller than the person who was at the Empire State Building. The guy on the subway platform has broader shoulders, too." He paused before asking, "Is there any way you can analyze video of the two suspects and compare their stature, Ashlynn?"

"Sure can, but you need to give me a few days."

"Any other thoughts?" the captain asked.

"The crimes are completely different for starters, which means that the ESB killer's motivation is different from the subway shooter's." Sinead spent a few minutes going over what she'd said before about the killer's MO. Wells watched her talk and he couldn't help himself, he was impressed. She concluded by saying, "My best guess is, the subway shooter has a personal score to settle with Wells."

The fact that she'd thought through the options was news to him. "What kind of score?"

She said, "There are a few possibilities. First, it could be someone who you arrested and has recently been released from jail. Or maybe there's a trial coming up where you're supposed to testify. Without you as witness, the case will fall apart."

"There are no trials on the docket for months," said Wells. "And as far as anyone I sent to jail?" He sat back on the sofa. "I haven't gotten notice of someone being paroled."

The captain rubbed her chin. "Ashlynn, can you search for people who've been recently released from jail and cross-reference that with anyone Wells arrested?"

"Of course." She pulled the laptop onto her knees again and began to type.

"While we wait for Ashlynn," said Wells. "We can fill you in on our visit with Edward Pendleton. He fits the profile for a potential victim perfectly. We tried to convince him to leave town for a week—even a few days."

"Tried?" Reeves echoed. "I'm guessing that you didn't get far."

"There's a project at the museum he doesn't want to leave. Says it's his life's work but that he'll be careful." Sinead gave a little shrug. "We really can't take him into custody and even if we did…" She shrugged again.

"Got it," said Ashlynn. "One man you arrested seven years ago was just released from the Fishkill Correctional Facility. He registered with his parole officer here in the city." She entered several keystrokes. "And I'm sending you his name and address now."

Wells's phone pinged with the incoming message. After pulling his phone from his pocket, he glanced at the screen. "David Atkins. I remember him. He was part of a bank robbery ring. His compatriots got sentenced to fifteen years for each robbery in the federal system. David cooperated and got a reduced sentence. Seven years in a NYDOC facility."

Sinead said, "We should pay him a visit."

He liked the way she thought. He liked the way she looked. Hell, there wasn't anything about Sinead that he didn't like. "Agreed."

"If he's shooting at you," said Reeves, "you are the last person who should go to this guy's house."

"No way," said Wells. "You aren't going to sideline me."

"I should send you home for the day."

"But you know I'd go and see David Atkins anyway." He smiled. Over the years Wells had learned that his smile often got him what he wanted.

"Don't try that crap with me," his boss snarled. "I'm immune to your charisma. But you are right. Someone needs to talk to Atkins. At the moment, you're the only one I have."

Wells stood. Sinead stood as well. "We're on it," he said.

"Just do me two favors," said the captain.

"Only two?" he joked.

"I want a report from you about what you find. I do not want another call from the media for a comment."

"Done," he said. "What's the second favor?"

Captain Reeves said, "Don't get shot this time."

Chapter 9

The address Wells had been given for David Atkins was just blocks from the Hudson River and near Columbia University. Despite the prime location, the neighborhood had yet to be gentrified. But expensive real estate was coming to the area. Only two blocks away the framework for what would be luxury condo units rose into the sky.

For now, the street was filled with small businesses. A Thai restaurant. A corner grocery store. A Laundromat that was closed.

A large Catholic church filled the block across the street. The building where David Atkins had registered with his parole officer was made of crumbling brick. A set of four steps led to a metal door. Affixed to the brick wall was a small blue sign. *Property of St. Ambrose Church. Diocese of New York City.*

"This is it," said Sinead, stopping on the sidewalk. "Looks like David moved into a halfway house run by the church or something."

"It would make sense if that's what this is," he said. "In the past seven years, I've worked hundreds of cases. But I do recall David Atkins. At the time I arrested him, he was a scared kid. Hell, he was barely old enough to be charged as an adult."

"And now?" she asked.

"And now we find out."

There was a single buzzer on the wall next to the door. Sinead pressed the button. The sound of far-off chimes came from inside the building. The door was answered a moment later by a Black man in a cleric's collar. "May I help you?"

Sinead and Wells had their IDs ready. They held them up for the priest to see. "I'm Special Agent Colton, FBI. This is Detective Wells with the NYPD. We need to see David Atkins. He registered this address with his parole officer."

The priest stepped back from the door. "Please, come in. My name is Father Charles and I run the rectory."

Rectory? Sinead wasn't a practicing Catholic, but she'd spent years in religious education and knew that the rectory was where the priest lived. Honestly, she was surprised to find an ex-con living here as well. "Can you give us an idea of David's role with the church?" she asked, crossing the threshold. Wells followed her inside.

The door from the outside led to a narrow foyer.

After standing outside in the bright sunlight, she found the vestibule dim. It took a moment for her eyes to adjust. A hallway led to the back of the rectory. On the right, a set of stairs led to the second floor. On the left was an open door. The room beyond was an office.

"If you'd like to step inside," Father Charles offered, "I can answer your questions about David Atkins."

The office was like many others. A desk. A computer. Filing cabinets. On the wall behind the desk were two pictures. One was of the current Cardinal for New York City. The other photograph was of the Pope in Rome. "Have a seat, please." The priest gestured to two chairs that sat opposite his desk. "Can I offer you a beverage? Water? Lemonade?"

"I'm fine for now, thank you," said Wells. He moved the conversation along. "What can you tell us about David? How long have you known him? When did he arrive at the rectory?"

Father Charles began, "I can answer your last question first. David arrived after his release from prison last week. He's been living here and helping with the cooking and maintenance ever since." He sat back in his chair, resting his hands on his stomach. "I met David about five years ago when I was assigned as the priest to several prisons in the state. He wasn't a Catholic when he was first sentenced to jail. Like what happens to some, during his incarceration, he found grace. Over the next several years, he came closer to God. Closer to the church. He went through the sacraments of RCIA. Eventually, he became a deacon who served other inmates. Truly, he's an inspirational story. For now, he's assigned as a deacon at Saint Ambrose while also on parole."

"Do you have any idea where he was this morning?" Wells asked. "From nine o'clock onward."

"We have a daily Mass at that time. He was with me at the altar." The priest leaned forward. "What is going on?"

Probably nothing to do with David Atkins. Sinead said, "Maybe we should talk to the deacon."

"If you'd wait here one minute—" Father Charles rose to his feet "—I'll find him."

The priest rounded the desk and exited the small office, leaving Sinead alone with Wells. A ball of disappointment dropped into her gut. She glanced at Wells. "Serving at Mass is a heck of an alibi."

Wells nodded slowly. "That it is." He paused a beat. "Still, we should talk to him. Maybe some of his old buddies are out for revenge."

The sound of footsteps in the hallway stopped their conversation. Sinead swiveled in her seat, looking over her shoulder. The priest entered the office. Another man followed. He had red hair, shaved close, ruddy cheeks and a long scar on the side of his face. He wore a black short-sleeved T-shirt, and black trousers. With each step, he dragged his left foot.

A folding chair sat in the corner. The priest set it next to Sinead.

David dropped into the seat with a sigh. "Detective Blackthorn." He reached across Sinead to offer his palm. "I'm surprised to see you here."

"Not as surprised as I am to see you," said Wells,

shaking the deacon's hand. And then, "This is Special Agent Colton."

He offered his hand to Sinead to shake. "David Atkins. Nice to meet you."

She took his palm in hers. "Likewise."

"Father Charles said you wanted to talk to me…"

The priest still stood. "I can give you privacy, if you need."

"No, Father, you stay," said David.

The priest rounded his desk and sat in the chair.

"There was a shooting on the subway this morning," said Wells.

"Oh no." The deacon went pale. In Sinead's estimation, David looked stricken. "I hope nobody was hurt seriously."

"There are no injuries reported," said Sinead. "But we need to know your whereabouts."

"I've been here all day. Up at five in the morning for breakfast and physical therapy…"

Sinead interrupted. "Physical therapy?"

David gripped his knee. "About six months after being sent to jail, I was in a fight. My kneecap was shattered. My face was sliced open. The injuries were so bad that I spent months in the prison hospital. I still have to do daily exercises for my knee."

She recalled those harrowing moments when the subway shooter picked up the child and threw her down the stairs. He then sprinted out of the station. Whoever had shot at Wells was stronger than the man who sat next to her.

It brought up an interesting question, though. "Are you still in contact with any of your old crew?"

David shook his head. "I haven't spoken to any of them in years." He looked at Wells and then back to Sinead. "Do you think they have something to do with what happened on the subway?"

There was no reason for Sinead to lie. "Wells—I mean, Detective Blackthorn—was the shooter's target. There's reason to believe that he was attacked in some kind of vendetta. You are the only person he arrested who's also been recently released from jail."

"Me?" The color came back to David's cheeks. "I didn't have anything to do with the shooting. In fact, I should be thanking Detective Blackthorn."

"You want to thank me?" Wells said, his tone skeptical.

David spoke to Sinead. "I was young and dumb when I was running around with those guys. We stole stuff all the time, which was wrong. But robbing banks..." He shook his head. "That's a whole other level of crime. When we were arrested, the detective told me that I could still have a life after serving my time. I'm not sure that I believed him then, but now I'm here. Ready to make my life mean something to the world."

Father Charles had been right. David Atkins was an inspirational young man. What's more, she knew that he wasn't involved in the subway shooting. But it brought up another question. If it wasn't David Atkins who wanted Wells dead, then who?

Edward Pendleton locked his office door and pulled it closed. He jiggled the handle to make sure that the latch had caught. It had. He slipped his messenger bag over his shoulder. The strap crossed his torso and back. The canvas pouch hung at his side.

His officemate was blessedly out of the country for the next ten days, but Edward knew how quickly those days would pass. As he walked down the narrow corridor, he admitted that several things were on his mind.

First was his work. He had to make a significant dent in the Eadweard Muybridge photographs or Jackie would come back from her trip, ready to take credit for everything he'd accomplished. Just like last time. The memories seared his gut.

As did the interruption to his workday.

He opened the door that led the public areas of the museum and crossed the threshold. He closed the door. The electronic lock clicked into place.

Sure, he understood that the museum held events for the hoi polloi for a variety of reasons. They were dedicated to the betterment of the greater New York area. In holding these events, they brought in money to the museum itself. That money helped to fund Edward's research. But how was he supposed to get anything done if he had to leave work in the middle of the afternoon?

He walked through the Egyptian exhibit, seeing nothing.

The sound of his footfalls echoed in the empty galleries.

Glancing at his watch, he saw that it was already 3:37 p.m. He was supposed to have been out of the building seven minutes earlier. He walked faster, ruminating on the final thing that weighed on his mind.

The visit from the detective and special agent had

left him rattled. It didn't help that the story was in the media. Typically, Edward ignored what was being reported. But today, he checked his phone again and again for news of the recent murders.

In short, his day had been a waste.

He crossed through the foyer. The ticketing booths were closed. Two security guards stood near a desk and silently watched Edward as he passed. He raised his chin in a silent greeting.

One of the guards nodded in return.

Edward pushed open the front door and stepped outside.

It was like going into a sauna. The air was hot and hazy with humidity. The sun beat down on the front of the building. He paused and opened his bag. He found his laptop. A file. Pens. A set of keys on a metal ring. Where were his damn sunglasses?

A man stepped out from behind one of the pillars. He was dressed in black. Black hoodie. Black jeans. Black sunglasses. Edward looked at him and went cold. He knew who the man was and what he wanted. "You're him," he said. "You're the murderer."

The man smiled and lifted a gun. The barrel was pointed right at Edward's heart.

"Is there anything I can say so you won't shoot me?" Edward asked. His heartbeat thundered, making him deaf to every other sound beyond his own fear.

The man shook his head. "No," he said. "There's not."

Then he pulled the trigger. There was a flash of fire. The boom of thunder. An agonizing pain that both stabbed him in the chest and knocked him off his feet.

He lay on the ground, bleeding, and the man loomed above him. Edward couldn't feel his hands. Or his feet. Or his face. "Why?" he asked, his word slurred.

"You know," he said. "It doesn't really matter. In fact, I'm not sure that any of this matters, at all."

Maybe, thought Edward as he stared at the sky, the man was right.

Wells sat in a booth of a pizza parlor that was located five blocks from St. Ambrose Church. A glass-and-chrome case sat near the door. It was filled with a dozen different types of pizza that could be reheated by the slice in the oven at the back wall. At the end of the case was a drink machine. Four booths lined one wall and a half dozen tables filled the middle of the floor.

At this time of the day, the restaurant was empty. Two employees stood behind the counter and scrolled through their phones. On the back wall, a boxy air conditioner blew a weak stream of cool air. It did little to fight the heat from the ovens and the heat outside.

It was 3:35 p.m. He hadn't eaten since breakfast and that had only been a piece of fruit. The heavy scent of tomato sauce and basil filled the small restaurant. His stomach contracted with hunger.

"I'm starved," said Sinead. She sat on the opposite side of the booth and lifted a waxed paper cup to her lips and sipped her soda. "I feel like we've accomplished a whole lot of nothing. We don't know who shot at you. And the one potential victim we spoke with didn't want to listen to what we had to say."

They'd both ordered slices of pizza—her plain cheese and him pepperoni—and drinks. Like all good New

York pizza, the slices were thin and bigger than the paper plate upon which they sat.

Sinead lifted her slice of pizza, folding it at the crust. She held the pizza and let the grease drip onto her plate. Using two hands, she turned the pizza's point to her and took a bite. "Delicious," she said, speaking around her food.

Wells reached for a glass shaker of shredded parmesan cheese. He tapped the bottom on the table and then shook cheese all over his pizza. He took a bite. "If heaven is a place where only good things happen, this pizza will be served."

Sinead wiped her mouth and took another sip of her soda. "I don't care that this will ruin my dinner."

Dinner. The one word dropped onto his back, like a boulder from the sky. It stole his breath and flattened him to the ground. When he got home, he'd have to feed Harry. True, the baby still ate food from a jar. But Wells hadn't thought about his nephew for hours. The kid deserved better.

He slipped his phone from his pocket and sent a quick text to Deborah.

How's it going?

She replied instantly.

Better since I got some teething gel.

He smiled, hoping that Harry was finally a happy baby again. He sent another text.

Thanks for taking care of him. I have a meeting. Will be home by 6:30 p.m.

Or so he hoped.

Deborah sent a thumbs-up emoji.

He put the phone back in his pocket. Sinead was watching him.

"Everything okay?" she asked.

"Yeah, just following up on something," he said, knowing full well that he was being evasive.

"Case-related?" she asked.

He shook his head and took a large bite of pizza. He chewed and swallowed. "Checking in on my nephew," he said.

Sinead slipped her tablet computer from her backpack. "I figure we should get a look at our shared document. See how the other teams made out today. Plus, I haven't updated anything about our meeting with Edward Pendleton."

As she tapped on the screen, Wells shoved the last bite of pizza into his mouth. He washed down the crust with a drink of soda. The phone in his pocket began to vibrate with an incoming call. He pulled out the cell and glanced at the screen.

Caller ID read: Colleen Reeves.

He cursed.

Sinead wiped her fingers on a napkin. "Everything okay?"

Wells hadn't taken the time to brief his boss on their visit to the rectory. At the same time, he'd left the church only moments earlier. "It's the captain." He swiped the call open and actuated the speaker function.

"Hey," he said. "Sinead and I just stopped to get something to eat. We're headed back to the precinct soon and I'll give you all the details. But David Atkins isn't the subway shooter."

"I hope that you've finished your meal," said Colleen, her voice stern. "Because it happened again."

Sinead leaned forward. "What happened again?"

"Another man's been shot. His body was just found at the Metropolitan Museum of Art."

"Do you have an ID?" he asked.

Wells knew what the captain was about to say, even before she spoke.

"We do." She paused. "It's Edward Pendleton, the man you spoke with this morning."

Chapter 10

At 3:45 p.m. traffic in the city was an absolute nightmare. Wells hoped that his SUV was fixed soon. Making his way through the city without a car was more than difficult. By the time Wells and Sinead arrived at Central Park, the crime scene had been cordoned off by the NYPD. A crowd had gathered, pressing up against the wooden sawhorses.

As Sinead and Wells made their way to the barricade, Nadeem worked his way through the crowd. "Detective. Special Agent. Do you have a moment?"

"Damn," Wells said. "How'd he get here before us?"

Sinead held up a hand to the reporter. "Not now, Nadeem."

A uniformed officer moved one of the sawhorses to let Wells and Sinead pass.

The reporter stood next to the sawhorse and asked his questions anyway. "Is it true that this victim is connected to the other murders? Are you any closer to having a profile for the Landmark Killer?"

She stumbled to a stop. "What did you call him?"

"The Landmark Killer. It's a catchy title, isn't it?" Nadeem continued. "I came up with it myself."

Wells gripped Sinead's arm and pulled her away from the reporter. "No comment, Nadeem." Talking over his shoulder as they walked, he said, "You know that already."

The reporter called after them, "If you change your mind, let me know."

"The Landmark Killer," she repeated, with a shake of her head. "It *is* a catchy title."

Wells said nothing.

Sinead continued, "You know that these killings are going to be in news stories all over the world. Which means that you and I are going to be under a microscope."

"It means that we have to catch this bastard before he kills again," said Wells, letting his hand slide from her arm.

The street had been blocked to traffic. The long sidewalk was eerily empty. Several police officers stood on the steps that led to the front doors. Near one of the Romanesque columns, a blue tarp was draped over a step.

Patrick Colton stood next to the cloth. He looked up as Wells and Sinead approached.

"What have you got for us?" Wells asked.

Patrick gave the basics. "We've used a driver's license to ID the victim. Edward Pendleton. Age thirty-four. Male. Caucasian. Blond hair, blue eyes. Shot once in the chest at close range."

Just hearing that the guy had been killed left Wells equal parts sick and furious.

"Any witnesses?" Sinead asked.

"There were several people who heard the gunshot. But those folks got a look at the perp." Patrick pointed to a group. Mother. Father. Two boys who looked to be in their teens. The family reminded Wells of his own. Then again, everyone was gone, except for him and Harry. His chest ached.

He cleared his throat. "What about a note?"

"I haven't checked the body yet," said Patrick.

"Do you mind if we take a look?" Wells assumed that this victim was related to all the other killings. But he needed to see if there was a note linking him to the previous murders.

"Here. You need these." Patrick held out two pairs of latex gloves. Sinead took both pairs and handed one to him. As Wells slipped on the protective gear, the crime scene investigator continued, "The family heard the shot and saw Pendleton fall. They also caught a glimpse of a person running into the park."

"Did they get a description of the shooter?" Sinead asked.

Patrick shook his head. "Not much. They all reported seeing a person wearing dark clothes."

"What about the security guard?" Sinead asked.

It was a good question. After all, there'd been one sitting near the door this morning.

"The murder took place after the museum closed. The security guards were all inside," said Patrick.

Wells knelt next to the blue cover that was draped over the body. Sinead took a knee beside him. He lifted the corner so they could both see the man underneath. She sucked in a quick breath.

"It's Edward Pendleton," he said before adding, "We met with him this morning. He fits the profile for victims of the Landmark Killer." Nadeem was right. The new title fit perfectly.

"What about a note?" Sinead asked.

Edward's shirt was stained red and wet with blood. There was no way the killer would have put a note in a breast pocket. A bit of white stuck out from the pocket of his trousers. Wells pinched the paper between finger and thumb. Slowly, he pulled it free. "I think I found something."

A crime scene tech approached. They snapped several photos of Wells as he worked.

He unfolded the note.

It read: *M, A and E down. V up next I will continue to kill in the name of Maeve O'Leary until she is set free.*

Wells handed the note to the tech. "Get this into an evidence bag."

After pulling the cover back over Edward's body, he rose to his feet.

Sinead stood and dusted her hands on the seat of her jeans. "I wish Edward would've taken his safety more seriously. I wish we could have figured out what to say to him…" Her words trailed off as she looked across the street. Her eyes were moist.

He imagined that her gut was filled with the same sludge of misery as his own. He wanted to take her in his arms and tell her everything would be okay, even if he knew it was a lie. But he couldn't offer her any physical comfort. Neither could he take any for himself. Instead, he said, "You can't blame yourself."

"If I'm not the one who's responsible," she snapped. "Then who is?"

"The bastard who killed him," he said. "It's our job to find him and stop him before he kills again." For Wells, that simple fact had become his mantra. Like all he had to do was say it over and over to solve the case.

"How are we supposed to do that?" He could hear the frustration in her voice. "All of these murders have been bold." She nodded toward the body on the ground. "This one especially. It means that the killer's getting more daring."

She folded her arms across her chest and chewed on her bottom lip. True, he hadn't known Sinead very long. But he'd been around her enough today to know what she was thinking.

He said, "So, the killer's getting more audacious. Do you think that'll lead to overconfidence?" If they were lucky, the murderer would make a mistake.

Sinead blew out a long breath. "Here's what bothers me the most—this killer is very careful. They do their homework. Like this morning, they knew when the cleaning crew would be taking out the trash. Or take this killing. The murderer knew when the security guards would be inside. They also picked today because the building had to be cleared for tonight's fundraiser, ensuring that Edward would leave by three thirty."

"What does all of this mean to you?" He stepped closer to Sinead, unable to keep from being drawn into her orbit.

"This killer has been thinking about these killings for a long time. He's planned them out and is just using Maeve O'Leary as an excuse."

Wells was confused. "You mean he's not just killing to get her out of jail?"

Sinead shook her head. "I think he feels an affinity to Maeve. She reminds him of someone important in his life—his mother, probably."

She had mentioned all this before. "Do you still think that the victims remind the killer of his father?"

"If we assume that Maeve is the mother, then yeah. The victims are his father. In his mind, he's protecting his mother from an abusive man whose description matches those of his victims," she said.

Her assessment made sense. "How does that help us to find the Landmark Killer?"

Sinead looked at Wells. Their gazes met and held. His pulse started to race. She licked her lips and he wanted to kiss her. "I'm not sure," she began, "that my assessment helps at all."

The crime scene had been processed. The body of Edward Pendleton had been taken to the morgue. The family of witnesses had been interviewed. The task force had helped with the investigation. The evening briefing at the precinct had been canceled. Wells had called for a meeting the following morning at 8:30 a.m.

The fundraiser for the museum had also been postponed. Sinead imagined that the world of social media was in an uproar over the cancellation.

The police barricade was still up, but even that would soon be taken down.

Sinead checked her watch. It was 7:42 p.m. and still, she had some theories she'd like to discuss with Wells. They stood at the top of the museum steps, near a towering column.

Pressing a hand to her stomach, she turned to Wells. "The pizza from our late lunch has been burned off. I'm hungry again. There are some things that I'd like to go over this evening with you. How about a working dinner?"

He swallowed. "I'd love to, but I can't."

His answer left her stunned. "Can't?" she repeated. "What's more important than this case? A murderer is loose in the city. He killed two people today and he's going to kill again."

"I just…" He sighed and ran a hand down his face. Stubble covered his cheeks and chin and Sinead's fingers itched with the need to touch him. "I just can't."

His answer, though firm, brought up more questions. "Why not? What is it that's keeping you from work?"

"I have a ten-month-old baby at home who needs me."

Now she was stunned. "You have a kid? I didn't know."

"He's not my kid. He's my nephew. I'm his guardian. So, I guess he is my kid now." He cursed. "This is all so new. I'm not used to having to think about someone other than myself. Before, I could focus on my job. Work all night if I had to. But now..." He shook his head. "I have to find some kind of balance."

All the puzzle pieces clicked into place. The baby was the son of Wells's deceased brother and sister-in-law. The small Blackthorn family was down to two members and all they had were each other.

"What's his name?" she asked.

"Harry," he said with a smile.

"Harry," she repeated. "That's a good name."

"I think he's teething. At least that's what Captain Reeves says." He held up his phone. The lock screen was a picture of Wells holding a smiling baby. The kid had the same dark hair and eyes as Wells.

"Oh my gosh, he's adorable," she gushed. "He even looks like you."

"He looks like my brother, so I guess he kinda looks like me, too." He glanced at his phone once more before slipping it into his pocket. "Poor kid."

"What if we ordered dinner?" she suggested. "My treat. I could get us some heroes. Then, you and I could work while you're at home with Harry."

"You'd do that?"

"It's not a problem at all. Besides, I love babies. As my mom would call it, I'll get my baby fix." She took her phone from her bag and opened the app for her favorite sub shop. She handed the phone to Wells. "Place your order and we can pick up the food on our way."

As he scrolled through the menu, Sinead tried to keep

her heartbeat steady. It was true that they had work to do. It was also true that she was flexible enough to work at a colleague's home if needed. But what she hadn't said to Wells—what she wouldn't say to him, either— was that Sinead wanted to see baby Harry.

Years ago, she'd wanted a child more than anything in the world. The fact that she never conceived ruined her marriage and during that time, it made her sad just to see an infant. Since the divorce, Sinead had been determined to live a rich and full life without a spouse or child.

For the most part, she did.

But there were days when she woke, and her chest ached.

There was a hole in her heart that only a baby could fill—even if it was just for the evening.

Wells still wasn't used to living in his brother's old apartment. The ornate woodwork that came straight from the Art Deco period. The high ceilings. The shiny parquet floors. The great views. But as he led Sinead up the staircase, his heartbeat resonated with a single word.

Home.

While holding a take-out bag filled with heroes and chips, he knocked on Deborah's door.

A shadow passed over the peephole as she peered into the hallway. There was a scraping as locks were unlatched. Then, the door opened. Deborah stood on the threshold. Harry was in her arms.

The baby smiled at Wells. His chest ached with love.

"Hey, little man," he said, opening his arms to his nephew.

Harry waved his fists happily and reached for Wells. He held the baby close to his chest and inhaled the scent of the child.

"I kept an eye on the news," said Deborah. "Looks like you've had an especially busy day. So, I gave Harry a bath already. And if you look closely—you can see a tooth coming through on his bottom gums."

"A tooth?" Wells peered into the baby's mouth. All he saw was drool. "Looks like you'll be eating steak soon."

Harry blew bubbles.

"I bought a tube of teething gel and stuck it in his diaper bag." She held up the bag. Wells grabbed the strap and looped it over his shoulder.

"Okay, buddy," said Wells. "We have company tonight. So, you gotta play it cool."

"Company?" Deborah looked behind Wells. She saw Sinead and smiled. "I'm Deborah. The neighbor and babysitter."

"And my guardian angel," he added. He realized he should've introduced Sinead to Deborah when they first arrived. "This is Sinead Colton. She's a colleague from the FBI."

"Pleasure to meet you," said Deborah.

"Likewise," said Sinead with a smile.

"You two enjoy your evening." Deborah held on to the door and sighed. "Me, I'm going to bed early."

"Thanks for everything," he said again. Although he couldn't say it enough. Without Deborah's help, Wells would be sunk for sure.

She closed the door and Wells pointed to his apartment. "That's me."

"Easy commute to the babysitter," Sinead joked.

"True, that," he said with a laugh.

Harry smiled and gurgled.

Sinead stroked the back of Harry's wrist. "You think I'm funny?"

Harry wrapped his chubby fist around her finger.

"He's a good judge of character," said Wells. "But let's get into the apartment so we can eat." Wells patted down his pocket for his apartment keys. Damn, they were in his suit jacket. Which was still covered in blood and stowed in Sinead's backpack. "You got my keys. Mind if I get them out?"

"I'll trade you for the baby," she said, reaching for Harry.

His nephew opened his arms to Sinead. She took the child and held him on her hip. The two gazed at each other.

Before Harry came into his life, Wells had only given a passing thought to kids. Eventually, he'd have a family once he met the right woman. But honestly, Wells wasn't even looking for her, either.

Sinead held Harry and his nephew looked at her with complete trust in his eyes. Wells wanted to stand in the hallway and watch the two of them forever. She glanced in his direction and her cheeks reddened.

"Sorry," she said, "I'm taken with this handsome guy. You need your keys." She slipped the bag from her back and held it out to Wells by a strap.

He took the backpack and unzipped the zipper. His

suit coat and shirt were still on top, creased and stained. He pulled them both out and found his keys. After unlocking the door, he turned the handle and pushed the door open.

Sinead stepped inside. "You have a lot of space here."

"It's a nice place," he agreed. He set both Sinead's backpack and the diaper bag by the door. "Not something I could ever afford on a cop's salary. I inherited the apartment when Dan and Julie passed. Or rather, Harry inherited it. Since I'm his guardian, I get to live here."

"Smart to keep him in an environment he already knows."

"That's sorta what I figured." He set the bag with their dinner on the counter. "I can take him if you want. Trust me, I know how heavy he can get—especially in the middle of the night."

"I'm good holding him and it sounds like you could use a bit of a break." Sinead blew a raspberry on Harry's neck. The baby squealed with laughter. "How's that sound? Me and you can look out the window and watch the sunset. Then Uncle Wells can have a minute to himself."

"After getting my scalp cut this morning, I could use a quick shower."

"Take your time. We're good."

Sinead stood by the window, her finger on the glass. "See those clouds?" she asked Harry. "Looks like we are about to get a storm."

Harry waved his arms in the air and cooed.

He watched the two of them for a minute and smiled.

Sure, it was ridiculous to think that after only a few hours he'd be thinking that Sinead was anything other than a competent and kind coworker. But he couldn't keep his mind from wondering, *what if*?

Chapter 11

Wells walked down the short hallway to the bedroom. The furniture in the apartment had all belonged to Dan and Julie—the bedroom suite included. Wells now had both an oak chest of drawers and a matching dresser. Along with a queen-sized bed with a coordinating headboard. The carved scrollwork and faux aging weren't exactly his taste. But it was better than what had been at his other apartment. He'd used an old chest of drawers that a friend had given away and a bed on a simple metal frame.

He stripped out of his suit pants, borrowed NYPD shirt and briefs. The bedroom had a small en suite bathroom. The towels and toothbrush holder coordinated with the dark blue and silver comforter in the bedroom. He entered the bathroom and turned on the shower to cool.

Plunging his head under the spray, he winced. The cut to his head still hurt. He backed out of the shower just enough to let water sluice over the rest of his body. After grabbing soap and a cloth, he washed. His soapy hand slid over his body and for a moment, he imagined Sinead in the shower with him.

His dick twitched and hardened.

True, he could use a release. But he'd already been in the shower long enough. What was he supposed to say if he was gone longer? He quickly washed his hair, careful not to scrub the scab and bruise on his scalp.

After rinsing, he stepped from the shower. He grabbed a towel and ran it over his body. Once dry, he redressed and made his way toward the kitchen. Plates, filled with the food they'd picked up, sat on the breakfast bar. Sinead held Harry on her hip. She filled glasses with water from a pitcher.

"You look like a natural with my nephew," he said, walking into the room.

"When Rory was first born, her mom used to invite me over. I got to help her take care of the baby." She gave a wan smile. "I guess caring for an infant is like riding a bike. Once you know, you never forget."

"So, you helped care for Rory as a baby and now the two of you aren't close. Obviously, I'm prying. But what happened?" he asked.

"To be honest, I'm not sure. One day, the invitations stopped." She placed her lips on Harry's downy head. "I've always worried that I did something wrong."

"I doubt that's the case," he said.

She glanced over her shoulder and smiled. His heart skipped a beat.

"I rummaged through your cabinets for plates and glasses," she said, changing the subject. "I hope you don't mind."

"I would've eaten the sandwich on the paper. This looks nice." He held out his hands to Harry. The baby reached for him. "You want to hang out in your swing while we eat?"

Sinead set the plates on the table as Wells strapped Harry into the baby swing. The swing moved back and forth. *Tick. Tick. Tick.* Sinead took a seat.

"I got your toes." She reached for his feet, her voice a singsong, each time the swing moved forward.

Harry squealed with glee. Wells took a bite of his sandwich. He chewed and enjoyed his food. The bread was fresh. The cheese was mellow. There was the perfect combination of turkey and ham. The lettuce was crisp, and the tomato was ripe. He swallowed his bite. "Damn," he said. "Now that's a hero."

"They're good, right?" Sinead picked up her own sandwich and took a bite. She chewed. Swallowed. "I order from the app once a week, at least."

Harry was happy. Wells's food was good. He was spending time with an attractive and smart woman. The moment was perfect. Too bad it couldn't last. "We need to figure out who might be next on the killer's list," he said, popping a potato chip into his mouth.

"Caucasian men in their thirties with blue eyes, blond hair and first names that start with *V*."

"Don't forget," he said, "a job at a New York City land-mark."

"There are a lot of databases that need to be cross-referenced. Sounds like another job for Ashlynn."

His phone sat on the counter. Wells rose from the table to get it. He typed out a text to Ashlynn.

We need a new list of possible victims.

She replied within seconds.

I'm already working on it. Will send it as soon as it's ready.

He sent a thumbs-up emoji.

She replied with a smiley face.

He set the phone on the charging station.

"She's on it already," he said, sitting back at the table. After picking up his hero, he took another bite. While chewing, he made a list of everything he needed to discuss with Sinead. Bringing up the most important item on his mental agenda, he said, "We need a plan to deal with possible victims who won't take their safety seriously." He meant those like Edward Pendleton, but he didn't need to say anything more.

"What other choices do we have besides protective custody?" She took a bite, chewed and swallowed.

A crumb of bread clung to her lips. Sure, he'd heard what she said. What's more, he didn't have an answer to her question. It would be hard—if not impossible— to keep anyone in protective custody for long. But he couldn't concentrate—not with the piece of bread cling-ing to her mouth.

He wanted to brush it off.

Or better yet, kiss it away.

He touched his own mouth. "You have something right there."

She licked her bottom lip. Her pink tongue on her red lips was erotic as hell. His dick twitched again. He regretted not taking matters into hand when he had the chance in the shower.

"Did I get it?" she asked.

"Yeah," he said, his word a groan. "You got it."

She drew her eyebrows together. "Are you okay?"

Picking up his glass of water, he took a sip. "Just got some food caught in my throat."

Sinead said, "We should consider talking with the media."

Wells shook his head. "Absolutely not. Once we speak to a reporter, we no longer control the narrative."

"Just because you had a bad experience doesn't mean that everyone in the news industry is bad." She popped the final bite of her sandwich into her mouth and chewed. "Besides, Edward might've reacted differently if he knew the facts before we showed up. Hell, he might've reached out to us personally because he fit the profile."

"He might've done all of that and more. Or, he might not have done anything differently. I will tell you this, once we talk to the media, we can't take back anything that's out."

"I just think it's something for you to consider."

"I'll think about it," he lied. "Until then, I'll check

with our legal department to see what options we have if any potential victims don't want to cooperate. You do the same."

Sinead wiped her mouth with a napkin. "I can reach out in the morning."

There was something else that was bothering him, though. "I want to revisit something you said at the museum."

In the swing, Harry fussed. Sinead rose from the table and took him out. She held him against her chest and swayed where she stood. "What did I say that you want to revisit?"

"You mentioned that the Landmark Killer had done his homework. That he knew all about his victims."

She placed a kiss on Harry's cheek. "Yeah. What are you thinking?"

"Well, I'm thinking it's taking us a while to find a list of potential victims and we're the police. How is some random person supposed to get access to all this personal information?"

Sinead stopped swaying. "What're you getting at?" she asked, though he guessed that she already knew.

"I think the killer has access to all the databases because he works for the city." He paused. "He might even be a cop."

Sinead's pulse thundered in her ears. Was Wells right? Was the Landmark Killer a police officer?

"We can't make your suspicion public, not until we have more evidence," she said.

"For now," he said, "it's just between the two of us."

Harry arched his back and yowled. Sinead started swaying again. She stroked the back of his head and made shushing noises.

Wells stepped forward, with his arms outstretched. "I usually give him a bottle around this time. I bet the little man is hungry."

"I can give him his bottle," she said. Maybe she'd spoken a little too quickly. "I mean, I don't want to intrude but I can help. It sounds like you've had a hard few weeks."

"You know, your help would be great. I can clean up while you feed Harry. Give me a sec and I'll make him a bottle."

The child was rigid in her arms. He squealed with hunger. Sinead walked to the window. The sun had set, and the clouds thickened, blocking out whatever light was left. It turned the window into a mirror. She could clearly see her own reflection and the downy hair on the baby's head. Behind her, Wells worked in the kitchen.

Funny how everything in the glass was slightly distorted. Like what she saw came from a dream. Then again, for Sinead, it was easy to look at the reflection and see her fantasy life. A home. A husband she loved—and who loved her in return. A baby that they both adored.

But that wasn't her reality.

Wells wasn't her husband. He was simply a colleague.

Harry wasn't her child. He was just a baby that needed someone to hold him.

In fact, she didn't belong in this apartment. She was a guest in the home.

None of this was for Sinead, not now and maybe not ever.

As if he'd read her mind, Harry screamed.

She tapped on the glass. "Can you see the handsome baby, Harry?"

His cries quieted and he reached for her finger.

There was more to worry about than her personal life.

"What if you're right?" she asked, speaking to the reflection of Wells in the window. "How do we investigate the Landmark Killer if he's getting inside information?"

Wells approached. "I trust everyone on our team. But we have to lock up our information tight. No leaks. No discussing the case with anyone else."

He handed her a filled bottle. Sinead sat on the sofa. She adjusted Harry so he reclined in her arms. He hungrily took the bottle, gulping down the formula. She glanced up at Wells. "We only discuss this with the team—and our bosses, correct?"

"Captain Reeves and ADIC Chang are obviously in the loop." Wells stroked the top of Harry's head. "You're okay feeding him while I clean up the kitchen?"

"I'm more than okay."

"You know, Harry really seems to like you."

"I like kids." She cooed at Harry. "And this one especially."

He smiled around his bottle and Sinead fell in love with the child a little bit more.

"But you don't have any of your own," Wells said from the kitchen.

She couldn't tell if that was a question or a statement.

"I don't," she said without looking up. "My ex-husband and I tried." She shrugged, summing up her painful past in a single gesture.

She raised her gaze. He held a dish towel in one hand and was watching her. For a moment, they looked at each other and said nothing.

He sighed. "Even the best marriages are hard."

She gave a wry laugh. "Trust me, my marriage was not one of the best."

"What about it—would you ever want to take the plunge again?" he asked.

Sinead didn't mind the intrusive question. After all, she was the one snuggling his infant nephew. "It's not that I disagree with the institution of marriage," she began.

"But who wants to live in an institution?" he said, finishing her joke.

"Hey," she said, the single word dripping with mock indignation. "You stole my punch line." She paused a moment, collecting her thoughts. "My first marriage was awful. Aside from the infertility, he wanted me to be something that I wasn't. In the end, I realized that I had to lose my marriage to save myself. If I were to commit to someone else, he'd have to be the right guy."

"What kind of guy is that?" he asked.

Was there more to his question? She wasn't sure how to categorize their relationship. True, they were more than colleagues. Hell, maybe they were even friends. But she wasn't interested in a romance with a coworker. Even if that man happened to be Wells Blackthorn. "Okay, it's time to stop analyzing the analyst. What about you? Single. Never married. Why's that?"

Dropping his gaze, he wiped the counter. For a moment, Sinead thought that he wasn't going to answer her question. He looked up at her. "I guess I'm single for the same reason as you, just from a different perspective. My parents had a great marriage. They loved each other. They were friends. They were both dedicated to me and my brother." He looped the towel over the faucet. "I guess they set a high bar. If I can't have what they had, I don't want a marriage at all."

Sinead wasn't sure how to respond. She looked down at the baby in her arms. Harry's eyes were closed. His lips had loosened from the nipple. She removed the bottle from his mouth. She placed him on her shoulder and gently patted his back. He gave a soft burp and snuggled into her.

"Looks like he's out," she said.

"You okay holding him for another minute?" Wells asked. "It'd give me a chance to take out the garbage."

Harry's heartbeat resonated with her own. "Take your time." She breathed deep, inhaling Harry's sweet baby scent. "We're good."

With a garbage bag in his hand, Wells left the apartment.

Then it was just Sinead and Harry. Her mind wandered to the days when she was allowed to be a part of her father's new family. At the time she really did love Rory. Maybe some of that caring still lived in Sinead's heart.

After she got married, she and her husband had tried

to have a child. But month after month was filled with disappointment when she failed to conceive. Then, her husband left.

It was as if both situations were separate streams of emotion. But today, they converged. All the feelings left her exhausted. Her eyes were heavy. She shouldn't fall asleep on Wells's sofa. But maybe she could let her lids close, just for a minute. Letting out a long breath, Sinead knew that this moment was perfect—and that it wouldn't last forever.

Chapter 12

Sinead woke, her heart hammering against her chest.

There'd been a shot and a scream.

Before she opened her eyes, she knew that she wasn't in her own bed—or even her own apartment. She was lying on a sofa with a blanket pulled up to her chest. Rain pelted a nearby window. But where was she?

A figure moved through the dark, and her heart ceased to beat. She held her breath and it all came back to her.

"Wells?" she said, her voice hoarse.

"Sorry we woke you," he said. "Harry's not a fan of the storm."

There was another boom. Lightning split the sky. It lit up the room like a camera's flash. There was a clap of thunder. It shook the windows. Wells stood near the kitchen. Harry clung to his chest. Tears stained the baby's cheeks and he squawked again.

"Poor guy." She sat up. "He really doesn't like the storm." Scrubbing her face with her hands, she asked, "What time is it?"

"A little after midnight."

Sinead stood. "Sorry that I dozed off. You should've gotten me up when you got back from taking out the garbage."

Even in the dark, she could see his smile. "You both looked so peaceful, I didn't want to wake you."

"Still," she protested. "It was unprofessional of me to just crash on your couch."

"I'd like to think we are beyond just being coworkers," he said.

In the dark, she was drawn to the sound of his voice. "Of course, we are."

Harry whimpered.

Wells gave a wry laugh. "I think he wants you."

Sinead's heart squeezed in her chest. As much as she loved Harry, she shouldn't allow herself to become attached after one evening. It wasn't good for either of them. And yet, she said, "I'll hold him. Do you think he's hungry again?"

"I tried to feed him, but he refused to take any formula."

"Maybe his teeth are bothering him."

"Damn," he cursed. He was still just a shadow in the darkness. But her eyes had adjusted enough to see Wells scratch the stubble on his chin. "He's getting a tooth, I knew that. I really am bad at this parenting thing."

"I think Deborah said that the teething gel was in your diaper bag."

"Here." Wells held the baby out to Sinead. "You hold him. I'll find the gel."

Sinead took Harry. He whimpered but sank into her chest. "Hush, little baby, don't say a word," she sang. "Aunt Sinead's gonna buy you some kind of bird. I don't remember the words to this song. If it makes you happy, then I'll sing all night long."

"Found it," said Wells. He approached Sinead and placed his hand on Harry's head. "I don't want to poke around his face in the dark, but I don't want to turn on a light, either. The light gets him all keyed up and he'll never go back to sleep."

"See?" said Sinead. "You are a good parent. You're learning what Harry needs."

"I might be learning, but they are all hard lessons." He paused. "Come with me. I have a night-light in the bathroom."

Sinead followed Wells. He led her not to the hallway bath but the one that was connected to his bedroom. True to his word, a small flat light was plugged into an outlet. It turned the bathroom an eerie shade of blue, but it was bright enough to see.

Wells unscrewed the lid off a small plastic tube. He placed a daub of the gel on his finger, filling the small bathroom with a medicinal scent. "Come here, little man, and let me put this on your new tooth."

Harry yowled and arched his back. Sinead felt him slipping and she held him tighter. Wells swiped his finger over the baby's gum. An instant later, Harry was silent.

"Wow," said Sinead. "That stuff works fast. I'm impressed."

"Me, too. I wish I'd known about it sooner." He set the tube on the bathroom vanity. "I haven't slept through the night since Dan and Julie died."

Harry nestled into Sinead's shoulder.

"I am sorry about what happened to your brother and that it turned your life upside down." The blue nightlight cast Wells in a silvery glow. It turned his dark eyes obsidian. His lips became the color of deep red wine. For a moment, she was overwhelmed with a ridiculous notion that Wells was an ethereal being. Her fingers twitched with the desire to touch him, just to make sure he was real.

"It's cliché to say, 'I can't remember what life was like before Harry.' But it's true." His words seemed to come from nowhere.

The baby was heavy in her arms. "I think he's asleep," Sinead whispered.

"I'll put him in his crib." Wells took Harry from Sinead and walked out of the bathroom. He crossed the bedroom floor and stopped at the door. Rain still fell outside and streaked down the window. A watery wedge of light stretched out across the mattress. "You should stay here tonight," he said. "I can't throw you out at midnight and in the middle of a storm."

"I am an FBI agent, you know," she joked. "Not a damsel in distress."

"Trust me, I know that you can take care of yourself," he said, his voice a whisper. "But even though you aren't a lady who needs saving, I can still be a gentleman."

Truth be told, the last thing she wanted to do was make her way home in the storm. "Thanks," she said. "I'll take the sofa."

"You can sleep in here," he said.

Was there more to his offer than simply being kind? Did Sinead mind?

"I can't take your bed," she began.

"It's not really my bed. I left all my furniture in Brooklyn when I sublet my other place. Everything in this apartment belonged to Dan and Julie." He paused. "I mean, the sheets are clean and everything. But I'm fine on the sofa. Besides, it'll be easier if Harry wakes up again."

She really was tired. The bed looked comfortable. "So long as you're sure." She paused. "I can always order a rideshare."

"At this time of night? In a storm? The prices for a ride will be highway robbery—literally."

She laughed quietly at his joke. "So long as you're sure," she said again.

"I insist," he whispered.

His words danced along her skin. "Okay, then. Thanks."

He backed out of the room and shut the door behind him. Sinead stood in the dark. The air in the room pressed against her flesh. Her blood rushed through her veins. There was no reason to invite Wells to share her bed, other than the fact that she wanted to have him inside of her.

In truth, she'd wanted him since the first moment she saw him.

She walked across the room, covering the floor in two

strides. She reached for the door handle and stopped. Sure, she wanted Wells as a bedmate. Who wouldn't? He was handsome. Funny. Intelligent. Caring.

But they had a killer to catch. Sinead wasn't sure that she could separate the emotional from the physical with Wells. In short, having sex with him would complicate her job and her life.

She refused to let that happen.

And yet, her hand still rested on the door handle, as she wondered—*what if?*

Wells stood in the darkened hallway. He still held the baby. Harry was nestled against his chest. Sure, taking care of his nephew had become his top priority. Yet at the moment, he wasn't really thinking about the child. Sinead was on his mind.

God, she was good looking. Better looking than anybody had the right to be. But there was more. Sinead was one of the smartest people he'd ever met on the job. Hell, she was one of the smartest people he'd met, full stop. Harry loved her. In fact, the baby seemed to like Sinead more than he liked Wells. That fact didn't bother him. He wasn't jealous, but it went to show what kind of woman Sinead really was.

Leaning on the door, he wanted only one thing: to go into the bedroom and make love to Sinead. Instead, he had to get his nephew into his crib.

The nursery was to the right of the master suite. The door was already open. He could see enough to find the crib. He set Harry down. The baby grumbled in his sleep. Wells stroked Harry's forehead until the child quieted.

With a sigh, he walked quietly out of the room.

He stood in the hall.

Damn. He should have offered Sinead a T-shirt to sleep in. After all, she'd been in the same clothes all day.

It wasn't too late to check on her, was it? Truly, she wouldn't be asleep already.

He knocked softly on the bedroom door. He waited a moment and turned the handle. He pushed the door open and stepped inside.

Sinead stood in the middle of the floor. Light from a streetlamp spilled into the room. It bathed her in a golden glow. She wore only her panties and shirt. Her fingers were wound in the hem of her shirt, ready to remove that as well.

He drank in the sight of her. She was more intoxicating than an aged whiskey. In the same instant he knew that it was wrong to ogle Sinead.

"Oh crap," he said. "I didn't mean to barge in." Dropping his gaze to the floor, he stared at the rug. But the image of Sinead was tattooed on his brain. "I was going to offer you something to sleep in," he continued, while backing out of the room. "There are other shirts if you want. Bottom drawer of the dresser."

"Wells." Her voice surrounded him and pulled him back to her.

"Yeah?"

"Don't go," she said.

He raised his eyes. She still stood in the pool of light. Raising her arms, she removed her shirt and let it fall to the floor. She wore only her bra and underwear. A line of cleavage separated her full breasts. Her waist was narrow, and her panties clung to her hips. She dragged her teeth over her bottom lip and smiled. "You can stay if you want."

Wells didn't need any other invitation. Crossing the room, he went to Sinead. He wrapped his arms around her waist and pulled her to him. Her breasts were crushed against his chest. Placing his mouth on hers, he kissed her hungrily. His dick was hard. She rubbed her pelvis against his hips. The slipstream of friction left him harder than before.

He moaned.

Sinead nipped his bottom lip. "You like that?" Her words mingled with the kiss.

"God, yes."

He lowered his mouth and kissed her soft neck. Her skin tasted of salt and yet she smelled like strawberries. He pulled the bra's cup down until her breast was exposed. He bent his head to her areola and ran his tongue over her nipple.

She sucked in a shaking breath. Her reaction left him wanting her more. To touch her more. To taste her more. He raked her flesh with his teeth.

She moaned. "Oh, Wells."

He kissed her mouth hard, wanting to claim her as his own.

She slipped her hands down the front of his shorts. Her touch ignited a fuse.

"Do you like this? Do you like when I touch you here?" she asked, her voice low and husky.

Her touch became his whole universe. "Like it? God, yes. I lo…" He bit off his final word. "I like it a lot."

She traced his tip, collecting a bead of moisture. She

ran her palm down his length. Wells's dick was so hard that he was ready to explode in her hand. "You are so close to perfect," he growled. "I like that you're taking charge."

A flash of lightning streaked across the sky. It filled his room with a burst of light. In that moment, he saw Sinead. She was sexy in her panties and bra. Her hand was in his shorts. The image flooded his brain. Just as quickly, he was back in the darkness. He could no longer see—just feel.

"What else do you like?" Her breath was hot on his neck. "What else do you want?"

His brain flooded with erotic images. "Oh, there's lots that I'd like to do to you."

"I want you inside me," she said. "Now."

He deepened his kiss. Gripping her ass, he lifted Sinead. She wrapped her legs around his waist. With one hand, he pulled down his shorts enough to free himself. Then, she slipped one leg out of her panties. He slid inside of her. She was hot and wet. He gripped her ass tighter. He drove into her harder. The pleasure was so intense that he forgot his own freaking name.

"Wells," she panted, riding him hard. She slipped her hand between them and rubbed the top of her sex. "Wells. Wells. Wells."

He dropped his gaze to the space between their bodies. Seeing her hand on her own sex was so damn hot that it left him dizzy. "Sinead," he growled. "You are so sexy." Even through the haze of his impending orgasm, he knew that she was much more than just sexy.

She tightened her legs around his middle and moaned with pleasure.

He wanted to be inside her all night. But his balls were already getting tight. He was going to come and soon. Sinead's innermost muscles tightened on him. She cried out with her climax. Wells couldn't hold back his ecstasy anymore. With a low growl, he came.

His pulse roared through his body. Every part of him throbbed with his racing heartbeat. Still holding Sinead, he stumbled through the dark and collapsed on the side of the bed. She was beneath him. He placed his lips softly on her mouth. Her cheek. Her chin. The spot right behind her ear. His pulse slowed.

Rain pattered against the window.

He was still hard and inside of Sinead. Already, he wanted her again.

"That was fabulous," she whispered into his hair. "You were fabulous."

In the dark, he could see her pulse fluttering at the base of her neck.

"You thought that was good..." Wells propped himself up on his elbows and began to move slowly inside of her. He gave her his best smile. "Then wait until you see what I'm going to do to you next."

Chapter 13

Wells was on top of Sinead—and still inside her. Sure, they'd had sex—something raw and primal. It was like a moment of insanity. But the fever that had burned her skin was over.

To take him again would mean something else.

Something more.

Yet, she was already moving her hips. She gripped his shoulders and kissed him harder. Wrapping her arms around his middle, she took him in deeper. Yes, she would take Wells again. In the morning? Honestly, that seemed like such a long way off it didn't really matter.

"Scoot up to the top of the bed," he said.

She did as he told her. Sure, she liked to take charge, but she could also take orders.

"Here?" Her head rested on the pillow.

He knelt at the foot of the bed. His gaze traveled from her feet to her legs to her sex. Her stomach. Her chest. Their eyes met and held. He gripped her foot with his strong hand and massaged her instep.

She groaned with pleasure.

"Now it's my turn to find out what you like."

"You're doing a pretty good job with that foot massage."

He hummed. "You like that?"

She bit her lip and nodded.

"What about this?" His hand moved up to her calf. His fingers worked away the cords of tension. "Do you like this?"

"Yes," she whispered. Her words mixed with the patter of the rain on the window.

"And this?" He kneaded her thigh.

"Mmm-hmm," she hummed. Sinead wanted Wells inside of her again and yet, she wanted this moment to last forever.

"Here?"

His touch was a delicious torture. "Yes."

"And here?" Wells slid his finger inside of her.

"Oh yes," she moaned.

He put another finger inside of her and moved back and forth. Sinead closed her eyes and let the sensations wash over her. Wells kissed her again. Using his thumb, he rubbed the top of her sex. His touch sent a shock wave through her body. She bucked on the bed, every inch of her tingling with pleasure.

He kissed her mouth. Her neck. Her chest.

She was awash in ecstasy. Her stomach tightened as

her orgasm began. She held tight to Wells. Pressing her lips to his throat, she cried out into his neck.

Her muscles went limp. She lay on the bed panting.

"I want you," he said. Their lovemaking was so frantic that he hadn't bothered to do anything beyond free himself from the fly of his shorts. He breathed in her ear, "Again. Now."

"Yes," she breathed. "Yes."

He pulled down her panties and dropped them to the floor. Then, Wells stood and stripped out of his shirt, shorts and briefs. He climbed back on the bed, and she parted her thighs. He moved between her legs. His skin was hot. The hair that covered his body was soft. He entered her in one stroke, and she clung to his back.

Wells moved inside of her. She met his tempo. Both took and received pleasure freely. It was more than a joining of the body, but of the spirit as well. It was as if, in this singular moment, she was no longer alone. What's more, she was good enough to be loved completely. Lifting one leg, she hooked it over his shoulder. He drove inside her deeper than before.

Somehow, he'd never be inside of her deep enough.

Her orgasm began to build again. It was a wave lifting her up and up and up. And then, it crashed, pulling her under. She broke the surface, breathless.

A sheen of sweat covered Wells's back and brow. He thrust inside of her hard. Once more and then once again. With a low growl, he came and then fell onto her stomach.

For a moment, neither said a word.

The staccato of the rain and their ragged breathing filled the small room.

He kissed her cheek, tenderly this time.

She reveled in the feeling of his lips on her skin. And yet, without the haze of passion to cloud her thinking, she knew that she'd been foolish to ignore the consequences of bedding a coworker—and one who she'd met only the day before. Wells seemed like a great guy. But she had no way to know how he'd react in the morning. Would he ignore her? Tell lewd jokes about their night together? Or worse, would he get clingy and jealous?

"Is it going to be weird between us tomorrow?" she asked.

He stood and put on his briefs. "Weird?" he echoed. "I mean, this is definitely the best get-to-know-you meeting in the history of the world."

She wanted to laugh but didn't. "Be serious."

He picked up his T-shirt. "You know, I came in here to offer you something to sleep in that wasn't your own clothes. You want this?"

"Sure. Thanks." She took the shirt. Sitting on the bed, she stripped out of her bra and put the shirt on. "The minute the bra comes off is usually the best feeling of the day. Today it's further down on the list."

He handed Sinead her panties. She slipped into those as well. "But I am concerned. How are we going to navigate work tomorrow?" And every other day until the Landmark Killer was caught.

Wells sat on the side of the bed. He reached for her hand and laced his fingers through her own. "I like you a lot. I want to spend more time with you. But it'd be foolish to think that an office romance wouldn't compromise the investigation."

"So, how do we act tomorrow?" Or maybe she should leave now. She could still order a rideshare—the cost be damned.

He slipped under the covers. "There's one thing I learned from Dan and Julie's accident."

"What's that?"

"There are no guarantees in life. Not for a year. A month. Even a day. We can only enjoy this moment because that's really all we have."

"That's profound." She slipped under the covers as well and lay back on the pillow. It really was too late to go home. Besides, after a few hours of sleep, she might have an answer to her question. *What now?*

She settled on the mattress and let her eyes drift closed. Wells moved in beside her. She laid her head on his chest. His arm lay across her back, his fingertips grazing the top of her butt. His warm breath washed over her hair. In the moment, she felt safe and cherished— even if it were just for the night.

"You really are almost perfect in every way," he said, his voice heavy with sleep.

His words resonated through her. *Almost perfect.*

Her entire life, she'd always tried to be perfect. The perfect daughter, so her father would take an interest in her. The perfect child, so her mother wouldn't be so damned sad all the time. The perfect student to get into the right school. The perfect wife, so her husband would stay. The perfect agent, so she could move up the chain of command.

She stared at the window, streaked with rain, and knew an important truth. She'd always been good—but she'd never been good enough.

Was it going to be the same way with Wells?

Sinead stretched out on the bed. Her limbs were loose and even before she opened her eyes, she knew where she was and remembered what she'd done. Wells lay beside her, his breathing slow and steady. She rolled toward him and watched him as he slept.

His eyelashes fanned out across his cheeks. It was totally unfair that a guy should have such thick lashes. His mouth was opened slightly, and he snored quietly. His lips still looked very kissable. A dark shadow of stubble covered his chin.

Her phone sat on the nightstand. 5:42 a.m.

She had to be at the office by 8:30.

She wanted to snuggle into Wells's arms and go back to sleep.

She needed to get out of his apartment before he woke.

Slipping from the bed, she found her discarded clothes on the floor. Sinead carried yesterday's outfit into the bathroom and redressed quickly and quietly. Holding on to her shoes, she tiptoed back through the bedroom. She paused at the door and glanced back at Wells.

Sure, sneaking out at dawn wasn't exactly a classy move.

But what were they supposed to say to each other? It was better for them both if the first time they saw each other again was at work. That way, what happened between them was already in the rearview mirror.

She pulled the door closed. The latch caught with a click. The nursery was next to the master suite. From his crib, Harry squawked. Sinead peeked into the room. Inside, she could see Harry's fists waving in the air.

"Hey, buddy," she said, walking to the side of the crib. "How're you doing this morning?"

He smiled and blew bubbles.

"That good, eh?"

He reached for her.

Sinead picked him up and held him to her chest. One hand was on his back and the other on his butt. His diaper was cold and wet. "Seems to me that you need a clean diaper and maybe some breakfast." A changing table was strapped to the top of a four-drawer dresser. Diapers and wipes were tucked inside a basket on the floor. True, she hadn't changed a diaper since Rory was a baby, but she imagined that the mechanics were all still the same. With a clean diaper and wipe ready, she unfastened the snaps on the legs of Harry's pajamas. She took off the wet diaper and threw it into the wastebasket. After a quick wipe, she put on a new diaper.

"That wasn't so bad," said Sinead. "Now we just have to get you back into your clothes."

Harry kicked and waved his arms.

She held on to the footie of his pajamas and tracked his chubby toes. "And I think getting you dressed is going to be a lot harder than getting you undressed."

He laughed in agreement.

Once she got him back in his pajamas, then what?

She couldn't just leave the baby unattended. She had to stay. It meant that she had no choice but to face Wells—to face what they'd done—now and not later.

Even before Wells opened his eyes, he knew that he was alone and in an empty bed. Sinead was gone. Rubbing his chest, he stared at the ceiling. He wanted to be mad, but he couldn't blame her for leaving before he woke.

The Landmark Killer case would force them to work together. So, he knew she was smart for leaving before the awkward morning-after chat. And still, her departure left him wounded.

He rolled to the bedside table and picked up his phone to check the time.

6:13 a.m.

His heart leaped to his throat. Harry had never slept this late in the morning. He jumped from the bed and threw the door open. It hit the wall with a clatter. He stumbled into the nursery. The crib was empty. His blood turned cold in his veins.

Then he heard them—Harry and Sinead. Their voices came from the kitchen.

"Here comes the airplane," she said. "Zoom. It's coming in for a landing. Open the hangar."

Harry giggled with delight.

"C'mon. Open the hangar."

He walked down the short hallway. Standing in the shadows, he watched.

Harry sat in his highchair and Sinead sat beside him.

She had a spoon lifted to his mouth and an opened jar of pureed sweet potatoes sat on the table beside her.

She pressed Harry's bottom lip with the spoon. The baby opened his mouth, and she slid the sweet potatoes inside.

"Atta boy," she said.

Harry cooed, spitting out half his food in the process.

"Let's get that cleaned up." She wiped his chin with a tea towel.

Harry leaned back and grumbled in protest. But his nephew wasn't upset, just being a baby.

He stepped back. The floor creaked. Sinead looked up. She wore yesterday's clothes. Her hair was tangled. She wore no makeup. She was the most beautiful woman he'd ever seen.

"Good morning," she said. "I hope you don't mind that I gave Harry breakfast. He seemed hungry. Oh," she added. "I changed his diaper. He was super wet."

Now what was he supposed to say? He ran a hand through his hair. "Thanks for taking care of him."

She scooped another bite of pureed sweet potatoes onto the spoon. "No problem." Then, she returned her attention to the baby. "You want to show Uncle Wells how good you can eat? Who's ready for the plane to land?" She swished in with the spoon. Harry gobbled down the bite.

The moment seemed all too familiar. His chest ached with nostalgia and something else. Was it hope for the future? "In my house it was a train pulling into the station."

Sinead looked up. "Excuse me?"

"Back when I was a kid, my mom used to get us to eat by saying the food was a train pulling into the station."

"In honor of your grandma Blackthorn," said Sinead, smiling at Harry, "The airport is now closed, and the train station is officially open." She scooped out another bite. "Unless you want to feed him. I mean, I should probably go back to my place and get showered. I need to get ready for work. The team leader I work with." She rolled her eyes. "You wouldn't believe."

She meant him. He chuckled. "Hard guy to handle?"

"Detective Wells, do I detect a double entendre?"

"Oh jeez, I hadn't meant to make a racy joke."

"Too bad. It was funny." She rose from the seat and held out the spoon. "I should get going for real."

The last thing he wanted was for her to leave. "You could stay for breakfast—it's the least I can do." Damn. He'd spoken too quickly and been too eager to have her stay. He paused a beat. "I make an outstanding Greek omelet."

"If it's really outstanding, then I'll stay." She dropped back into the seat.

Harry babbled happily.

Wells still wore only his briefs. "Give me a second to put on something less comfortable."

"Take your time. If my task force leader gets an attitude, I'll blame you."

Shaking his head, he walked down the hallway. He slipped inside the bedroom and shut the door. With a minute alone, he had to admit that an affair with a coworker was always a bad idea. But Sinead had been too much to resist.

The shirt she'd slept in was on the floor. He picked it up and held it to his nose, breathing in her scent. He had to get a grip. Sinead was dredging up feelings that Wells wanted to avoid. More than that, he had to think of Harry. Obviously, the baby was besotted with Sinead. But how would Harry feel when the office affair inevitably ended, and she was gone?

The kid had already lost his parents.

He couldn't let Harry love Sinead only to have her leave, too.

Maybe he shouldn't have offered to make them breakfast. He slipped into the shirt and knew one thing for certain. Whatever feelings he had for Sinead had to stop.

It was best for everyone.

Sinead scraped her fork across her plate and licked the tines clean. Her stomach was pleasantly full, and the food was enough fuel for her to start the day. Wells sat in a seat next to hers at the table.

"I'll admit, you do make an outstanding Greek omelet," she said to him.

He finished the last bite on his plate. "It's nice to have someone to cook for," he said. "Soon, every meal will be for two."

She glanced at Harry. The baby sat on a blanket that had been laid out on the floor. A colorful baby gym was set next to him. Stuffed elephants and plastic giraffes hung from crisscrossed padded beams. He batted at the dangling toys.

"He'll be a lucky guy when he starts to eat table food." She stood and picked up her plate and silverware. She grabbed his, too, and placed both in the sink. The clock on the microwave read 6:55 a.m. "I really should get going. I still need a shower and to change clothes."

He rose from his seat. "I'm not sure what to do now. Do I kiss you? Shake your hand?"

She opened her arms. "How 'bout a hug?"

"Sure."

He stepped into her embrace and wrapped his arms around her back. God, it felt good to be held by Wells. So good that she never wanted to let go.

Maybe that was the best reason of all for her to leave.

Inching back, she created space between herself and Wells. "I'd better," she said. Whatever else she was going to say caught in her throat. She coughed. "I guess I'd better go."

"Yeah, I guess so. I'll see you at the office." He stepped back. "I promise, this doesn't have to get weird."

Sinead had a long list of reasons why their single night together shouldn't cause any problems. They were both adults. Neither one had made any promises. It was all about lust, not love. Too bad she thought the list was crap.

Still, she nodded her head. "I know."

Now there was truly nothing else for her to say or do. Except...

She knelt on the floor next to Harry. "You be a good guy for your uncle Wells. He works hard to keep us all safe."

He reached for her and rolled over. He hit the baby

gym and started to cry. Sinead knelt next to Harry and picked him up. He leaned into her chest and wailed. She knew how he felt. She patted his back.

"It's okay. You'll be all right," she soothed, speaking as much to herself as to the child.

Harry's cries went quiet.

"He likes you," said Wells.

She rose to her feet. "The feeling's mutual."

Wells walked down the hallway that led to the door. Sinead held Harry and followed. Her backpack sat on the floor. She picked it up and slipped a strap over one shoulder. Now there was nothing more for her in the apartment.

Wells pulled open the door.

Sitting on the floor in the hallway was a delivery box.

"Did you order something?" she asked, although it really wasn't her business. And was it odd that the package had been left at his door? She hadn't noticed a doorman the night before—which meant that the packages delivered to the building should be kept in the lobby.

"I didn't." He paused. His pallor went gray. "Maybe it was ordered by Dan or Julie before..." His voice trailed off.

Sinead knew what it was to have a sibling and not be close. That described her relationship with Rory in a nutshell. In a lot of ways losing her sister now would be worse than if they ever developed a relationship—not that reconciling was part of her plan. It's just that to lose Rory now would leave her with a future that would be filled with nothing but regrets instead of any happy memories.

She watched Wells. Those regrets were etched into each line of his face.

No wonder she'd tumbled into bed with him last night. They'd gone through so much of the same heartache. Even after spending just one day with him, she must've sensed that they were kindred spirits.

They'd stood in silence for too long, both staring at the box.

"Do you want me to check?" she asked.

Wells shook his head. He bent to the box with his arms outstretched. He stopped. "Huh. That's odd."

"What's odd?"

"It's a handwritten label, not a printed one, and it's made out to me—not Julie or Dan."

"That is odd." Despite the air-conditioning that circulated through the building, Sinead started to sweat.

Then, in Sinead's mind, four separate events occurred. In reality, it was a continuous moment, like the current of a rushing river. Wells nudged the box with his toe. Sinead reached for his shoulder and pulled him back. A flash of light and noise filled the hallway. The concussion of the blast threw her back into the apartment.

Chapter 14

Wells lay on his back, not sure how he'd ended up on the floor. His vision was blurred, and a high-pitched ringing filled his ears. Acrid smoke filled the hallway. It burned his eyes and made it hard to breathe. Yet in and around the confusion he knew one thing.

"Bomb."

Rolling to his side, he held on to the wall. The smoke rose to the ceiling and dissipated. He drew in a single breath before rising unsteadily to his feet. He was propelled into his apartment as if shoved from behind by the hand of a god. There, on the floor, lay Sinead. Her eyes were closed. Her limbs were loose. Harry lay on her chest. Red-faced, the baby bawled.

"Sinead." He dropped to her side. His words echoed in his head. There was no blood on her clothes or the floor. Then again, the absence of blood meant little. All her injuries might be internal. He took Harry and held him to his chest. "Sinead, can you hear me?"

Her eyelids fluttered.

"Can you hear me?" he asked again, his throat tight with emotion.

"What in the hell was that?" Her words were slurred.

"A package bomb," he said.

From the hallway came Deborah's voice. "Wells, are you okay? I heard an explosion and swore I was back in Beirut."

"Will you be okay alone for a minute?" he asked Sinead. "I've got to get Harry to Deborah."

"Yeah," she said, her voice hoarse. "Take him. I'll be fine."

"Don't move." He glanced once more at Sinead and rose to his feet. With the squalling Harry clutched to his chest, he exited the apartment. Deborah, clad in a T-shirt and a pair of black-and-red USMC sleep pants, stood in the hallway. "Can you take him?" He held out Harry. She took the baby and kissed his head. "Stay in your apartment. Don't open it for anyone unless it's me. Got it?"

"Got it. But what's going on?" she asked.

"You were right about Beirut," he said, his tongue thick in his mouth. "Someone sent me a bomb."

"Who? Why?"

That was exactly what he planned to find out. But for now, he had to ensure that Harry was kept safe. "Take him, please. I'll be over when I can."

The retired Marine must've known that the situation was dire. "Will do," she said. "You can count on me."

He knew he could.

"I'll call 9-1-1," she said, retreating into her apartment.

Wells sprinted back to his apartment and Sinead. In his absence, she'd sat up, her back against the wall.

"You should still be lying down," he said. "That bomb knocked you on your butt."

"It knocked you on your butt, too," she said. "And you're on your feet."

"Yeah," he said. "But I have to be in charge."

"Looks like the blast broke your filter. Stop being sexist and help me get to my feet." She held her palm out to Wells. He gripped her hand and pulled.

The need to protect Sinead had nothing to do with her being a woman. He knew she was smart and capable. Hell, she was an FBI agent. At the same time, the deep desire to care for her had everything to do with her being *his* woman.

How was he supposed to explain all of that—especially since he didn't understand himself? He pushed all emotions aside and focused on the facts.

Her hand still in his, he asked, "Are you okay? Is anything hurt?"

She worked her jaw back and forth. "Now that the ringing in my ears has stopped, I think I'm fine." She squeezed his hand once and let her palm slide from his grip. "How's Harry?"

"Mostly scared." Without her hand to hold, he balled his fingers into a fist. "He's with Deborah."

The screeching of a siren could be heard in the distance. Sure, Deborah called emergency services, but he imagined that other neighbors had reported the explosion, too.

A minute later, the sound of footfalls on the stairs could be heard. A pair of uniformed police officers rushed onto the landing.

Wells didn't have his badge with him, but Sinead had her FBI credentials. She held up her ID and introduced herself. "I'm Special Agent Colton and this is Detective Blackthorn. A bomb was left in a package at the detective's door. There are several things we need to do. First, a CSI team needs to be contacted. More uniformed police officers need to be brought to the scene. Tenants will have to be escorted from the building and interviewed once they're outside."

Wells had a few more items to delegate to the cops. "Contact the bomb squad as well, this device has to be removed safely. And find the building's manager. He'll be able to access footage from last night's security cameras."

It took only a few minutes more for Patrick Colton to arrive. "I heard about the explosion on my way to work," he said. "How are you two doing?"

Sinead shrugged. "I've been better."

"Do you need to see a doctor?" Patrick rubbed her back.

She said, "I need to figure out who's trying to kill Wells—and stop them."

Patrick wore a pair of black jeans and a windbreaker. He took a knee next to the remains of the bomb. The box had exploded, destroying the cardboard completely.

But the explosive device—wires, a bag of black powder, and a mechanism of some sort—was still intact.

He said, "It's a pretty rudimentary device. Unfortunately, anyone can look up the blueprints for this online." He continued, using the end of a pencil to point out the different parts of the bomb. "A switch is used to ignite the black powder. The switch is controlled by movement. Basically, it was supposed to blow your head off when you picked it up."

It made sense to Wells. "I touched the thing with my toe before it blew."

"Good thing you did that," said Patrick. "It malfunctioned, but there was enough powder in here to kill you." He looked up at Sinead. "And anyone within twenty feet of where you were standing."

The CSI tech's words sent a chill down his spine. It meant that if the bomb had functioned properly then both Sinead and Harry would be dead, too.

Sinead said, "You said that it malfunctioned. Why's that?"

"The charge got wet," he said. "It looks like some of the powder's wet, too."

"You think whoever left this also stood outside in last night's storm?" Sinead asked.

"Your guess is probably right," said Patrick. "But for now, we need to wait for the bomb squad to safely remove what's left of this device. Then, we can process the rest of the crime scene without anyone getting hurt."

Hurt. The one word slapped Wells in the face. He had to get Harry to see a doctor. Sure, the baby didn't have any visible wounds. But just like his concern with Sinead, his nephew could have internal injuries.

"You take care of the bomb squad when they get here," he said to Patrick. "I need to check on my nephew. Meet me at the precinct building at ten o'clock."

"Will do," said Patrick. He walked down the hallway and spoke into his phone.

Sinead was still with Wells.

He had a plan. He was ready to act. "I need two minutes to put on actual clothes." The building was being evacuated. But more than getting people out, the premises would have to be searched to make sure there was only one device. He didn't have a lot of time to waste. "Then, I'm going to see if Deborah can take Harry for a quick checkup to make sure there's nothing wrong. She has a sister who lives near Union Square. Maybe they can spend the day with her until it's safe to come back home." He stepped toward his apartment.

"Wells, wait."

He stopped and faced Sinead.

She placed her hand on his arm. "How are you?"

He didn't have time to ask himself that question. "Once I know that Harry will be safe, I'll be better."

"What can I do?" she asked.

"Will you help Deborah get Harry ready to spend the day out of the apartment?"

"Of course," she said. "I'd do anything for that little guy."

Wells knocked on Deborah's door. Before she even had a chance to unlatch the locks, he spoke into the jam.

"It's me. I have Sinead with me. She's going to help you get out of the building while the bomb is removed."

Deborah opened the door. Her eyes were wide with excitement. She reached for Sinead and pulled her into the apartment. "Come in and tell me all about what happened."

After Deborah closed her door, he returned to his own place. He changed into a suit, shirt and tie quickly, thankful for the shower the night before. He didn't bother shaving, even though his beard was starting to get thick.

By the time he left his apartment, the bomb squad had arrived. The whole building needed to be evacuated. All available police officers were going from unit to unit. But for now, Wells had only one concern—making sure his nephew was safe and healthy.

He knocked on Deborah's door. Sinead answered. She'd pulled her golden locks into a ponytail at the nape of her neck. Just seeing her left his mouth dry and his palms damp. But he didn't have time to be love-struck now.

"They ready?" he asked.

"Ready," said Deborah as she approached. Harry was in her arms. He looked at Wells with wide-eyed confusion, but at least he wasn't crying anymore.

He took the steps down to the ground level two at a time. Both Sinead and Deborah followed.

A uniformed police officer stood on the sidewalk. He motioned to her. "Can I have a minute of your time?"

"What can I do for you, Detective?"

"I need an officer to take my nephew and his baby-sitter to Union Square."

"I have a car. I'll take them myself."

At the end of the block, a wooden barricade had been set up outside the building, but news vans clogged the road. Onlookers pressed up against the sawhorses from either side. Thankfully, the cruiser was waiting at the curb. Wells opened the back door. He scanned the crowd as Deborah and Harry slid into the patrol car. The patrol officer stood next to the front fender. Wells gave her the address for Deborah's sister. "Take care of these two," he said to the officer.

"I'll protect them with my life."

Wells hoped it wouldn't come to that. "Thank you."

She rounded to the driver's-side door and slid behind the steering wheel.

He bent to look in the back window. Harry gazed at him. Wells pressed his hand to the glass. With the lights atop the car flashing, the cruiser wove through the crowd of onlookers and the media. Once it rounded the corner, Wells turned back to the building, but it was too late. The reporters had seen him. They began to yell questions in his direction.

"Detective Blackthorn, is it true that you were the target?"

"Detective Blackthorn, was the bomb planted by the subway shooter?"

"Detective Blackthorn, is this bomb connected to the Landmark Killer?"

He waved away all their questions. "No comment."

There was one final question that came from the

crowd. "Special Agent Colton?" It was Nadeem Alvi who spoke. "What are you wearing? It looks like you're in the same clothes as yesterday."

Sinead had expected that her single night with Wells would remain a secret. But Nadeem's pointed questions destroyed that hope.

"With cases like the Landmark Killer, we work odd hours." She tried to give a charming smile—just like the one Wells always used. The expression hurt her cheeks. "It was a late night followed by an early morning."

Nadeem raised one dark eyebrow. "I'll bet. Was it a late night for you too, Detective?"

Wells glared at the reporter. "No comment." He reached for her arm and guided her toward the front door of his apartment building. "Let's go."

"One last question," Nadeem called after them. Stopping, she turned to face him. "How'd you arrive at Detective Blackthorn's apartment so quickly? The call about an explosion came in less than ten minutes ago."

Sinead was starting to see the wisdom in how Wells handled reporters. "No comment," she said, striding up the steps.

Wells reentered the building. She was right behind him. Several uniformed officers stood guard in the tiled foyer.

He stopped at the base of the stairs that led to the upper stories. A vein throbbed at the base of Wells's throat. "I could choke Nadeem for throwing that question at you."

"Now, that would make some headlines," she said,

trying to make a joke. "I need to get back to my place. Shower. Change. I can't go to the office like this." She paused. "But I don't know how I'm supposed to get out of this building, much less back to my apartment, without being followed by a pack of rabid reporters."

"I'll take you," he said. "We can leave through the back door." He waved a hand to one of the uniformed officers.

The officer was a young man with a thin mustache and bright blue eyes. His name tag read Lutinski. Officer Lutinski trotted to where Wells and Sinead stood. "What can I do for you, Detective?"

"I need access to an unmarked police car. I'll leave the vehicle at the 130th and the keys with the desk sergeant," he said. "Have it delivered to the back door of this building."

"I'm on it," said the officer.

"The NYPD is quite the car service for you," she said, almost teasing.

Wells regarded her with his eyebrows drawn together. "What?"

"You have one car take Harry and Deborah to stay with relatives. Now you're commandeering another vehicle." She paused a beat. "It's not a criticism, just an observation."

"Getting around the city is a nightmare. I can't do my job if I can't travel. I need to use other cars until my SUV is fixed." He shrugged.

"I get it." And she did. The NYPD not only respected Wells Blackthorn, they revered him. He was their hero. The golden boy.

Before Sinead had to say anything else, Officer Lutinski approached.

"The car's waiting out back."

Even Wells seemed impressed. "That was fast."

He led Sinead to the back of the building. There was a door that led to a narrow alleyway. An unmarked sedan waited. A police officer handed Wells the keys. "Thanks," he said, opening the driver's-side door.

Sinead slipped into the passenger seat.

"Where to?" he asked.

"27th and Ninth, just a block up from FIT." The Fashion Institute of Technology was the premier fashion school in the world. It occupied a three-block campus in the heart of Chelsea, a quaint New York City neighborhood.

Soon, they were parked in front of her building. Her apartment was on the third floor of the six-story structure. An upscale consignment store took up the street level. The rest of the building was subdivided into residences, with eight units on each floor.

As Wells slipped a card, NYPD on Duty, onto his dash. He turned off the ignition and opened his door. She got out of the car as well. "This way." She pointed at a door that was located to the left of the fancy thrift store.

The lock was always kept latched. Sinead inserted her key and opened the door. A bank of mailboxes was attached to the wall. A set of stairs circled upward. A small elevator was tucked behind the stairwell. Sinead always took the stairs and began to climb. Wells followed.

She passed the second-floor landing. That was when she noticed that her back hurt, and her right ankle was sore. The aches were probably from getting flattened by the bomb. "You know," she said. "We were just damn lucky that the bomb didn't kill us all."

"I know." He paused. "The one thing I keep thinking is—what if I had died? What would happen to Harry?"

It was a good question—one that Sinead couldn't answer. Instead, she said, "But you didn't die."

"Not this time at least." He paused. "This is a dangerous job. I've always known that fact. But it never really mattered if I lived or died. Until now, nobody ever counted on me."

They'd reached the third floor. The air in the corridor was hot and sticky. She stopped on the landing and turned to face Wells. "What are you saying?"

He waved her question away. "Nothing. I'm just thinking out loud is all."

She walked down the hallway. "My apartment is over here."

He followed and stood at her side.

After unlocking the dead bolt, she opened the door. Holding on to the door, she let Wells pass. "Welcome."

The apartment opened to combo living room/dining room/kitchen. A large set of windows overlooked the street. Bright morning light reflected off the wood floors. At the back of her apartment was her bedroom. A small bathroom sat at the back of her bedroom.

"This isn't as fancy as your place, but make yourself comfortable," she said, pointing to a tan sofa. "I'll be back in a minute."

Sinead entered her bedroom and closed the door behind her. Sure, she thought of inviting Wells into the shower with her. But now was not the time for another session of sex. First thing, she set her phone on a charging stand that sat on a bedside table. She stripped as she crossed the floor, dropping clothes behind her like breadcrumbs in a fairy tale. In the bathroom, she turned on the shower to hot and stepped under the spray. She washed her hair, rinsed and applied conditioner.

Having finished her shower, she turned off the water. After wrapping a towel around her chest, she stepped from the shower. On the best day, Sinead's beauty routine was minimal. Cleanse, tone, moisturize. But today, she only slathered sunscreen on her face, neck and chest. She ran a comb through her hair and let her wet tresses hang over her shoulders. In her bedroom, she pulled a clean pair of underwear and a bra from her chest of drawers. In her closet, she found a pair of darkwash denim jeans and another golf shirt with the FBI's seal. She dressed in record time. Sinead typically wore her holster on her hip. After threading the rig through her belt, she put on both.

She checked her sidearm, a Sig Sauer, to make sure it was properly loaded before sliding it into her holster.

Finally, she donned her FBI windbreaker. True, with the heat, she hardly needed to wear a jacket. But the windbreaker helped to hide the gun on her hip.

Sinead was ready to go. She lifted her phone from the charging stand and froze. There was a single text message on the screen.

With the phone in her hand, she strode into her living room.

Wells stood at the window, presumably admiring the view. He turned as she approached, that languid smile on his lips. He glanced in her direction and the smile faded. Drawing his eyebrows together, he stepped forward. "What's wrong?"

"We have a very big problem." She held out her phone for him to read.

He glanced at the screen and cursed. "When did this come in?"

"Just now," she said.

"Let's get to my office. I'll contact Ashlynn and have her meet us there. Hopefully, she can figure out who sent this to you."

Sinead gave a terse nod. She glanced at the screen once more, before tucking the phone into her pocket. The message was burned into her mind.

How are you supposed to catch me if you're so focused on your love life?

Chapter 15

Wells walked into the conference room on the fifth floor of the police station. Sinead followed. She took a seat near the head of the table, depositing her backpack on the floor next to her chair. After pulling the door closed, he moved to the front of the room. He uncapped a dry-erase maker and wrote two words on the whiteboard.

Edward Pendleton.

The newest victim's name was added to the list with the other two.

He had to maintain focus on finding justice for those who were murdered. But it was hard to remain single-minded when so much had happened in the past twenty-four hours both professionally and personally.

The text that Sinead had received was at the top of

the agenda for this meeting. He stood at the head of the table and looked around the room. Only half the chairs at the table were filled. Aside from him and Sinead, there was Captain Reeves, ADIC Chang and her ever-present assistant, Xander Washer. Ashlynn Colton was also present, along with another of her brothers, Brennan, who was a fellow FBI agent.

Recapping the marker, Wells began the meeting. "You all know why we're here this morning. Someone reached out to Sinead, claiming to be the Landmark Killer. We need to know who contacted her and if they're our man." He sat and turned to Ashlynn. "What do you have for us?"

"In a word," she said. "Nothing." While driving to the 130th, he and Sinead had contacted Ashlynn and given her the phone number associated with the text. "I was able to find the phone that contacted you, but it's a burner. According to the purchase information, it was bought at a drugstore in lower Manhattan. But it looks like the phone was bought with cash and never registered before being used."

"We'll send a team to the drugstore to talk to the employees," said Wells.

Brennan raised his hand. "I can take care of that."

"Thanks, man. We also have to find the next victim. We know the profile. Male. Caucasian. Mid to late thirties. Blond hair and blue eyes. Initial of first name will be *V* and he'll work at a New York City landmark. Our list from yesterday worked. Sinead and I both talked to Edward Pendleton." The feeling of failure stabbed him in the chest. "He refused to leave the city or accept any kind of protection. What are our options if we run into this issue again—legally speaking?" He looked to both Chang and Reeves. "Any ideas?"

"I'm not entirely certain. We can't just take people into custody because we think it's best for them." Chang glanced at her assistant. "Make a note to talk to the legal department. See what we can do."

Xander held a tablet computer. Using the tip of his finger, he scrawled a note onto the screen. "Got it."

"What else?" Reeves asked.

Ashlynn said, "If I can have Sinead's phone, I can dump her hard drive onto my computer. Then, I can look and see if there's anything from the burner phone that leads to the Landmark Killer."

"Can you do that?" asked Xander. "I mean, will there really be something that leads us to the killer?"

"I hate to be such a downer, but probably not," said Ashlynn.

"Find what you can," said Chang. "At the moment, we don't know anything about this man. And what's more, I don't like that he can reach out to my agents."

"That brings up an interesting question," said Sinead. "How'd he get my number in the first place? He texted an unlisted cell phone that was given to me by the Bureau. I mean, I give out my number to colleagues or friends, but that's it. How does the killer know so much about all his victims? We have Ashlynn, a cyber-whiz, and she still digs on the internet to find information the killer already has."

"Do you have any ideas?" Chang asked.

Last night Wells mentioned his fear/theory that the

killer was linked to the city, or specifically the NYPD. He didn't want to share his thoughts openly because his words would become media gospel. If that happened, there would certainly be an uproar in the city.

At the time, she'd agreed to keep his secret. Was she about to break her promise?

Then again, so much had happened. Maybe now, it didn't matter.

"It sounds to me like the killer is smart," said Xander. "A genius, maybe."

Sinead nodded slowly. "He's above average intelligence certainly. But he also seems to know things that the average person shouldn't. I think." She glanced at Wells. He gave a slight nod. After all, she wasn't talking to a reporter. This was a closed-door meeting with the top brass of the NYPD and the FBI. She drew in a breath and began, "We think that the killer has connections to law enforcement in the city."

For a moment, nobody spoke.

"It would make sense," said Reeves. "How he can find men who fit a very specific profile."

"I think you've missed something important," said Brennan. "The Landmark Killer only needs to find one victim who fits what he's looking for. We're the ones who need to know everyone because the victim could be any one of a dozen people or more who fit the profile."

He was right.

"Still, we should see if anyone has accessed the same sites as Ashlynn," said Chang.

"I made a note," Xander added.

Sinead held up her phone. "I guess you need this," she said to Ashlynn.

The IT expert took the device. "It will only take a minute, I promise."

The phone pinged with an incoming text. Ashlynn glanced at the screen and turned pale. "Uh, you need to see this."

"What is it?" Sinead asked, alarm evident in her voice.

Ashlynn handed the phone to her cousin.

Sinead glanced at the screen. "It's from a former classmate," she said, looking Wells in the eye. "He says he might know the Landmark Killer's identity."

Her words sucked all the air from the room. For a moment, Wells couldn't breathe. "Who's the classmate?" he asked.

"His name is Frazer Parker. We went to high school together and had lots of the same classes. I wouldn't have passed Intro to Calculus without him."

"Forget that," said Brennan. "Who's the killer?"

"Who do you think is the Landmark Killer?" Sinead said, typing her response as she spoke. "And how did you get this information?"

She glanced at her boss. Doubtless, she was looking for approval of her text. ADIC Chang gave a slight nod.

Sinead hit Send. The message was sent with a whoosh.

Wells stared at Sinead while she stared at her phone.

A moment later, the response came back. *Ping.*

"He says that he doesn't want to give me the information in a text."

"Have him come down to Twenty-seven Fed," said Chang, mentioning 27 Federal Plaza, the home of federal law enforcement in New York City.

"Come to my office, we can chat," she said, relaying the message. She hit Send.

His reply was instantaneous.

Sinead raised her eyes from the screen. "He said no."

Wells wasn't in the mood to play games. "Let's send a unit to his house and bring him in. A few hours in custody will change his mind about when and where to talk."

"We can't just arrest someone because they might know something but don't want to go to an FBI office," said Sinead.

Just because she was right didn't mean that Wells had to like it.

She sent another text. "When can we meet?"

He replied. Sinead read the message out loud. "Tonight. 7:00 p.m. There's an Italian place on 87th and Ninth. Amore."

A hard knot dropped into Wells's stomach. "I don't like it."

All eyes turned to him.

Reeves spoke. "Why not?"

He knew why but preferred not to say. To him, it sounded like the guy was asking Sinead out on a date. He dropped into a chair next to Sinead.

Brennan spoke up. "I don't like it, either. We're the FBI. This guy should come to our office and speak to agents in a controlled environment. What's more, we shouldn't have to wait until this evening to hear what he has to say. What if the killer strikes again today? Mr. Parker should speak to us right freaking now."

"Talking to informants on our terms isn't always possible," said Sinead. "You know that as well as anyone here. Sometimes we have to meet people where they're comfortable."

"What do you know about this guy? You said he was a classmate and good at math," Chang began. "What else do you remember about him? And how'd he get your number?"

"As far as getting my number, I'm still in contact with some of my old classmates." Sinead sighed. "Maybe he got it from them. Do you want me to ask?"

Chang shook her head. "I'm more interested in what you know about him."

Sinead said, "Frazer and I graduated together. He was a nice guy. Quiet. I think he played the trombone for the pep band."

"Let me guess," said Wells. "You were a cheerleader."

"Actually," said Ashlynn, "she played forward for the girls' basketball team. Was it your junior or senior year that your team won All-City?"

And then, Brennan said, "Remember that game against Saint Mark's? There was the girl who kept throwing elbows at everyone. Then she tried to drive through you, but you wouldn't move. It was like she hit a brick wall."

Oh yeah, Wells was in a room filled with Coltons. For a moment, he let the friendly banter of the cousins swirl around him. He wondered what it would be like to belong to a large extended family.

"I wish I could've seen you play," said ADIC Chang with a rare smile. "But we have to get back to the question of whether you should meet with Mr. Parker—or not. How well did you know him in high school?"

"Like I said, we had classes together," said Sinead. "We were friendly but never friends."

"So, he wasn't your boyfriend?" *Way to play it cool, Blackthorn.*

"He asked me to a school dance once. I already had a date, so I declined. He seemed to take it well. Like, 'Oh, I should've guessed that someone had asked you already.' But he didn't seem mad or anything." She paused and placed her hands flat on the table. "I have a question. Are we really going to ignore this guy because an old classmate wants to talk to me over spaghetti? If he called the office, we'd make an appointment and send agents to his house—or anyplace else he wanted to meet."

"Okay, that's true, too," said Brennan. "You wouldn't believe some of the places where I've talked to confidential informants."

"Fair enough," said Chang. "We're all on edge because of the two assassination attempts on Detective Blackthorn. Sinead, meet with Mr. Parker. Obviously, you'll report back whatever he tells you."

"Will do," she said. She spoke as she typed out her text. "Sounds like a plan. See you there." She hit Send. Her phone pinged with his reply.

"What'd he say?" Wells asked. His stomach churned and he regretted having made omelets for breakfast. But it wasn't the food leaving his stomach upset—it was the fact that Sinead was going out with someone else. Sure, it was all part of the job. And true, he had no reason to be jealous at all. But that didn't mean he had to like the plan, either.

She held up her phone so he could see the screen.

There was a smiley face emoji.

Great.

"That brings us to the next item on the agenda—the subway shooting and the bomb," said Reeves. "You met with David Atkins yesterday. I know that you said he wasn't the assassin. But if not him, then who?"

It was a great question. Wells said, "I don't have an answer."

"For now," she continued, "I'll keep you as the leader of the Landmark Killer task force. You'll work from the office. No more running down leads until we find whoever is after you."

"No way," said Wells. Indignity bubbled up from his middle. He was the one who took care of all the problems, not the one who hid behind a desk when things got dangerous. "I'm not going to be sidelined from my own investigation."

"You aren't being sidelined," she said. "You're still the lead. It's just when your team reports to you, you'll be here."

He gave her his best smile—the one that always got him what he wanted. "C'mon, Captain, we can work something out."

"I'm not risking the lives of any of my officers—not even yours," she said, making a small joke. "Besides, leadership comes with responsibilities. You can't manage a team if you're dodging bullets and bombs."

"You know I don't care about my own safety," he began. But he should care about himself now that he had to be around for Harry.

"I do know," said Reeves. "And that's part of the problem."

His mind filled with images of his nephew. Yet giving in went against his nature. In the end, Harry won out. "Fine," he grumbled.

"Agent Colton, you'll be working out of the Federal Building for now. But you'll keep the NYPD apprised of anything you learn this evening," said Chang.

Wells couldn't help but wonder if the new assignment had to do with Sinead being at his apartment this morning. At least he knew enough not to question his boss about it.

Reeves stood, ending the meeting.

Everyone else stood and filed out of the conference room.

Sinead sat at the table, yet she remained silent.

"Say something," he said.

"I was just wondering how you're holding up."

He shrugged. "I'm okay."

"Are you lying to me?"

He was. "Of course not."

How had his day turned upside down so quickly? It was only a few hours ago that he and Sinead had been eating breakfast. Harry had been safe and happy. More than his day starting off right, his life had felt complete.

"I don't want you to go to the meeting tonight," he

said, blurting out the words before he'd even decided what he wanted to say.

"Not go?" Her tone was filled with steel. "You're kidding. Right?"

He wasn't. "I don't like it."

"What's not to like? An old classmate contacted me with possible information. This happens all the time."

"I bet you a hundred dollars that this guy has an agenda. What's more, it has nothing to do with helping us find the Landmark Killer."

"Bet me?" she echoed. "What are you, five years old?"

"There's no reason to be nasty," he said. "Or call me names. I just don't like that he wants to meet you at a restaurant is all."

"What don't you like about the scenario?"

"It just seems off…" He knew his explanation was insufficient.

"Why is that? Do you not like that it's me who's meeting with Frazer and not you? Are you afraid that someone will steal your glory?"

"Of course not. All I want is for the killer to be caught." He paused a beat and waited for Sinead to say something. She didn't. "I could go with you, though."

"No way. I'm not sure where all of this is coming from, Wells. Maybe you think that because I'm a woman I can't do my job. Or maybe you think because we had sex last night that you somehow own me. Or maybe it's as simple as you don't want to be stuck behind a desk and coming with me is a way to escape." She rose to her feet. "But I can't help you out."

He watched Sinead as she walked to the door. Wells turned back to the table.

"Aren't you going to say anything?" she asked.

"Seems to me like you said it all." The thing was, he regretted the words as soon as he spoke. He wanted to tell her that after one day, he cared for her—and that level of emotion scared him. He was worried that if she stayed in his life, Harry would get attached to Sinead. Then, when things ended, the baby would be upset. What's more, Wells himself would be crushed.

So yeah, he knew he was being a jerk. But it was all for the best to stop the burgeoning romance before it got a chance to grow.

He could feel her gaze on the back of his neck.

He wanted to turn and face her. He needed to apologize.

Instead, he stared at the table.

After a moment, he heard her footfalls as she walked out of the room and down the hall.

Then Wells was alone, like always.

Chapter 16

After leaving the conference room, Sinead visited Ashlynn's workstation. There, her cousin had spent only a few minutes downloading the memory from her phone. That important task complete, there was nothing left for her to do but get back to the Federal Building.

She walked down a narrow staircase in the bowels of the 130th Precinct. Her eyes burned. Her chest was tight. She'd spent only one day with Wells, but already he was under her skin. She needed to forget all about him. But how?

Her feet clanged on each step, the noise echoing in her head.

"Sinead?"

She looked toward the sound of the voice. Rory stood on the next landing down.

For a moment, neither woman spoke. She wasn't in the mood for another awkward conversation with her sister. Swallowing, she clutched the strap of her backpack. "Hey, how are you?"

Rory said, "I should be asking you that instead. I heard about what happened this morning. A bomb? Cripes, that's scary."

Sinead's eyes watered. She wiped them with the back of her hand. "The thing is—it was just a package in the hallway. We didn't know anything was wrong until it exploded."

"And you weren't hurt or anything?" Rory's eyebrows were drawn together in concern.

"I was knocked down, but that's all. Wells and I were just lucky that the thing was defective."

She wondered about Harry, too. Had he been seen by the doctor yet?

"When I saw it in the news…" Rory's eyes were wet. She blinked several times. "Well, I was so scared. I started to call or text. I didn't because I wasn't sure if you wanted to hear from me."

Sinead was struck by her sister's confession. She swayed on the steps and reached for the railing.

Rory rushed to her side and held her arm. "You aren't okay. Maybe we should get you to a doctor."

"You can always call me," Sinead said. "You know that."

Rory let her palm slip away from Sinead's arm. "It's just that we've never been super close. I know what happened—how I happened—ruined your life."

Reaching for her sister's hand, Sinead said, "You

never ruined my life." She paused. "Wells is his nephew's guardian. He's a cute little guy named Harry."

"If he's related to Detective Blackthorn, I'm sure that one day he'll be more than cute." Rory gave a wry smile.

"Anyway, I was over at his house yesterday and I got to take care of Harry a bit. It brought back memories of when you were a baby. Your mom used to let me come over and help take care of you. You were actually cuter than Harry. You laughed a lot."

"Really? Obviously, I don't remember. I wish I did."

"Yeah, that's too bad. We used to have a great time playing peekaboo."

Rory laughed. Sinead laughed too and some of the tension in her chest eased away.

"Can I ask you a question? Why'd you stop coming over?"

Sinead shook her head. "Honestly, I'm not sure." Although she suspected that their father loved Rory more than he loved her.

"Just because we didn't spend much time together as kids doesn't mean that we can't get to know each other better now," Rory said. "Maybe we could grab dinner sometime."

"That would be nice," said Sinead. She hated for the moment to end, but she needed to get back to her office at Federal Plaza. She walked down a few steps and stopped. Turning, she looked at her sister. "And Rory?"

"Yeah?"

"I mean it. You can call me anytime."

It was almost noon. Wells had spent his morning meeting with the task force. He'd given assignments to each of the members, and they were out completing their missions. And him? He was stuck in the office waiting to hear back from those who were on the street.

What a waste of time.

His phone sat on the conference table. After opening his contact app, he found Sinead's information. For a moment, he thought about sending her a text. But to what end? They weren't partners anymore. After their argument, he wasn't even sure if they were friends, either.

Maybe it was best if he stopped worrying about her. If he wanted to move up the ranks in the NYPD, he had to act like the boss. It meant turning in paperwork that was due and filling out reports that he needed to file.

Before he got started, he wanted to check on Harry. After finding Deborah's contact in his phone, he typed out a message and hit Send.

How's the little man?

She replied.

Just left the Dr. office. Clean bill of health. Gained two lbs since last visit.

Was gaining two pounds a good thing for a baby? There was still so much he didn't know.

She sent another message.

How are you?

He replied.

Physically fine.

She sent another message.

And emotionally?

Emotionally, he was a mess. He wanted to see Sinead again. He needed to find the subway shooter and the Landmark Killer. And beneath it all, he worried that his being a single dad and a cop wasn't the best combination for Harry.

Wells was a killer's target. Because of that, Harry had literally ended up as a target. Sure, he was thankful that his nephew hadn't gotten hurt this morning. But what about the next time? Or what would happen to the kid if one day, Wells didn't come home?

He replied to Deborah.

Emotionally, fine as well.

She texted him back with one word.

Liar.

He typed a reply.

???

The minute it was delivered, his phone began to ring. It was Deborah. Since he was alone in the conference room, he could speak to her freely. He swiped the call open.

Before he could say hello, she started to speak. "You probably weren't even born when I was stationed at the embassy in Beirut. A suicide bomber drove a truck filled with explosives right through the front gate. A lot of Marines who stood guard were killed that day. Being a woman and all, I was stuck in an office. But still, those men who lost their lives were more than my colleagues. They were my family. So, I know you aren't okay emotionally."

How was he supposed to answer that? He'd heard enough about the Beirut embassy bombing to know it had occurred, but not much more. "I'm confused about a lot of things."

"Like what?"

He sat and said nothing. A full sixty seconds passed. He knew that Deborah was waiting for him to speak. "I'm not sure that me being a cop is best for Harry. First of all, it's a lot of late nights at work. That means you're the one taking care of him, not me."

"I don't mind at all. I love the kid to bits."

"I'm glad to hear that, sincerely." His thoughts swirled quickly. He couldn't catch a mental thread long enough to follow it to the end. "It's just I don't know if I can do this anymore…"

"So, what, do you plan to quit?" she asked. "It's being a cop or being Harry's only family?"

Both options left him ill. "That's pretty blunt of you."

"What'd you expect? I'm a Marine." She paused a beat. "You know what you need? A woman to help you raise this little guy." He could hear Harry babbling in the background.

"Isn't that sexist of you? Or are you proposing?"

"Har-har," she laughed. "A young pup like you couldn't handle a seasoned gal like me."

"Trust me, I know," he said, teasing her in return.

"You know who Harry really responds to?" Deborah asked. She didn't wait for an answer. "That cute FBI agent you had at your place last night. She loves him, too. I can tell."

"I know." He sighed.

"If you know, then do something about it. Don't just talk to me on the phone and bellyache."

"I think that you're blunt, even for a Marine."

Deborah snorted. "Call it a gift."

"I have to go. I've got work to do. Let me know if you need anything." He paused. "Once it's safe to go back to the apartment building, I'll let you know."

"You take care of yourself," she said before hanging up the phone.

Now Wells had to turn his attention to finding the Landmark Killer. In a city of nearly nine million people, someone had to know something. Sure, Sinead's former classmate might be the key to finding the suspect. But he wouldn't know what kind of intel she'd gotten for hours.

He had to do something.

His phone vibrated with an incoming notification. It was from the *Daily Herald*. There was a picture of Wells and Sinead as they stood in front of his building, along with a headline: *NYPD Detective Target of*

Killer. Of course, Nadeem had the byline. The story had been posted only minutes earlier. Already, it had over two thousand clicks. In an hour, tens of thousands more would have read the story. By the end of the day, who knew?

Wells gave a disgusted sigh and tossed his phone onto the table.

He looked at the whiteboard and the names of the victims. He looked back at his phone. Leaning forward, he picked it and placed a call.

Nadeem answered after the second ring. "This is Alvi."

"It's Wells. Do you have a minute?"

"Hold on and let me check my weather app. Nope, it doesn't say anything about hell freezing over…"

"Very funny. Do you want to talk about the Landmark Killer—or not?"

"Is this on the record or off?" the reporter asked.

"On," he said.

"Are you sure?" Nadeem asked. "You're usually the king of 'no comment.'"

Wells hadn't put much thought into his plan. Still, he knew that the Landmark Killer was no typical criminal. If he wanted to catch the bastard, he had to do something different. "I'm sure."

"Then, I'll be recording this conversation to ensure accuracy."

Wells drew in a deep breath. "You were right to notice that all the victims are the same race, roughly the same age, all the way down to looking alike. You also made the connection between the killings and the New

York City landmarks. What you didn't know was that a letter has been found with each of the victims. The killer is murdering men to get the Black Widow Killer freed from jail. The initial of each victim's first name corresponds with a letter in Maeve O'Leary's name."

"Can I have a copy of the letters?" the reporter asked.

Wells wasn't ready to share all the details. "There's some information I'll be keeping back. The exact wording of those letters is one of those points."

"I get it," said Nadeem. "Someone might confess. If they really killed all those men, they'll know what the letters say."

He was right but Wells said nothing.

"What do you know about the suspect?" the reporter asked.

"We have video of him outside the Empire State Building. He's pretty well covered from head to toe. But I'm going to share it with you because you never know. One of your readers might recognize the way this person moves or walks." He turned on the speaker function and found the file on his phone. He attached the video to a message and sent it to Nadeem.

"I got it." And then, "I heard about what happened to your brother over the Fourth of July. Pretty tragic. I am sorry, man."

"It was tragic." Wells hadn't called Nadeem to have a personal conversation. He wanted to get off the phone. "Thanks for your condolences. I gotta get back to work."

"Can you hang on for a minute?"

"I guess."

"Listen, the last time we got together things went from bad to worse. I'm sorry for the role I played."

Wells's throat tightened. "Are you apologizing? Maybe I should be the one checking *my* weather app to see if hell really has frozen."

"Listen, I am trying to apologize. It's been years. I'd like to move on from our shared animosity."

For a moment, Wells couldn't decide what to say. The thing was—Nadeem's betrayal had scarred Wells. But he missed having the guy as a friend. "I'd like that, too. But now, I do have to get back to work."

"Yeah," said Nadeem. "I really have to thank you, man. This is a great scoop."

"Don't thank me," said Wells. "Get the story out there and help me catch this bastard."

At 6:50 p.m. Sinead arrived at Amore, the Italian restaurant, ten minutes before the scheduled meeting. The restaurant was tucked into the basement level of an old brownstone near Harlem. Small white lights were strung across the ceiling. A dozen tables were scattered across the floor, almost all of them filled with patrons. A long mahogany bar sat at the far side of the room. Frazer already sat at the bar. She recognized him at once.

"I thought that was you," she said, walking toward him.

"Hey, stranger," he said with a smile. He held a glass filled with amber-colored liquid. He took a quick sip and set down his drink before standing. "It's great to see you. You look terrific, by the way."

Frazer hadn't changed much since they were in high school. He was still tall and had dark brown hair. Then again, the last time she'd seen him, he'd been a lanky kid. As a man, he was muscular. His shoulders were broad and stretched the fabric of the golf shirt he wore. The muscles in his arms were well defined and large. To her, it looked like the Mathlete had become a regular gym rat. "It's great to see you again." She held out her hand for him to shake. Her bag was slung over one shoulder. It slipped forward and hung from her arm.

Gripping her palm, he looked deep into her eyes. His booze breath rolled over her in a wave. Now that she was closer, she could see that his eyes were glassy. She imagined he wasn't having his first drink of the evening.

"It is so great to see you."

Sinead felt a tickle at the back of her neck. She didn't recall his being a heavy drinker when they were in school. Was there something she'd missed—or forgotten? Or maybe it was simply that Sinead was having a bad day. In fact, she'd arrived early to get a few minutes alone to think. Now she had to deal with her former classmate.

"I thought we were meeting at seven," she said. "I hope I didn't mess up the time."

"No. I work nearby. My last meeting of the day got out sooner than expected. Instead of starting a new project, which would probably make me late, I just decided to come here and get a drink." He gestured to the bartender. "What can I get for you?"

"Just a water," said Sinead.

"Nothing stronger?" he asked.

"Can't," she said, readjusting her backpack to her shoulder. "I'm working."

"One water," said the bartender. He filled a glass and handed it to Sinead.

She sipped, taking a minute to collect her thoughts. She hadn't spoken to Wells since leaving the 130th that morning. She was desperate to know how his day had unfolded. Were there any leads for the subway shooter? She was also curious how Harry's doctor appointment had gone. But mostly she just wanted to hear his voice.

"Riiiight," said Frazer, drawing out the word. "Your job is why you're here. I was surprised when I saw your picture in the *Herald* yesterday. I didn't know you worked for the FBI." He clamped a hand over his mouth. "Or is that a secret?"

"It's not so secret since my picture's been in all the local media outlets."

Frazer laughed. "I guess you're right." And then, "Let's see if our table's ready."

They approached the hostess stand. A woman with black hair looked up and smiled. "May I help you?"

"Reservation for two. Frazer Parker."

She glanced down at a tablet computer. "I have you right here. Follow me." She led them to a table set for two that was tucked into a corner. "How's this?"

"It's perfect." Frazer pulled out a chair for Sinead.

After setting her bag in the corner, Sinead removed her phone from the backpack's front pocket. Frazer still held her chair and she sat.

The hostess set down a pair of menus along with a drink list. "Enjoy your meal."

Sinead waited for the hostess to leave. Then, she leaned forward. "This is a nice restaurant. We didn't need to meet at a place where reservations were required. I would've been happy with a hot dog from a vendor."

"Like I said, my engineering firm is right down the street. I've been interested in this place since it opened last month. Getting together with you just gives me an excuse to eat here." He took a long swallow of his drink. "Besides, I'll be honest, I'm a little nervous to talk to a fed about a killer. I figured a good meal would help me relax."

"Take your time," she said. The last thing she wanted was for Frazer to get spooked. "I'd like to know what you know. But I understand if you have some reservations. It's been a while since we were friends, so I get it."

"Is that what we were in high school?" he asked. "Friends. You were so popular. Star of the girls' basketball team. And me? I was a band kid."

"Hey, we loved having the pep band at all our games. You were the ones who brought the school spirit."

"Yeah, that was fun."

"Yeah, it was." Sinead wondered how long she was going to have to make small talk with her former classmate. Then again, if he really did know the Landmark Killer's identity, all the awkward conversation would be worth it.

Chapter 17

Sinead knew it was going to be a long and tedious night. She'd already spent over twenty minutes reminiscing with her former classmate. During it all, Frazer hadn't mentioned the real reason they were meeting. He was supposed to tell her what he knew about the Landmark Killer.

"Remember that time I asked you to the winter formal? You turned me down flat," Frazer said with a quick laugh.

"The way I remember it, I had a date already." She was already tired of the conversation, so she put a little steel in her tone.

"I guess that's right," said Frazer. He lifted his drink and finished it in a single swallow. He set the glass back on the table with a *thunk*. "But what about if you hadn't had a date? What would you have said then?"

In all honesty, Sinead wasn't sure if she would have accepted his invitation or not. But there was only one answer she could give now. "Of course, I would have gone with you."

He smiled. "That's good to know."

The waiter approached. "How're we doing this evening, folks? What can I get started for you?"

"I'll take another bourbon," said Frazer, holding up his glass. "What do you want, Sinead?"

"I'm fine with water."

"Oh, come on," he said. "You can't pair a nice meal with nothing other than water."

"Iced tea, then." She smiled at the waiter.

"Are you two ready to place an order?" he asked.

Sinead hadn't even opened the menu. "I need a minute."

"Me, too," said Frazer.

"I'll get your drinks and be back."

The waiter left. Sinead glanced over her shoulder. Since they were seated in a corner, no other tables were nearby. Leaning forward, she said, "In the text you sent this morning, you said you have some information about the Landmark Killer."

"I do." A set of silverware was wrapped in a white cloth napkin. He unwrapped the cloth and draped it over his lap. "It's someone I've known my whole life, so I sorta feel like a jerk for ratting them out."

Sinead needed to know what Frazer suspected. "I get that you feel loyalty to this person. But lives have already been lost and more people will die unless the killer is stopped."

"I know," he said. "It's just..."

His words trailed off as the waiter approached. Two glasses were balanced on a tray that he carried. After setting the drinks on the table, he tucked the tray under his arm. "Have you decided what you'd like for dinner?"

Sinead summoned her patience. It was going to take all her skills to pull the information from her former classmate. She opened the menu and scanned the entrees. "I'll take the chicken parmesan with linguini," she said, picking the first item that caught her eye. She closed the menu and handed it back to the waiter.

Frazer ordered cheese ravioli.

"I'll get your order to the kitchen right away," the waiter promised.

Sinead picked up her tea and took a sip. Setting down the glass, she asked, "You were telling me about who you suspected of being the Landmark Killer."

Frazer took a gulp of his fresh bourbon. "Honest to God, I've known him my entire life. This is hard."

She knew that he was struggling to give up the name of his lifelong friend. Sinead decided to try a new tactic. "Maybe you could tell me why you have your suspicions."

Frazer took another swig of bourbon and set the glass on the table. "This person hates Manhattan. He had a lawsuit against the city and feels like he got screwed— even in court."

That wasn't something that Sinead had ever considered. Was the Landmark Killer trying to get even with

New York City? "Do you have a sense why the victims have a matching profile? And what's the connection with Maeve O'Leary?"

"To be honest, I've never thought about the common profile. In fact, I didn't know there was one until I saw the story in the *Daily Herald* this afternoon. But the connection to Maeve O'Leary makes sense. They were obsessed with the case. I kinda thought it was childish, but now?" He lifted his glass and took a drink.

There had to be a reason that all the victims looked alike. Sinead reminded herself that Frazer wouldn't have access to all the pertinent information about the killer or their motives. And still, she needed a name.

The waiter delivered bread and salads. "What else can I get for you?"

Frazer finished the last swallow of his drink. He held up the empty glass. "I'll take another."

"I'll be right back with your bourbon, sir," said the waiter.

Sinead took a few bites of her salad. The house dressing, a balsamic vinaigrette, had the perfect tangy bite. The croutons were freshly baked. The lettuce was crisp. The tomatoes were sweet. "This is an excellent salad," she said.

And it was, but she couldn't help but compare last night's dinner to the one she was eating tonight. Sure, she and Wells had eaten take-out heroes in his apartment. But they'd laughed. They'd shared ideas.

"What did you say this person does for a living?" she asked, recalling Wells's theory that the killer worked for the city. She hadn't considered a disgruntled employee as a possible suspect, but it would make sense...

"I didn't say." Frazer stabbed a lettuce leaf with his fork and took a bite of salad.

As he chewed, Sinead asked, "What can you tell me?"

Frazer swallowed his bite. "What can I tell you?" he echoed. "To be honest, I'm not sure."

The waiter dropped off the drink and left. Frazer picked up the glass.

Sinead reached for his wrist, stopping him before he could get the glass to his mouth. "Remember, you were the one who called me. There's a killer on the loose in New York City. If you know his identity, you need to tell me now."

Frazer took a long swallow of his drink. He set the glass on the table. "I know I must seem ridiculous to you. But reaching out was difficult. I'll tell you, I just need some time, ya' know?"

Sinead certainly understood hesitancy and the need for others to feel comfortable. She also knew that pushing Frazer for information he wasn't ready to share might scare him away. It didn't matter that she was eager. She drew in a long breath, lowering her expectations for the moment. "How about we change the subject. Tell me about yourself. You obviously stayed in the city. You mentioned that you're an engineer—good for you. You were always good at math. What else? Are you married? Kids?"

"Never married. No kids." He gave a disarming smile. "Just waiting for the right woman for both. How 'bout you?"

"Married once. Divorced. No kids," she said, giving a succinct rundown of her life over the past few years.

"There's nobody special in your life right now?"

Immediately, Wells's face flashed through her mind. "No, not really—unless you mean the FBI. Seems like all I do these days is work."

"I saw you on the news this morning. A bomb being delivered to your friend's apartment must've been scary."

Sinead hadn't taken the time to process what'd happened. "This morning seems like it was a month ago," she said, honestly.

The waiter approached their table with two plates balanced on his forearm. He set Sinead's meal down in front of her. "We have chicken parmesan for the lady. For the gentleman, cheese ravioli." He cleared away the salad plates. "Enjoy."

She took a bite of her meal. The tangy sauce filled her mouth. The chicken was tender and flavorful. The pasta was light and homemade. She chewed and swallowed. Pointing with her fork, she said, "This is really good."

"I'm glad you like it." He stabbed a ravioli with his fork and lifted it to his mouth. He took a bite and chewed. With an exaggerated eye roll, he hummed, "Mmm. That is good."

"Thanks for insisting that we come out for dinner. Usually, my dinner comes out of a delivery bag. What's more, I'm sitting at my desk while eating."

"Is that what happened yesterday?" he asked. "You were working late with the NYPD detective?"

"Excuse me?" Her tone was defiant.

Frazer leaned back in his chair. His change in posture was almost a surrender. "It's just that I saw your picture online from the Empire State Building. And then, from this morning. You were in the same clothes."

Plus, there was the video of Nadeem asking her about wearing her outfit. The moment had gone viral.

True, she'd thought about how to handle the subsequent questions. Her first notion was to tell everyone who asked to piss off. But that wouldn't work. She decided instead on a version that wasn't exactly true, but truth adjacent. "With a case like the Landmark Killer, there are a lot of moving parts. I never made it back to my apartment at all."

He stared at her. The look in his narrowed eyes said what his mouth never would. *Liar.*

She glared back. Sinead didn't owe her old classmate—or anyone else, for that matter—more of an explanation.

After a moment, he dropped his gaze back to his dish. "This food really is fantastic."

Good. He'd returned to neutral territory. She took several more bites, eating in silence.

After a moment, Frazer spoke. "I feel like I ruined our meal by asking you such a sensitive question."

"You didn't ruin anything." He'd given her the perfect segue into returning the conversation to what he knew—or thought he knew—about the Landmark Killer. "But we aren't here to talk about me. Or you. Or high school. Although I've enjoyed getting caught up, if you know something about all these murders, you need to tell me now."

He lifted his drink and took a sip. "I don't know…"

"Can I be honest with you?" she asked, although she didn't expect him to answer her question. "I'm not sure if you know anything about the Landmark Killer at all. Maybe you have been following the case in the media. That's how you came across my face and name after all these years. Then, you decided to call. Why? I don't know. Could be that you want to insert yourself into the investigation." She also thought it was possible that he wanted to reconnect with her personally and used this ruse as an excuse. But she knew enough not to say so. "Whatever the reason, it's become apparent that you don't have any idea of who the killer might be— and what's more, you've wasted my time." She looked around the restaurant. "Where's the server? I need to pay for my meal and get out of here."

The waiter stood next to the bar. Sinead caught his eye and lifted her hand. He nodded and held a single finger while mouthing the words, "One minute."

"My cousin James." Frazer's voice was little more than a whisper.

Turning back to the table, she asked, "What'd you say?"

"I think the Landmark Killer is my cousin James. He's always been troubled, even as a kid. One time, I caught him trying to choke our family dog…" His eyes were wet. He sniffled and picked up his drink. He took a swallow, finishing the amber liquid. "His dad was really loud and had quite the temper. He scared me as a kid.

There were times when I saw bruises on James's arm. At the time, I wondered if it was his dad. But we were little, and I never said anything. You've got to know, James wasn't always bad. We used to play spacemen and superheroes as kids. I was best man at his wedding. But after he got divorced a few years ago, he changed."

The waiter approached. "Looks like you're done with your meals. Are you interested in dessert? Or are you ready for the bill?"

Frazer glanced at Sinead. "Are you ready to get out of here?"

Sure, she had a name for the killer. But this was just the beginning of the investigation. There was so much more information she needed—and Frazer would be a prime source.

"I'll take a refill on my tea," she said.

"Another drink for the gentleman?" the waiter asked.

"No, I'll switch to water."

Sinead imagined that all the drinking Frazer had done was simply to build up some liquid courage. Now that he'd shared his suspicions about his cousin, there was no need for alcohol-fueled bravery.

"Anything else?" the waiter asked.

"Actually, yes. Where's your ladies' room?"

"Around this corner," he said, pointing behind their table.

Sinead stood. Adrenaline coursed through her veins until her palms itched. "I'll be right back."

Frazer smiled. "I'll be right here."

She followed the waiter's directions and found a door marked *Ladies' Lounge*.

A large mirror hung on the wall behind a long counter with two sinks. There were also two lavatory stalls. Both doors were open. The bathroom was empty. Sinead leaned her shoulder against a wall. After pulling her phone from her pocket, she placed a call.

Wells sat on his sofa. The NYPD had increased patrols on his street and the building manager had hired a guard to monitor the building. Whoever had gotten in last night, wouldn't be able to return to his apartment.

Because of the increased security, he'd come back home. Harry was sleeping in his room. For the first time in weeks, the apartment was quiet. He tried to count the nights that he'd gotten a full night's sleep since his nephew came into his life. Then again, he knew the number—it was zero.

With that in mind, he should be getting ready for bed now. If Harry were true to form, he'd wake in the middle of the night.

Or Wells could be working. After Nadeem published his story about the Landmark Killer, along with a photo, the task force had been inundated with calls.

But at the moment, he was neither sleeping nor working. Instead, he was scrolling through his phone and torturing himself with thoughts of Sinead. She'd met the informant at 7:00 p.m. It was after 8:30. Had she learned anything about the killer? Or was she simply enjoying dinner with an old friend?

He pulled up a review of the restaurant. The headline read: *Amore. Celebrity Chef Opens Restaurant.*

Features Italian Food like Grandma Used to Make—if Grandma's Kitchen Had a Romantic Ambiance.

Clenching his jaw, he closed the story.

Wells laid his head back on the pillows and closed his eyes. The phone vibrated in his hand. He looked at the screen. Caller ID read: Sinead Colton, FBI.

His heart began to race. He swiped the call open.

"Hey." He was breathless, and the one word came out as a wheeze.

"I only have a second, but I have a name for you. James. I don't have a last name, but he's cousins with Frazer. You could start with Parker, but I sense my classmate isn't related to the father by birth. They're approximately the same age—around thirty-two. So he shouldn't be too hard to find. James has a pretty typical background for someone who becomes violent. Early childhood trauma by way of an abusive father. Torturing animals. I'm not sure where he works, but he did sue the city and felt he got a raw deal, even in court."

Wells stood and walked to the kitchen. In a drawer, he found a pen and stack of sticky notes. "James," he repeated. "Cousin to Frazer Parker. Sued New York City." It wasn't a lot, but it was something. "What's your gut tell you? You like this guy, James, to be the Landmark Killer?"

"I like him enough to excuse myself to the ladies' lounge and give you a call." She paused. "I'm going to go back to the table and see if I can get more information. A last name. An address. An employer. But I figured you could get started with what I've gotten so far."

She figured right. "I'll reach out to Ashlynn."

"Okay, I'll let you go."

"Hey, Sinead." He spoke quickly, before she had a chance to hang up.

"Yeah?"

"How's it going? Other than getting a name, which is great. Did he bring up the time you wouldn't go with him to the dance?"

She laughed. The sound was music to his soul. "Actually, he did. It was hella awkward. He's been drinking a lot, so honestly the dinner's been painful. I'm not saying that I'll never have a drink, but being around someone who's tipsy while I'm sober isn't fun." She paused. "How's Harry?"

He said, "Harry's sleeping. The apartment is quiet. It's kinda boring."

"Sometimes boring is good."

Was she brushing him off? God, he hated the idea. Still, he wasn't going to beg someone to care for him—even if that person was Sinead. "Can we talk sometime about what happened?"

"Sure, I'd like to talk."

She hadn't said no. For now, he'd take it. "I'll let you get back to work."

"Take care of yourself. And give Harry a kiss for me." She ended the call.

Her comment made him smile, even though Wells would rather have the kiss from Sinead for himself. He opened his contacts app. After finding Ashlynn's number, he placed the call.

She answered before the first ring stopped. "You got a name for me?"

"I got a name for you." He spent a few minutes outlining everything Sinead had shared.

"That's plenty of information. If James is out there, I'll find him."

"I'll let you get to work." He hung up the phone. His heartbeat was strong and steady. Wells could tell they were on the right track.

Chapter 18

Sinead returned to the table. The waiter had delivered a fresh glass of iced tea. Frazer now had a glass of water sitting in front of him.

She sat down. He smiled.

"You know, I feel better for having talked to you. I thought I'd feel guilty, but I don't." He paused a beat. "I'm not sure why."

"It's because you don't have to handle the problem of your cousin on your own. And you did the right thing. It's best to let the professionals handle the investigation from here out."

"What will happen to James?" he asked.

Sinead picked up her glass and took a sip. The tea tasted like syrup. She gagged. "What's wrong with this?"

"Sorry. The waiter asked if you wanted sweet tea

or unsweetened tea. I couldn't remember what you ordered, so I just guessed."

Funny, Sinead didn't remember being given a choice of tea when she ordered. She'd just assumed the tea was served unsweetened.

"I can order you another one," he offered.

"No, it's not that bad." She took a sip, as if to prove that the tea was potable. But it was awful. Now, what had they been talking about? Oh yeah: "We'll start off by talking to your cousin. See if he has alibis for the time of the killings." What else happened with an investigation? "You know, having a big meal and not much sleep is starting to get to me. I'm exhausted."

"Try the tea," Frazer suggested. "The caffeine might help."

Caffeine. "Good idea."

She took a long drink from her glass. Her tongue was thick. Her vision was blurry. The tea seemed to ooze through her veins. She blinked several times, trying to clear her head. It didn't work. Her bag, which had been sitting in the corner, now lay on its side. Several packets of artificial sweetener were next to her bag. Sinead never drank sweet tea. It seemed like an important detail, but she couldn't follow the thought.

"What's wrong with that tea?" she asked, struggling to form each word.

Frazer smiled. "Wouldn't you like to know?"

Wells hadn't moved from his spot on the sofa. While waiting to hear back from Ashlynn, he'd tried to find the elusive James—cousin to Frazer Parker—on the internet. So far, he'd come up with nothing.

The phone rang. Snatching it from where it sat on the cushion next to him, Wells stared at the screen. Caller ID read: Ashlynn Colton.

His gut contracted with regret that it wasn't Sinead. After swiping the call open, he said, "Hello."

"Hey. I have news for you," she said.

"Good," said Wells. "Because I've tried to find James on social media. But no luck."

"That's just the thing," said Ashlynn. Her words held a hint of alarm. "I've accessed all the databases I can. Frazer has cousins, just none who might be James."

"It might be a nickname." Sure, it'd be an odd moniker, but who knew?

"I thought of that, too. But I don't think it's the case. Frazer has four first cousins. None are close to his age. Three are female and only one lives in the tri-state area—and she actually lives in New Jersey. The single male cousin is name Samuel. Samuel Francis, to be precise, before you go asking about his middle name. He's a forty-seven-year-old neurosurgeon who practices medicine at a hospital in San Francisco. At the time that Edward Pendleton was murdered, he was speaking at a conference in London—as in England."

"That's a pretty good alibi," said Wells.

"The best one I've run across lately."

"Maybe James is a second cousin. Or he could be a neighbor. Maybe someone who he was close to as a kid, and they just claim a family relation." Sure, he was grasping for an explanation.

Ashlynn sighed. "Any of those are possible, but all the scenarios will take time for me to investigate. What I need is more information. I tried to call Sinead. She didn't answer."

"She didn't answer?" he repeated. The apartment suddenly became frigid.

What would keep Sinead from taking a call during an important investigation? A million different reasons came to mind—like she was possibly getting all the details Ashlynn needed to find James. "I'll reach out to her myself."

"That's what I was hoping you'd say. Have her call me back when she can," Ashlynn said, ending the call.

Wells called Sinead's cell phone. It rang three time before being answered by voice mail. "You've reached Sinead Colton. Leave a message and I'll call you back."

He didn't bother with a voice mail. She'd see his number on caller ID and reach out. Did she wear a smart watch? He thought she did. If he sent her a text, she'd see it and know to call back.

He typed out a message.

Need more information on James to make an ID. Call me ASAP.

He hit Send and waited for a reply.

A minute passed.

A minute more.

He sent a second message.

You there?

He waited another minute. It seemed like an hour.
No reply.
He sent another text.

Let me know if you're getting these messages.

The message field on his phone remained blank.

Wells felt many things. Frustration. Concern. Down-
right worry.

He knew that Sinead might not be answering him for
a variety of reasons. The most likely reason was that
she was doing her job. But part of her job was staying
in contact with the team.

He didn't like that she was now incommunicado.

After closing his messaging app, he opened his
phone's history. He found the article he'd been reading
about the restaurant.

There, at the bottom of the write-up, was a phone
number for reservations. He used the hyperlink and
placed the call. It was answered after the second ring.

"Amore. This is Marc. How can I help you this evening?"

"Marc, this is Detective Wells Blackthorn with the
NYPD."

"No kidding," said Marc, interrupting. "The guy
from the papers?"

For once in his life, he was thankful for the notoriety.
"The same. I'm looking for a colleague of mine. Sinead
Colton. Female. About five feet seven inches. Shoulder-
length blond hair. Early thirties. She was meeting with

a male. I don't have a description for him, but his name is Frazer Parker. Have you seen them?"

"Yeah, I saw them," said Marc. "I'm the bartender here. I see everyone."

"Saw them?" Wells echoed. His pulse skyrocketed. His hands shook. He drew in a deep breath and calmed his racing heart. "You mean they're gone?"

"They left just a minute ago. And to be honest, I didn't know that your coworker was the one throwing back all the drinks. I mean, I just fill the orders that the waiter brings to me. When she showed up, she ordered a water. But when she left…" The bartender whistled. "She was so drunk that she could barely walk straight."

The bartender's comments left Wells stunned. For a moment, he was numb. Then, the feeling came back into his hands and feet. He mumbled his thanks and hung up the phone.

Wells had placed another call before he even realized that the phone was ringing.

"It's late," said Deborah as she answered the phone. "Everything okay?"

He ignored her question. "I hate to do this, but can you come over here and watch Harry? He's asleep. But I have to go to work."

"Again? I'm all for putting service above self, but you've had a hell of a day. You need to stay home—not just for Harry's sake but your own as well."

He didn't have time to argue with Deborah. That meant he had to tell her the truth. "It's Sinead." His voice caught on her name, breaking with emotion.

There were several facts that Wells knew to be true.

Sinead had been meeting with an informant, whose information hadn't been verified. She wasn't answering her phone—neither calls nor texts. When she'd called him earlier, she'd claimed that Frazer had had several drinks. But the bartender said that she could barely walk when they left the restaurant. What's more, he knew that until then, she hadn't been drinking.

It meant only one thing. "Sinead's been drugged and kidnapped."

It took Deborah only seconds to get to his apartment. Wells was ready as soon as she showed up at the door.

"Thanks a million," he said, stepping out into the hallway.

"You go find Sinead and bring her back," said Deborah as she entered his apartment. "That's an order."

"That's exactly what I plan to do."

"Keep me posted."

He gave her arm a gentle squeeze. "Sincerely, thank you."

He took the stairs two at a time. The phone jostled in his hand, but he pulled up his call log and contacted Ashlynn once more. It rang once and she answered. "Hey," she said. "I'm really not finding anything to connect Frazer to another person named James—relative or otherwise."

Wells wasn't surprised. In fact, now he was certain that the dinner meeting had been a ploy from the beginning. He couldn't help but wonder why. Although the why of the matter was something to be figured out later.

"I don't think there is a James," he said. "But I do

think that Sinead's been drugged and kidnapped." He was sick with fury.

Ashlynn gasped. "Are you kidding?"

"I wish I was." He made it to the ground level of his apartment building. After jogging through the foyer, he pushed the front door open. The night air was heavy and hot. He began to sweat.

"What do you need from me?"

"I need Frazer's address."

"That should be easy. Anything else?"

There was—and what's more, it was going to be a big ask. "I need to know what kind of car he drives. And I need you to find him via traffic cameras."

"Usually, I need a warrant for this kind of search," she began.

It was true. In the state of New York, police had to go before a judge and prove they had probable cause to find and follow people. The thing was, Wells didn't have the luxury of time. It meant that he wasn't following protocol. But if Sinead was in danger, nothing else mattered. "A federal agent is missing. If the shit hits the fan because we tailed him without authorization, I'll take complete responsibility." Wells knew that if there were issues, it could cost him his job. Ashlynn's, too.

She said nothing.

"She's your cousin, damnit," he growled. "Help me to help Sinead."

"I want to, it's just that I don't want to do anything that'll land me in jail."

Wells wanted to curse. He knew it would do no good. He ground his teeth together and remained silent.

After a moment, Ashlynn said, "Let me see if I can find her phone. I've got her contact information in my personal cell," she said. "I might be able to track her."

"Anything you can do." Wells stood on the sidewalk. His shirt clung to his sweat-dampened skin.

"That's odd," she said. "Her tracking's been disconnected."

Disconnected? His stomach dropped to his shoes. "Are you ready to help me now?"

"Okay, fine. Give me a few minutes and I'll call you back."

"I'll be waiting," he said before hanging up.

The damaged tire on his SUV had been replaced. He'd been able to drive his vehicle home and it sat at the curb across the street. Wells jogged to the driver's side. Using the fob, he unlocked the door and slid inside. He started the engine and put the gearshift into Drive.

His phone began to ring, the call coming through his in-car audio system. Caller ID flashed on the dashboard screen. Ashlynn Colton.

Using the controls on the steering wheel, he answered the call. "What've you got for me?"

"I have an address for Frazer." She gave Wells a street name and number.

"That's only a few blocks from the restaurant." Pulling away from the curb, he continued, "I'm headed there now."

"I'm still working on getting into the DMV's site for his car registration. When I get the information, I'll contact you." She ended the call.

There was still more for Wells to do. But for now,

he had to wrestle with his own feelings. In the middle of his chest was a hard knot. It was the cold, hard feeling of fear. Sure, he wanted every member of his task force to be safe. But with Sinead, it was more. In just one day, she'd become important to him personally.

He couldn't let it end like this for her—for them.

Turning on his sirens and lights, he dropped his foot onto the accelerator. Cars moved to the side as he thundered past. In the gathering darkness, their brake lights shone like the eyes of evil creatures. It was easy to imagine that he was headed straight to hell.

By breaking so many rules, Wells was putting more than his career or livelihood at risk. Being a cop was more than a job, it was a calling.

Was he willing to throw it all away for Sinead?

He knew the answer.

Using the voice controls in his SUV, he sent Sinead a text message. "Sinead," he said. "If you can read this, just know that I'm on my way."

Ashlynn called back.

He flipped a toggle switch that was set next to the gearshift and quieted his siren. Next, he pressed a button on his steering wheel to answer the call. "What've you got for me?"

"Frazer drives a black sedan with NY license plates. You're in luck, he was just caught on a traffic camera for running a red light."

That was good news. "Where?"

"He was heading toward the FDR."

"But that means he's going east." Wells was confused. That wouldn't get Frazer back home. "Besides, there's nothing beyond the FDR, except for the river." The notion hit him like a brick to the face. His head throbbed and his jaw ached. "He's trying to get Sinead out of the city."

Ashlynn sucked in a breath. "Where would he take her?"

"Once he gets out of Manhattan, Frazer can take Sinead anywhere. And that's a huge problem."

"You need to call Captain Reeves," said Ashlynn. "It's more than the legality of the situation—though what we've done is questionable. We need every cop in the city looking for Sinead and that car."

He didn't disagree with Ashlynn. "I'll call her."

"Now?" she pressed.

"Now," he said, trying to keep the annoyance from his voice. It didn't work very well. And then, "Thanks for everything."

"Contact Reeves," she admonished once more before hanging up.

Wells would reach out to the captain. But first, he was headed in the wrong direction. His mind filled with a map of the Manhattan streets—many one-way. He thought of a route, not direct, but one that would get him to the FDR and one step closer to finding them.

He took a right at the next block. At this time of the evening, the road was all but empty. The light ahead was green. He blew through the intersection without taking his foot off the gas. At the next intersection, a line of traffic waited for the light to change. He had to turn right, and he didn't intend to wait.

Flipping the switch again, Wells turned on his sirens. The piercing wail filled the night. The cars closest to him inched to either side of the road, giving him room to pass. But soon, the cars stopped moving to the side. He pressed his hand into the center of his steering wheel, giving a blast from the air horn that had replaced the factory horn. The cars slid to the side, barely giving him enough room to pass. He rolled forward.

Then, the traffic stopped. He was able to see into the intersection. Up the street, there was a long line of red and glowing taillights. He cursed.

His SUV was equipped with a radio. He adjusted the frequency to the transit authority and picked up the mic. He depressed the broadcast button. "This is Detective Blackthorn with the NYPD. What's the holdup on Park Ave?"

He released the button. The speaker gave a bark of static. "Detective Blackthorn, be advised of a lane closure on Madison," said the MTA dispatcher who answered his call.

"I'm at the corner of Park and 57th Street. What's my ETA to getting past this mess?"

"Ten minutes," she said.

The metallic taste of panic coated his tongue. From where Wells sat, it looked like it would take him an hour to travel a block. And by then, would it be too late for him to save Sinead?

Chapter 19

Wells maneuvered his SUV through the traffic snarl. The large vehicle inched forward, the cars moving to one side or another to let him pass.

"C'mon," he said, talking only to himself. "Move over." His tires rolled slowly, but at least he was making progress. He gained a foot and another foot. And then he'd gone a few yards. The snarl loosened and he wove through traffic. He still hadn't crossed the street, but he was closer.

Keeping his promise to Ashlynn, he called Captain Reeves. The phone rang once. Twice. After the third ring it was answered by voice mail.

"You've reached Collen Reeves, Captain at the 130th Precinct. Leave a message and I'll contact you at my earliest convenience."

He began, "Sinead's been kidnapped." Ashlynn had been right. Reeves should have been the first call he made. How could he have been such a cowboy? He filled the captain in on what had happened as he slowly moved through the traffic. He maneuvered around the grille of a luxury car. The driver gestured wildly and rudely at Wells. He ignored the antics. His front tires lifted onto the curb. He rolled down the other side.

Then, like the cork from a bottle of prosecco, *pop*. He shot forward.

He finished his story with, "According to Ashlynn, Frazer's vehicle is headed toward the FDR. I just made it through a jam on Park. But I don't know if I'll be able to catch him." He dropped his foot onto the accelerator. The cars in front of him moved to the side. It was just like the story he'd heard as a kid, Moses parting the Red Sea. He would have been pleased with the power to control traffic, if it wasn't for the bone-deep worry over Sinead.

Soon, the captain would get the message. He imagined that she'd get an APB on Frazer and his car. For now, he'd done all that he could to notify his superiors. He had to focus on finding Sinead. Saving her was more than just work. It was personal.

Sinead was slow to wake. Sure, she was conscious, but it hurt too damned much to open her eyes. Her head throbbed with each sluggish beat of her heart. Her shoulders ached. There was a pain in her side.

The time before falling asleep was a blank slate, black and endless.

More senses came to her. Like the rough carpeting under her cheek. The hair that covered her face. There was also a nearby rumbling sound. Was it the whirring of an engine?

She opened her eyes. They were dry and her vision was blurry. Her tongue felt thick in her mouth. She tried to wipe the hair from her face, but her arm wouldn't move. Her hands were bound behind her back. Her feet were tied as well. Plastic cuffs bit into the flesh on her wrists and ankles.

Her pulse went up like a rocket. Then, she remembered everything—including her final thought before losing consciousness—that Frazer had put something in her tea. She struggled to flip onto her back and realized that she was on the floor of a car. Above her, she could see the back of his head.

He'd drugged and kidnapped her. Why?

"Hey," she called out. The single word came out as a croak.

From the driver's seat, Frazer glanced back at Sinead. His eyes were wide with surprise. He turned back to look out the windshield. "You're awake. I'd hoped that the sedative would've kept you out for a little longer. It'd be easier for both of us that way. No matter." He glanced at her again and smiled. "We're together now—and we always will be."

Sinead's stomach turned. She feared that she would retch. The pounding in her head became a thunderous roar. It was hard to think, harder even to speak. But she needed to know what was happening. "What have you done to me?"

He glanced over to the rear seat again. "I've never forgotten about you. I can tell that you haven't forgotten about me."

"I remember who you are," she said from the floor of the back seat. She struggled to sit up. The exertion left her nauseated. She lay back and drew in a deep breath. "But I haven't thought about you for years. In fact, it took me a minute to remember who you were when you texted."

"Liar," he yelled. Slamming his palm on the steering wheel, he screamed. The sound was feral and savage. His screams faded and his shoulders heaved, as he drew in several labored breaths. "See what you did? You made me lose my temper. You can't lie to me, not now and not ever."

Sinead knew two important things. Frazer was like a loaded gun, and he could go off at any moment. She couldn't reason with a person who was irrational. If she wanted to escape—and for her, there was no other goal—she had to be very careful.

The car was moving slowly. The sky was dark. When she had arrived at the restaurant, it was still light outside. Now it could be any time. What's more, he could have taken her anywhere.

Lying on her back, she stared out the window. The illuminated iron arches that spanned a bridge were visible. There were 21 bridges that led to or from Manhattan and were accessible to cars. She could be on any one of them.

Another thought came to her, one that left her sick with worry. Did anyone even know that she was missing? She immediately thought of Wells. Where was he? She regretted their quarrel from this morning. Sinead hoped she'd have a chance to make amends.

Then again, Wells might be the only one who could find Sinead. Certainly, he'd get worried when she never contacted him. Then Sinead could be tracked by her phone, or watch, or even her tablet computer. She relaxed a little.

"You won't get away with this, you know. The FBI is very good about finding missing people—especially if those people are one of their agents."

"Do you mean you'll be located by finding your electronic devices?" he asked. "I used your face to open the lock and turned off all tracking. I still have all your stuff—including your backpack. That's where I found a pair of flex-cuffs."

She tried again. "Where are we going?"

Frazer chuckled and gooseflesh covered Sinead's arms. "I bet you'd like to know."

Sinead wasn't about to give up—or give in. Sure, she'd been drugged and kidnapped. But as long as she could draw breath, she'd continue to fight.

She watched Frazer for a moment as he drove. She hadn't seen him for years—and back then, he'd been an awkward and scared kid. But in truth, they'd all been awkward and scared. What had changed to make him the man he was today? And why had he fixated on Sinead—a woman he hadn't spoken to in more than a decade?

Her head still rested on the floorboard. The road noise

was deafening. "You said you saw me the other day. Where? When?" She had to yell to be heard.

"Your picture was in an online article." He let out a sigh of frustration. "I told you that already."

It seemed unlikely that he saw her once and began to obsess. To her it felt like the article was just the impetus for his plan to kidnap her. "That was it?" she asked. "You never saw me before yesterday morning?"

He glanced over his shoulder. His gaze met hers and he smiled. Sinead had to fight the urge to shudder. "Maybe I've been keeping track of you." He looked back at the road. "I thought about reaching out to you when you got divorced. Since you never started dating, I wasn't sure if you were ready for a relationship. But when I saw you in the paper, I knew."

"You knew what?"

"How you felt about that other cop."

Other cop? "Do you mean Wells?"

"Wells," he scoffed. "I could see how you felt about him by the look on your face. You lusted after that guy, even though you'd never met him before. That's when I knew…"

Sinead had to keep Frazer talking. Her only hope of escaping was to discover his motivations and use those against him. "You knew what?"

"That's when I knew that Wells Blackthorn had to die."

Wells's gut still told him that Sinead was being taken to Queens. But even that borough had more than two million people living in an area that covered over one hundred square miles. Unless he got more information, it'd be damned near impossible to find either Sinead or the car.

His phone rang, the call coming through his speaker systems. Caller ID flashed on the radio's screen. Colleen Reeves. Finally, she'd heard his voice mail. He used the controls on the steering wheel to answer.

Before he got a chance to say anything, she asked, "What in the hell is the matter with you? You'll never get promoted acting this way. In fact, you'll be lucky if you don't get terminated."

For the first time since becoming a cop, he didn't care about his job. "I don't care if you fire me right now. I'm going after Sinead."

"Be careful what you say to me, Detective. You're on very thin ice right now." She continued, "I want you to come back to the 130th. You can work the command center with me."

"No way," he said. "I'm not sitting behind some desk."

"You're the leader of a team, damnit. Act like it."

But he was more than just a cop. He was a man who wanted to protect the woman he… His thoughts unraveled. How did he feel about Sinead? He respected her. He cared for her. Her touch made his blood boil—but in a good way. But his feelings for her were more than liking or even lust.

Aww, hell. Now was the worst time to parse his emotions—especially since he hadn't known her long at all. He said, "Let me amend my statement, I'm not sitting behind some desk while Sinead is out there."

"I'm not blind. I can see that you've become attached

to Special Agent Colton over the past twenty-four hours. But you need to ask yourself if the risks are worth the rewards." She paused. The silence stretched out, a gulf between the two phones. "You could be a captain one day."

Ahead was the entrance ramp for the Queensboro Bridge. He had to make a choice.

Did he follow an order that was given to him by his superior?

Or did he follow his heart?

Follow your heart.

Even thinking such a sentimental thought made him want to gag. Then again, Sinead really had gotten to him.

There was only one thing for him to do.

"You're right," he said. "I am fond of Sinead. But it's more than that. If anybody in this entire city was in her situation, I'd slog through hell to find them." He turned on his emergency lights. They strobed red and blue, throwing multicolored beams into the night.

"There's more for you to do than sit behind a desk. Brennan Colton is in front of a federal magistrate right now, getting a search warrant for Mr. Parker's residence. We've got his license plate and we're looking for the car. We'll get Sinead back. I promise."

"I'm going to Queens."

"You don't know that's where Sinead's being taken," said the captain.

She was right, he didn't know. "There's no place for Frazer to hide in Manhattan. He has to get off the island—and fast. This is the only thing that makes sense."

With the speedometer climbing, he crossed several lanes of traffic. Fifty miles per hour. Sixty. Seventy. By the time he swerved onto the entrance ramp, his SUV was going seventy-five miles per hour.

Traffic pulled to the side as he approached. He had a clear shot straight into Queens.

"You don't know where she's gone," said the captain again.

"Then get me some intel," he said. "And quick, because if I'm right, this guy isn't going to kidnap an FBI agent and stick around. Getting out of Manhattan is only step one. Once he's off the island, there's no telling where he'll take Sinead."

Brennan had been tasked with executing a search warrant at Frazer Parker's apartment. He stood in the hallway right outside the door. He was accompanied by his brother Patrick with the crime scene unit and his cousin Sean from the NYPD.

They all wore tactical vests with ceramic plates inside.

A SWAT team was on standby in case things went sideways.

Tension pinched his shoulders together. Who the hell was this guy to kidnap a federal agent? And what's more, Sinead was also his cousin.

Brennan had spoken to the building's manager already. Frazer hadn't been seen since he'd left for work that morning. So nobody expected him to be home, but laws had to be followed before entering any private residence.

He held the warrant in his left hand. With his right hand, he beat the door with his fist. "Open up, Mr. Parker. This is the FBI," he said, announcing their presence. He waited a minute. Then, he waited a minute more.

"Try again," Patrick suggested.

He knocked. "This is the FBI. I have a warrant to search these premises and for your arrest, Mr. Parker. Open the door."

Nothing.

Sean held a battering ram. It was a black tube, three feet long and nine inches in diameter, with two metal handles. The steel cylinder was used to knock down doors.

He tucked the warrant into a pocket on the front of his bulletproof vest. At the same time, he removed a gun from a holster at his hip. "Maybe it's time for you to knock," he said to Sean.

The cop smiled. "I was hoping you'd say that."

Sean swung the battering ram back and slammed the blunt end into the lock. The jamb shattered and the door swung open.

Brennan was already on high alert. He held his gun out as he stepped into the apartment. "FBI," he said. "Put your hands up."

The door lead straight to the living room. Books and papers sat on a coffee table. There was a sofa and a chair. Other than the furniture, the room was empty.

"Clear," he said, alerting his team that it was safe to enter the room.

Sean followed.

There was a door to the left. Brennan inclined his head. Sean nodded and strode across the room. Brennan pressed his back against the wall as his cousin opened the door from behind. He stepped forward and gasped.

The wall above the bed was papered with pictures of Sinead. They'd been taken at different times, in different seasons. In one picture, she wore a wool coat with the collar turned up. Falling snow had been captured in the photograph. In another, she walked through Central Park. He recognized Strawberry Fields. In that picture, she wore a denim jacket and the trees had turned from summer's green to the gold and red of autumn. In another, she was in a sundress and sitting at a sidewalk café. Her dining companion was a dark-haired woman. Even from the back, he recognized Ashlynn.

And as bad as all the pictures were, there was one that really turned his blood cold.

In the center of the wall was a recent photograph. It was a picture of Sinead and Wells that had been taken from the *Daily Herald*'s website. The photograph had been blown up until the image appeared to be little more than a blur. Using a red marker, Frazer had drawn a circle around Wells several times. Then, he'd drawn a slash through the middle.

Sean and Patrick stood next to Brennan.

"What in the hell is wrong with this guy?" Sean asked.

"He's got our cousin and it's up to us to get her back."

"Then let's process this crime scene by the book," said Patrick. "I'll call in my team. Until they show, you two can help me look for anything that might give us a clue as to where he'd take Sinead."

"Well, they aren't here," Brennan said.

"Parker was last seen running a red light on Riverside Drive. He was heading toward the FDR," said Sean.

Sean stowed his firearm. "What do you want us to do, Patrick?"

"You both check the living room. Tag anything that might be evidence. I'll start in here."

The two cousins returned to the living room. A box of ammunition sat on a shelf. Under the box was a page of instructions, printed from a site on the dark web, that gave directions for making a bomb.

Sean whistled through his teeth. "Patrick said to tag everything that might be evidence—that's everything in this place."

"I couldn't agree more." In the kitchen, a garbage can sat under the sink. A stack of papers had been shoved into the container. Brennan donned a pair of latex gloves and pulled out the pile. He scanned the first item, just a small slip of paper. "Bingo," he said.

Sean had removed the cushions from the couch. He looked up as Brennan spoke. "Did you find out where he's taken Sinead?"

It wasn't going to be that easy. "I don't know where he's going. But I know where he's been." He held up the receipt. "This is for a coffee shop in Long Island City from this morning."

Brennan grabbed his phone and dialed.

Chapter 20

Wells made it out of Manhattan in record time. The bridge ended, bringing him into Queens. But the thing was, he didn't know where to start looking for Sinead. His phone rang. Caller ID appeared on the screen. Brennan Colton.

He answered the phone. "Please tell me that you found Sinead."

"There's a lot I did find, but not Sinead."

To Wells it was a mixed blessing. He had to come to terms with the fact that the outcome might be disastrous. What was more, when Sinead was found, she might be dead.

Brennan continued, "I did find a receipt at Frazer's apartment. Looks like he visited a coffee shop in Long Island City this morning." He gave Wells the address.

"What time was he there?"

"About seven thirty," the FBI agent said.

It wasn't much but it was more than he had before. "Thanks, man. I'll check it out."

The call ended.

Wells had never worked in Queens. It wasn't his borough. Using his phone's GPS, he found the coffee shop. It was only minutes away. It sat on a corner, next door to a ladies' clothing store. The store was closed, but lights from the coffee shop spilled onto the sidewalk. Three people sat at a booth by the window. An illuminated open sign hung on the door.

After parking at the curb, he turned off the engine. Wells fished his phone from his pocket. He opened his own social media app and searched for Frazer Parker. He found the other man's profile and took a screen capture of the photo. After cropping the picture, he opened the SUV's door. The hot and humid air washed over him. He strode up the sidewalk. Sweat trickled down his back.

He opened the door to the coffee shop. The air was cool and smelled of freshly ground coffee beans. A man stood behind the cash register. He looked up as Wells entered.

"Evening," he said. He picked up a menu from a stack. "You want a table or a booth?"

"Neither," said Wells. He held up his NYPD badge. "I'm Detective Blackthorn. I was wondering if you've seen this man?" He slid his ID back into his pocket and removed his phone. He pulled up the picture of the kidnapper. "He would have been in your shop around seven thirty this morning."

The man behind the cash register wore a name tag. Moe. He leaned toward Wells's phone and squinted. "He don't look familiar, but my brother and I run this place. He works mornings. I work the nights." He paused. "I can call him if you want. But at seven thirty in the morning, this place is pretty busy. The warehouses open at eight and a lot of the workers stop by for breakfast or coffee."

"Warehouses?"

He pointed to the left. "There's a bunch of warehouses for online retailers down there. The drivers start delivering at eight in the morning."

"Do they operate twenty-four/seven?"

"Best I can tell," said Moe. "All the trucks return at six in the evening—that's when we get a dinner rush. Then, big trucks make a delivery. The shelves are restocked. Those workers are done by nine thirty. Some stop in for pie. Some get a late dinner."

Wells's pulse raced until it echoed in his ears. If Frazer wanted to truly kidnap Sinead, he'd need a car other than his own. An empty parking lot would be the perfect place to stow a getaway vehicle.

"That man on your phone work at the warehouse?" Moe pointed to the trio at the table. "Those fellas stock shelves. They might know him."

"No, he doesn't." Wells backed away from the counter. "You've been very helpful. Thanks so much."

Turning for the door, he rushed back into the hot and

humid night. While jogging to his car, he took out his phone and called Captain Reeves.

She answered after the second ring. "You better be calling to tell me that you're on your way to the precinct." Each word was filled with irritation.

"I think I know where's Frazer's taken Sinead." Wells used the fob to unlock his door. He slipped into his SUV and started the ignition. The call automatically transferred to the in-car audio. Setting his phone in a cup holder, he continued, "A receipt was found at his apartment for a coffee shop in Queens from this morning..."

"I know about the receipt," she said, interrupting. "I also know about the box of ammunition that was found. I know, as well, that the ammo matches the bullets that were fired at you yesterday morning. You want to know what else was found? Directions for a homemade bomb—as well as the materials."

It took a moment for all the pieces to fall into place. "Frazer is the subway shooter?"

"Looks like it," said Reeves. "And the subway shooter was definitely targeting you."

Then Wells had two reasons to find the bastard and bring him to justice. "I think he's taken Sinead to a complex of warehouses in Long Island City. They aren't far from the bridge. I'm going there to check it out. I need backup."

"I suppose it won't do me any good to tell you to stand down, will it?" she asked.

"You know it won't."

"Then, I'll tell you to be careful."

He wasn't worried about himself. In fact, Wells would do whatever it took to find Sinead and bring her home.

Sinead remained on the floor of the car. She was still bound and unable to do anything other than watch a sliver of the sky through the car's window. The car slowed and the sky outside of the window turned dark. Frazer applied the brakes and the vehicle stopped. He turned off the engine. After having her ear pressed to the floorboard, the silence was welcome. It was like the first cool breeze of autumn. But it also meant they'd arrived at their destination. Where had he taken her, and would she have a chance to escape?

He opened his door and got out of the car. He closed the door again, leaving Sinead alone. Without the distractions of her kidnapper in the driver's seat and the continual droning of road noise, she finally had a moment to concentrate.

Her situation was awful, she knew that. She also knew that the longer she was held captive, the less likely she was to escape. The door above her head opened. She looked up. Frazer loomed above her. The view from her back changed her visual perspective and he looked like a giant.

"I'm going to lift you out of the car now. I don't want to hurt you, but if you fight me, I will." His voice was calm and all the more chilling for his control.

"I won't fight you," she said, keeping her voice meek. But she was far from compliant.

"That's what I was hoping you'd say." He reached

into the car and gripped her under the shoulders. She was dragged out of the car and lifted to her feet. She leaned on the bumper and waited for the feeling to return to her legs. Looking around, she assessed her situation. If it had been bad while she was stuck in the back seat of his car, it had definitely gotten worse.

She stood in the dark corner of an abandoned parking lot. Parked two spaces away was another car. The lid to the trunk was open. Despite the sultry night air, she went cold.

He obviously meant to stow her in the trunk. She couldn't let that happen.

It was just that she didn't know how to stop him.

"All right," he said, heaving in a sigh. "Let's get out of here."

He slid an arm around her middle. His touch made her sick to her stomach.

"You won't get away with this, you know," she said. "To you, I might just be a girl from high school who you used to like. But in real life, I'm an FBI agent. The authorities will never stop looking for me."

"You might work for the FBI. The feds might keep looking for you. But I've watched you. I know all about you. I know that more than living alone—you're lonely. Once we're together, you'll see that I was right to save you from yourself."

Frazer really was unhinged. "If we're meant to be together, why not ask me out? Why not woo me yourself?"

"It was part of my plan. Watch. Wait. But then, you met *him*." He spit out the last word. "He would only hurt you in the end, you have to understand that."

"Funny that you're worried about Wells hurting me. He never tried to blow me up with a bomb."

"You weren't supposed to be there," Frazer snarled.

A fleck of spit hit her in the cheek. For Sinead, what happened next was less of a plan than a reaction. She arched her back. Then, she snapped forward. Her forehead connected with Frazer's nose. She felt the satisfying crunch of bone and cartilage giving way.

He cursed. Blood spurted from his nostrils.

He gripped his face, letting go of Sinead.

She lost her balance and fell to the ground. Her skull slammed into the pavement. For a moment, her vision filled with a flash of light. And then, she saw nothing but black.

Wells drove on a frontage road. On either side of him were warehouses that were larger than sports stadiums. So far, there was no sign of either Sinead, the kidnapper, or his car. He clenched his jaw. "Damnit," he grumbled.

There was no way he could fail.

But it looked like this hunch hadn't been right.

Was now the time to turn around? He wasn't quitting, but he needed to regroup. Maybe he should have stayed in Manhattan. He could have helped search the kidnapper's home. Certainly, there had to be something in the apartment that was a clue...

That was when his headlights reflected off the glint of glass. He peered into the night. At the far end of a parking lot, there was a car. He dropped his foot onto the accelerator. The SUV's powerful engine pushed him back into the seat as the auto sped down the road.

He drew closer. Just like he'd sprinted the last one hundred yards of a race, his heart hammered in his chest. Was that a dark sedan?

It was.

What's more, a second car was parked next to the first.

The beams of his headlights caught a figure. The person appeared to be male. They held their hands to their face. He'd never seen Frazer in person, but he knew that was who he'd found.

Where in the hell was Sinead?

The kidnapper let go of his face. It was covered in blood. He looked toward the SUV, coming up fast, and bent to the ground. When he stood again, he held a body in his arms. It was Sinead, Wells was sure of that. But she was limp. Was she even alive?

He lifted the radio's mic and chose an emergency broadcasting band. "This is Detective Wells. I need all available units." He gave the address. "Subject is trying to flee with Special Agent Colton. She's unconscious and unresponsive."

Still holding the mic, he flipped a switch and turned on his PA system. "It's time to give up, Frazer. Put Special Agent Colton on the ground and step away from her. Keep your hands in the air."

The kidnapper hesitated only a minute. Holding her close to his chest, he dumped Sinead into the trunk of the second car and slammed the lid closed. Rounding to the open door, he slid into the driver's seat. He started the engine and began to pull away.

Wells refused to let him get out of the parking lot.

Gunning the engine, he aimed straight for the fender. He hit the smaller car, sending it spinning like a top. One of the tires blew and the car came to a stop.

The driver's door opened. Frazer sprinted into the night. Wells put the SUV in Park and jumped out of his vehicle. He wanted to check on Sinead, but he needed to catch the kidnapper. He chased the other man. With only a few feet separating them, Wells dove forward. He grabbed the kidnapper around the middle. They tumbled to the ground. Wells punched the guy in the face. Damn. It felt good. In the distance, the sound of sirens tore through the night.

He hefted Frazer to his feet.

Wells had a pair of flex-cuffs looped over his belt. "You're under arrest," he said, sliding the cuffs over Frazer's wrists.

He patted him down quickly to make sure he didn't have any concealed weapons. He didn't.

The kidnapper struggled to break away. That was the last thing Wells would let happen. Holding tight to Frazer's shoulder, he walked to the car. The engine was still running. Inside the open door was a button to release the trunk latch. He pushed it and the trunk sprang open with a click. At the same moment, a first police cruiser pulled up.

Two uniformed officers rushed forward. They took custody of Frazer. Wells sprinted to the back of the car.

Sinead was in the trunk. She lay without moving. Her hair was matted with blood. In the dark, he couldn't tell if she was breathing—or not. He found the artery under her chin. Her pulse was strong and steady.

She moaned.

A wave of relief washed over him.

"Sinead." He shook her shoulder. "Can you hear me?"

She blinked. "Wells?"

"Yeah, it's me." His eyes began to burn, and he blinked hard. "You're safe now."

"I guess I owe you money. You were right. There was something wrong with Frazer."

It had to be a good sign that she had her sense of humor. "I shouldn't have told you how to do your job." He paused. "I'm sorry."

An ambulance sped up the frontage road. The siren pierced the night. "I'm going to let the EMTs check you out. Anything hurt?"

"I hit my head on the pavement. And my arms and legs hurt like hell. That bastard tied me up with my own flex-cuffs."

Wells wished he'd hit the guy a little harder when he'd brought him to the ground. "Can I lift you out?"

"Please do," she said.

He scooped her up and held Sinead to his chest. With her in his arms, he placed a kiss on her head. An EMT waited with a stretcher. Wells placed Sinead on the mattress.

"She hit her head," he told the woman. "And her wrists and ankles are bound with flex-cuffs. You gotta get them off."

"I can speak for myself," said Sinead, giving him a gentle censure.

"I know that, but I also want to take care of you. Not because I think you aren't capable—but because keeping you safe is all that matters." Until he spoke the words, Wells hadn't known the depth of his feelings for Sinead.

"We've got her, Detective," said the EMT.

Several other cars, with emergency lights flashing, raced through the empty parking lot. One was an unmarked sedan. It stopped. Captain Reeves exited from the passenger door. She strode to where he stood. "I don't know whether to fire you or give you a medal, Detective."

"I'd prefer the medal, if it's all the same to you." He gave her his best smile.

"For the record, that grin has never worked on me."

His smile faded. "With all respect, Captain, I know I didn't follow protocol or orders. But, if given the same set of circumstances, I'd do it all over again." He let his gaze drift toward the ambulance. The plastic cuffs had been removed from Sinead's wrists and ankles. One EMT examined her head wound. The other applied a bandage to her arm.

He knew how he felt about her. He was also wise enough to know that when the passion of a new relationship burns like an inferno, it tends to run out of fuel quickly. He shouldn't hope for something more—something permanent—with Sinead.

But he did.

A patrol officer approached. "While searching the suspect's car, I found this." He wore gloves and held up a dark blue vial.

"What's that?" the captain asked.

Wells leaned forward to read the label, but he already

knew. "It's a prescription sleep aid. My guess—that's what Frazer used to drug Sinead."

Reeves said, "Take that to the EMTs. They'll need to know what might be in her system."

"Will do, ma'am," said the officer.

Neither spoke as the patrolman left. Then, Captain Reeves said, "I'm putting you on paid leave for the next two weeks."

His head snapped around. "Leave? With the Landmark Killer at large? No way."

"Think of it as a vacation. After everything you've been through, you can use some time off to bond with your nephew."

For the first time in his working life, he liked the idea of a break. "Thanks, Captain. That's nice of you."

"I'm not trying to be nice," she said, obviously lying. "You're being reprimanded for not following orders, Detective. But over the next two weeks, you take care of yourself. That is an order I expect you to follow." She walked away.

"Hey, Captain," he called after her.

She turned.

"You gotta admit," he said, "the smile works sometimes."

"Never," she said, before turning her back on him.

He couldn't help but laugh. He looked back at Sinead. She was being helped off the stretcher by the EMT. He walked to her side.

"I guess I should thank you for saving me," she said.

He reached for her hand. "There's nothing I wouldn't do for you."

A police cruiser drove past, leaving the scene. Frazer sat in the back seat.

"What's going to happen to him?" she asked.

"You know better than I do. He's going to go to jail for a long time." He kissed the bandage that was wrapped around Sinead's wrist. "What'd the EMT say?"

"She said I should go to the hospital and be evaluated. But I promised to see my doctor tomorrow and I was released."

"I guess you need a way to get back home, then."

"Yeah, I guess I do."

"I can give you one." He glanced over his shoulder. The grille of his SUV was broken. The front fender was bent. "My car looks bad, but it's still drivable. I can give you a ride back, if you want."

"Sure. Thanks."

He squeezed her hand. "Stay with me tonight. I can sleep on the sofa. I just don't like the idea of you being alone."

"If I stay with you tonight, what does that mean for tomorrow?"

Wells pulled her to him. "Let's make a deal. We can start with now and figure out the rest later."

She placed her lips on his. "Done."

Chapter 21

Sinead dozed as Wells drove. At this time of night, there was little traffic in the city and in less than thirty minutes, they were parking at the curb next to his apartment. From the street, she could see the lights coming from his living room. The glow was inviting, and one word came to mind.

Home.

She slowly climbed the steps to his apartment. Wells worked the key into the lock and opened the door. He held it for her as she passed.

She gave him a wan smile. "Thanks."

As she'd noticed from outside, the lights were on in the living room.

Deborah sat on the sofa. The Marine stood as they entered. "Thank goodness you're okay."

True, she hadn't spent much time with Wells's neighbor. But Sinead already liked the woman. "Thanks for coming over to take care of Harry. If Wells hadn't realized what was happening and come after me..." Her voice trailed off as her mind filled with a flash of being bound, helpless, in the back of Frazer's car.

"I'd do anything for these two guys. Harry's been asleep the entire time that I've been here." Deborah paused a beat. "How are you?"

"Exhausted," said Sinead, honestly. But there was more. She had yet to lose the feeling of being vulnerable and defenseless. Then again, she knew that the traumatic event was likely to stick with her for a while.

"You take care of yourself, you hear?" said Deborah. "Don't try to be tough. Take some time off. You'll need it."

It hadn't occurred to Sinead to do anything other than show up at work in the morning. After all, the Landmark Killer was still terrorizing the city. A few days off seemed scandalous. "I'll think about," she promised.

"I'm gonna get out of here and let you two rest. If you need anything, call. Otherwise, I'll see you in the morning when you drop off Harry."

Wells stood next to the breakfast bar. "I'm not going to the office in the morning," he said. "I don't know my schedule for the next few weeks, but I'll let you know when I do."

"I'm not going to lie," said Deborah as she crossed the living room floor. "I'll be happy to sleep in."

She left the apartment and then, it was just Sinead and Wells.

"What can I get you?" he asked. "Are you hungry?"

Her mouth was dry. Her head ached. "Just some water."

He found a pitcher in the fridge and poured water into a glass. He brought the drink to Sinead. "Here you go."

She took the water and finished in a single swallow. "Thanks," she said, breathless. "That was perfect." She handed him the glass. "Crap," she said. "I left my phone and backpack in Frazer's car."

"You want me to call someone at the scene? I can have them bring them to you."

"I'm too tired to work tonight. If I'm needed, they can find me." The last word stretched out with a yawn. Her legs were tired. Her arms were sore. She wanted to lie down and not get out of bed for a week. "Man, it just hit suddenly. I'm exhausted."

"I'll sleep here on the sofa. You can take the bed."

After everything that she'd been through, Sinead wasn't in the mood for sex. But she also wasn't in the mood to be left alone, either. "You don't have to stay out here, unless that's what you want."

"I want to be—and do—whatever it is that you want."

It was a pretty significant invitation. "Let's start with just sleeping tonight and then see how things unfold."

"Sounds good to me."

Wells turned off all the lights in the apartment. In the dark, he reached for her hand. They walked down the short hallway. At the door to the nursery, they stopped. Enough light filtered in from the windows that she could see Harry sleeping in the crib.

His eyes were closed. A fringe of lashes spread out above his cheeks. "Just like his uncle Wells, he has those beautiful and thick eyelashes."

He smiled, "He's a great kid. I just want to do right by him, you know?"

"You will," she said. "You are."

Wells placed his lips on her temple. She wrapped her arms around his waist and pulled him closer. They stood in the dark hallway, watching the baby sleep. It was easy for her to imagine that this was her life, even though she knew that it wasn't. But was there any harm in living the dream just for a moment?

Sinead woke in the middle of an erotic dream. In it, her hands were tangled in Wells's thick hair. His lips were pressed against her neck. She was beneath him. He was hard. She was wet. She kissed him deeply and realized that this was no dream.

She didn't know who had reached for who in the darkness. But really, she didn't care.

He licked her earlobe and pulled the soft skin between his teeth.

"Oh Wells," she gasped.

His mouth moved lower. He kissed her neck. She wore one of his shirts for sleeping and he reached inside the hem. His touch was hot against her skin. But she wanted more of Wells. She needed him.

Sinead gripped the ends of the shirt and drew it over her head. She dropped it over the side of the bed.

Wells only wore his briefs. Now they were skin to skin. Her breasts were pressed onto his chest. She spread her thighs. He settled his hips between her legs, and she kissed him deeper.

He pulled away from the kiss and pressed his forehead into hers. "I want you, Sinead. I want to be inside of you so bad that I can taste it." His words mingled with his labored breathing. "But you had a rough night. I don't want to do anything that would hurt you. Emotionally or physically."

"The only way you'll hurt me is if you don't take me now."

"Are you sure?"

She traced his chest with the tip of her finger. Collar bone. Sternum. Nipple. "Frazer said he only wanted to kidnap me because he knew that he and I were meant to be together. Make no mistake, when he realized how wrong he was, he would've killed me. I survived, Wells, mostly because of you. But from here on out, I want more than to just move through life. I want to live."

Until she spoke the words, Sinead hadn't admitted the feelings to herself. It was as if in the darkness, she understood what had been missing. Since she was young, she'd focused only on being perfect. And all the while, striving for perfection had kept her separated from anyone who might care. Because what happened if she cared about them, and she wasn't good enough? Or what if they disappointed her in the end?

No more.

She kissed Wells again. "I want to live my life. And tonight, I want to be with you."

He ran his hand over her stomach and up to her chest. He cupped her breast. His touch danced along her skin.

He dipped his head and ran his tongue over her areola, scraping his teeth on her nipple.

"Oh, Wells," she moaned.

He moved his hand lower now. Slipping his fingers inside the waistband of her panties, he found the top of her sex. She was swollen with want. He rubbed her and a wave of pleasure began to build in her middle. She gripped his wrist. "I want you inside of me when I come."

"I can manage that," he said.

Wells pulled down his briefs as Sinead wiggled out of her panties. He moved so that he was pressed against her. Driving his hips forward, he entered her in one stroke. When he moved inside of her, it was like the tide crashing against the shore. She raked her fingers over his back and wrapped her legs around his middle.

He slid his hand between them and found her most sensitive spot. He began to rub. The pleasure was intense and instantaneous. Her climax came crashing down on her. She held tight to his shoulders as she came. As if she let go of Wells, she'd somehow lose him and herself.

He kissed her deeply. His hips moved harder. Faster. The blankets had fallen from his shoulders and torso. They now pooled around his legs.

She looked between them and watched as he slid inside of her, so deep that the two of them were fully connected. "God, seeing you inside of me is so sexy."

"You're sexy," he said, kissing her again. Sweat dampened his hair and the ends curled.

Throwing back his head, he came.

He collapsed on top of Sinead. His breath was ragged. He kissed her slowly before rolling onto his back. He wrapped his arm around her middle. She rested her head on his chest. His pulse was rapid, and his breaths were shallow. She traced the smooth skin on his nipple.

Placing a kiss on his chest, she snuggled deeper into his embrace. With Wells's arm around her waist and her heartbeat matching his own, she slipped back into a deep sleep. But as consciousness slipped away, Sinead finally felt that she'd found someone she could fully trust.

Wells sat on the floor of his living room. His back rested back on the front of the sofa. Bright sunlight streamed through the windows and reflected off the wooden floors. A blanket was spread out across the floor. Harry lay on the blanket and happily blew bubbles. It was 6:15 a.m. His nephew had slept through the night.

Funny, a month ago, getting out of bed before 7:00 a.m. would have been unthinkable. Now he was pleased with the extra rest.

Sinead was still in bed. The midnight sex had been mind-blowing, but he'd been honest with her. The past two days had been a lot for her. He figured she could use all the sleep she could get.

An open laptop sat on his legs, and he read the online edition of the *Daily Herald*. The front page was filled with a picture of Frazer Parker's mugshot, along with the headline "Subway Shooter Captured." The attached story had been written by Nadeem.

For the past two days, the city has been living on the edge. Amid blistering temperatures, three men have been murdered at Manhattan landmarks. Yesterday, a gunman targeted one of New York City's finest, Detective Wells Blackthorn, while he stood on a busy subway platform. Through a joint investigation between the NYPD and the FBI, the identity of the subway shooter has been determined. Frazer Parker, a civil engineer who lives in Manhattan, was apprehended last night in the borough of Queens. According to the arrest report, the arresting officer was Detective Blackthorn.

The police have no comment on whether Parker is connected to the Landmark Killer. Nor have they commented on Parker's motive in targeting the NYPD Detective. A press conference has been scheduled for later this morning.

With a smile, he closed the article. Next, he opened a search engine. He entered the words *House Rental/ Finger Lakes.*

It was too much to hope that his old home would be listed and available. But even if it wasn't… "Hey, little man. I figure it's about time for me and you to make some of our own traditions. What do you think about getting out of the city for a few weeks?"

Harry looked at his uncle and made a motorboat noise.

Wells decided to take that as a yes.

He scrolled through the listings on the screen. There

were several homes available for the next two weeks. Now he just needed to find the perfect place.

Harry gave a happy squawk. Wells looked up from the computer. Sinead stood at the end of the hallway. "So this is where you two have gotten to. Can I join you? Or are no girls allowed?" she joked.

Sinead wore one of his old T-shirts. It hung down to her thighs, giving him the perfect view of her long and toned legs. The collar was wide on her, too. It hung off one shoulder. In short, she looked perfect.

"What do you say, little man? Should we let Sinead join us?"

Harry squawked again.

"He said yes."

Sinead lay down on the blanket next to Harry. The baby saw her and smiled wide. He waved his hands in the air as she kissed his forehead. "How're you this morning? It looks like you slept through the night."

"He did," said Wells. "How are you?"

"Better," she said. "I had weird dreams."

He knew that Sinead was tough. But he also knew that it would take some time to get over what had happened. "Any time you want to talk—even if it's in the middle of the night—I'm available."

"Thanks. I appreciate that." She glanced at him and smiled. Then, she looked back at the baby. "Oh my gosh! Is that a tooth?" She pulled gently on his bottom lip. Harry gurgled. "That is a tooth. Come here!"

Wells dove forward. "A tooth?" He looked in the baby's mouth. There, in the middle of the smooth pink gums, was a white line. "That is a tooth. No wonder you slept so well last night."

His phone began to ring. Wells pushed off the floor and walked to the kitchen. His cell sat on the charging station. Caller ID read: Colleen Reeves.

He answered. "Morning, Captain. What can I do for you?"

"You sound chipper. Only one day on vacation and already you're more relaxed. I have some items that need to be returned to Special Agent Colton. Any idea where they can be delivered?"

It seemed like a waste of time to be coy. "She's here right now. You can drop them off at my apartment."

"I'm on my way to the office. Mind if I stop by in about ten minutes?"

"See you then," he said, ending the call. He returned to the blanket. "Did you hear what Captain Reeves said?"

"I did." She stood and held out the hem of the shirt. "I should probably shower and change."

"I don't know, you look pretty good to me." He smiled.

"Don't give me that grin," she said, walking away.

He propped Harry up with a bolster and put some blocks within reach. The baby reached for his toys, chewing on them one at a time.

Wells returned to his internet search. He found the perfect place on Cayuga Lake. It was a two-bedroom cottage, complete with a dock and a large porch that overlooked the water. The price didn't matter, and he booked the rental.

Sinead came down the hall. She wore the same

clothes as she had the day before. But her hair was damp. The ends hung down her back. With a sigh, she sat on the floor. "I could've stood in your shower all day."

He liked the idea of her naked and wet. "Glad you feel better." He tried to think of something else to say, but his mind was filled with images of Sinead in the shower. The silence was cut off by a knocking at the door. He rose from the floor. "That's probably the captain."

He walked to the door and glanced through the peep-hole. Captain Reeves stood in the hallway. She was already dressed in a navy blue suit. Sinead's bag was slung over her shoulder. He unlatched the locks and opened the door. "Thanks for stopping by," he said, pulling the door open further. "Come in."

She followed him into the apartment. "I know it's early, but I wanted to get this bag back to Sinead. Also, I'm glad to stop by because I haven't met your nephew yet."

"He's got a tooth," said Wells, his chest filled with pride. "I think that's why he was so cranky. But we both survived all the sleepless nights."

"You do know that babies have twenty teeth."

Obviously, he knew that kids had more than one tooth. It was just he hadn't thought through the fact that he and Harry would have to deal with teething another nineteen times. He was suddenly exhausted. "Twenty teeth, eh?" The thing was, if he could get through teething once, he could get through it again. And again. And again… "Harry's in the living room with Sinead," he said, walking down the hall.

Reeves followed. They entered the living room. Sinead stood near the window. Harry was in her arms. "Thanks for bringing my bag to me," she said.

"Your phone is inside the front pocket." She set the backpack on the floor near the sofa. "We checked both for evidence. Nothing was kept."

"Thanks for letting me know."

"And who's this handsome man?" the captain asked. She held out her finger to Harry. The baby grabbed Reeves. "Ow," she teased, shaking her head. "You've got a strong grip. Are you going to be a police officer one day like Uncle Wells?"

Harry squealed with laughter.

"I'd take that as a no," said Wells.

"He might want to follow in your footsteps," said the captain.

"I have a question about last night," said Sinead. "You didn't find anything useful in my bag, but what *did* you find? Any idea what Frazer will be charged with?"

Reeves sighed. "Obviously, there's kidnapping you. Because you're an FBI agent, he can be charged both with federal and state crimes. He confessed to shooting at Wells and leaving the bomb in the hallway. That means he's likely to get charged with two counts of attempted murder. He'll go to jail for a long time. You won't have to worry about him bothering you again."

"That's good to hear." Sinead worked her bottom lip between her teeth. She was thinking about something, he could tell. "I know that I said the subway shooter and the Landmark Killer were different people. But I need to ask, is there any evidence linking him to the other three murders?"

"Actually, we checked. Frazer has an alibi for the murders of Mark Wheden and Edward Pendleton—he was at work both times. He says he was sleeping when Andrew Capowski was killed. It's hard to verify that he was in his apartment and alone. But we don't have any evidence that he left his residence that morning."

"So, we're still no closer to finding the Landmark Killer," said Wells. "Too bad that Frazer wasn't responsible for all the crimes. It would have been nice to wrap up both cases with one arrest."

"You're on vacation," Reeves chastised. "Remember that."

"I thought you put me on leave," he said.

"Call it forced rest and relaxation." She glanced at her watch. "I have to go. The mayor wants to hold a press conference." Then to Harry, she said, "You keep your uncle out of trouble, okay?"

Harry smiled and reached for Wells. He took his nephew from Sinead's arms. Balancing the baby on his hip, he walked the captain to the front door. "Thanks for stopping by."

Harry opened and closed his hand.

"Bye-bye," said Reeves, tickling the baby's foot.

Harry gave a big smile.

"Oh no, not another Blackthorn with a smile like that," Reeves joked.

"Hey, little man, the captain is immune to your charms."

"I didn't say that. In fact, this guy can have anything he wants." She tickled Harry's foot once more and left.

Wells shifted the baby to his other hip and walked back to the living room. Sinead stood next to the breakfast bar. Her backpack was draped over one shoulder. She held her phone and scrolled through the screen.

"Did you miss anything important last night?"

"ADIC Chang messaged me. I can take off all the time I need from work."

That was good news—at least to him.

"Anything else?"

"It looks like Rory called several times."

To Wells, it seemed like the two sisters were forming a connection. He hoped that Sinead and Rory could have the kind of relationship that Wells and his brother, Dan, had not.

She continued, "I'll reach out as soon as I get home. I can't thank you enough for everything, but I'll start by getting out of here and letting you get back to your morning."

His pulse spiked. She was leaving? "Can I get you to stay for a minute? I want to show you something."

"Sure."

"Hold him for a minute." He held out Harry.

The baby reached for Sinead. "Come here," she said, taking him into her arms.

Wells found his laptop where he'd left it on the floor. He brought it back to the kitchen and set it on the breakfast bar. He opened his email and found the confirmation message from the cottage he'd rented. He pulled up a photo of the property. "This," he said, turning the computer so the screen faced Sinead, "is the place I've rented for the next two weeks."

She looked at the laptop and back at Wells. "Is that the place your family used to own?"

"Unfortunately, no. But it's close by, so there are places I remember from when I was a kid." He paused. "Anyway, I figured that Harry and I needed to start our own traditions."

"That's great," she said. Her smile faded. "So that means that you'll be gone for two weeks. I was hoping we could chat and figure out, well, us."

"Come with us," he said. "Harry loves you. You can have some time away from the city. Your boss told you to take off time if you needed."

"I can't just leave," she protested. "I have…" Her words trailed off. "I suppose I could leave. But what if we get sick of each other after two weeks together?"

"We won't," Wells promised. "C'mon. It'll be an adventure."

Sinead turned to Harry. "What d'you say? You want me to come along with you on your adventure?"

Harry clapped his hands.

"He says yes," said Wells.

"In that case…" Sinead moved closer to Wells. "I'll go."

He wrapped his arm around her waist. The three of them were together—and complete. Sure, he knew that life wouldn't always be perfect. But he was ready to see what happened next.

Epilogue

Two Weeks Later

The sun shimmered off the waters of Cayuga Lake. In the distance, a bird called. Its song was answered by a mate. Sinead sat on the dock and sipped her morning coffee. Her legs dangled over the rough wooden boards and the water swirled around her toes.

It was her last day of vacation, and she was determined to enjoy her final morning. The past two weeks had been bliss. Sinead started each day drinking her coffee at the lake's edge as the sun rose. Then, she went inside to make breakfast. Harry had settled into a routine of sleeping until 6:30 a.m. At that time, Wells got up as well.

They spent every morning at the cottage. Then, after

lunch, they explored the area. So far, they had visited three wineries and four quaint upstate New York villages. They'd also taken hikes to seven waterfalls.

Dinner was takeout from one of a dozen different restaurants. Harry went to bed promptly at 8:00 p.m. Then, Wells and Sinead spent time together. They watched movies or played board games. Once they were in bed, they made love every night. At first, the sex had been frantic, but now it was tender and loving.

Behind her, a board creaked. She glanced over her shoulder. Wells approached with Harry in his arms. Her chest filled with love as she watched the duo. Oh sure, she had yet to share her feelings with Wells. But she could wait. After all, she wasn't sure how life would turn out once they were back in the city.

"Morning," said Wells with a smile.

Harry clapped his hands and smiled as well.

"How are my two favorite men?" She rose to her feet and walked up the dock to meet them.

"You ready to head back?" he asked.

"I was just thinking that the past two weeks have been as close to perfect as I'll ever get. But, yeah, I am ready." In the two weeks since they'd been gone, the Landmark Killer had gone silent. But Sinead doubted that he was done killing. Even if he was, there were three murder victims who deserved justice. "We have jobs. What we do is important to the city."

Wells nodded. "I think that Harry's going to miss all of this attention."

"He probably will, but I imagine that Deborah will happily give him extra snuggles."

He chuckled. "True."

Harry reached for Sinead. She took him from Wells's arms. More than Harry would miss the attention, she was going to miss being around the baby. And his uncle. Her eyes burned and a single tear ran down her cheek. She wiped it away with a laugh. "Maybe I'm not as ready to leave as I thought I was."

Wells moved in close. He wrapped his arms around her waist, connecting them in the circle of his embrace. "Harry loves you. You know that."

She kissed the baby's head. "I love him, too."

"Sinead." He whispered her name. "I love you."

She looked up to meet his gaze. "I love you, too."

"I don't want this to end. When we get back to the city, move in with me—with us. I want us to be a family for good."

Sinead thought about all those years when she had nothing but her job and doubts that she would ever be good enough. With Wells and Harry, she'd have everything she ever wanted. A man she loved—and who loved her in return. A child she adored. A job that was more than employment, but a calling.

"Yes," she said. The tears began to fall and there was no way she could stop them now. "Yes, Wells, let's see where this goes."

He kissed her. True, it was the end of their perfect vacation. But it was the beginning of their life together.

It was almost 11:00 a.m. Checkout time for the cottage. Sinead shoved her toiletry bag into the top of her duffel bag and pulled the zipper closed. The bag bulged.

She hefted it off the bed. Wells stood at the door. Harry was in his arms.

"I'll trade you," he said. "You carry Harry and I'll get the luggage."

"Deal," she said. Before she could reach for the baby, her phone pinged with an incoming text. "Work," she groaned. "We haven't even gotten back to the city and already they're reaching out."

Her phone was in an outside pocket on her duffel bag. She dropped the bag back on the bed and pulled the cell from the pocket.

She read the text once. And again. Her heart skipped a beat and then her pulse began to race. It was from the same untraceable number as the first message she'd received from the Landmark Killer.

"What is it?" Wells asked.

Sinead swallowed and held out the phone.

He took the cell and read the message out loud. "See you on Broadway."

"The Landmark Killer's ready to strike again," she said. "This time we know where. The question is, can we stop him before he kills again?"

* * * * *

*Don't miss the next exciting story
in The Coltons of New York:*

Chasing a Colton Killer
by Deborah Fletcher Mello

Available from Harlequin Romantic Suspense!

#2243 CHASING A COLTON KILLER
The Coltons of New York
by Deborah Fletcher Mello

Stella Maxwell is one story away from Pulitzer gold, but when she becomes the prime suspect in the murder of her ex-boyfriend, those aspirations are put on hold. FBI agent Brennan Colton suspects Stella might be guilty of something, but it isn't murder. Between his concern for Stella's well-being and the notorious Landmark Killer taunting them, Brennan never anticipates fighting for his heart.

#2244 MISSING IN TEXAS
by Karen Whiddon

It's been four brutal years for Jake Cassin, who finally locates the daughter who's been missing all that time. But his little girl is abducted before he can even meet her. Despite his reservations and an unwanted stirring of attraction, he must work with Edie Beswick, her adoptive mother, who is just as frantic as he is. How can they stay rational on this desperate search when they have everything to lose?

#2245 A FIREFIGHTER'S HIDDEN TRUTH
Sierra's Web • by Tara Taylor Quinn

When Luke Dennison wakes up in the hospital with amnesia, he doesn't know why a beautiful woman is glaring down at him. He soon learns he is a firefighter, a father and someone wants them both dead. After engaging the experts of Sierra's Web, Luke and Shelby are whisked into protective custody. Could this proximity bring them to a greater understanding of each other...or finally separate them forever?

#2246 TEXAS LAW: SERIAL MANHUNT
Texas Law • by Jennifer D. Bokal

For more than twenty years, Sage Sauter has been keeping a secret—her daughter's biological father is Dr. Michael O'Brien. Michael has never forgotten about his first love, Sage. So when Sage's daughter shows up at his hospital—presumably after being attacked by a serial killer—he offers to help. Sage knows that Michael's the best forensic pathologist around, but she's terrified that he'll discover her secret if he gets involved with a very deadly investigation.

Get 3 FREE REWARDS!

We'll send you 2 FREE Books plus a FREE Mystery Gift.

FREE Value Over **$20**

Both the **Harlequin Intrigue®** and **Harlequin® Romantic Suspense** series feature compelling novels filled with heart-racing action-packed romance that will keep you on the edge of your seat.

YES! Please send me 2 FREE novels from the Harlequin Intrigue or Harlequin Romantic Suspense series and my FREE gift (gift is worth about $10 retail). After receiving them, if I don't wish to receive any more books, I can return the shipping statement marked "cancel." If I don't cancel, I will receive 6 brand-new Harlequin Intrigue Larger-Print books every month and be billed just $6.49 each in the U.S. or $6.99 each in Canada, a savings of at least 13% off the cover price, or 4 brand-new Harlequin Romantic Suspense books every month and be billed just $5.49 each in the U.S. or $6.24 each in Canada, a savings of at least 12% off the cover price. It's quite a bargain! Shipping and handling is just 50¢ per book in the U.S. and $1.25 per book in Canada.* I understand that accepting the 2 free books and gift places me under no obligation to buy anything. I can always return a shipment and cancel at any time by calling the number below. The free books and gift are mine to keep no matter what I decide.

Choose one:
- ☐ **Harlequin Intrigue Larger-Print** (199/399 BPA GRMX)
- ☐ **Harlequin Romantic Suspense** (240/340 BPA GRMX)
- ☐ **Or Try Both!** (199/399 & 240/340 BPA GRQD)

Name (please print)

Address   Apt. #

City   State/Province   Zip/Postal Code

Email: Please check this box ☐ if you would like to receive newsletters and promotional emails from Harlequin Enterprises ULC and its affiliates. You can unsubscribe anytime.

Mail to the **Harlequin Reader Service:**
IN U.S.A.: P.O. Box 1341, Buffalo, NY 14240-8531
IN CANADA: P.O. Box 603, Fort Erie, Ontario L2A 5X3

Want to try 2 free books from another series! Call 1-800-873-8635 or visit www.ReaderService.com.

*Terms and prices subject to change without notice. Prices do not include sales taxes, which will be charged (if applicable) based on your state or country of residence. Canadian residents will be charged applicable taxes. Offer not valid in Quebec. This offer is limited to one order per household. Books received may not be as shown. Not valid for current subscribers to the Harlequin Intrigue or Harlequin Romantic Suspense series. All orders subject to approval. Credit or debit balances in a customer's account(s) may be offset by any other outstanding balance owed by or to the customer. Please allow 4 to 6 weeks for delivery. Offer available while quantities last.

Your Privacy—Your information is being collected by Harlequin Enterprises ULC, operating as Harlequin Reader Service. For a complete summary of the information we collect, how we use this information and to whom it is disclosed, please visit our privacy notice located at corporate.harlequin.com/privacy-notice. From time to time we may also exchange your personal information with reputable third parties. If you wish to opt out of this sharing of your personal information, please visit readerservice.com/consumerschoice or call 1-800-873-8635. **Notice to California Residents**—Under California law, you have specific rights to control and access your data. For more information on these rights and how to exercise them, visit corporate.harlequin.com/california-privacy.

HIHRS23

HARLEQUIN
PLUS

Try the best multimedia subscription service for romance readers like you!

Read, Watch and Play.

Experience the easiest way to get the romance content you crave.

Start your **FREE TRIAL** at
<u>www.harlequinplus.com/freetrial</u>.